HOME IN ALFALFA

HOME IN ALFALFA

Stories by
Hugh Cook

To Fan —
welcome to Alfalfa!
Hugh Cook
(SPU Oct 2000)

Mosaic Press
Oakville, ON - Buffalo, NY

Canadian Cataloguing in Publication Data

Cook, Hugh, 1942-
  Home in alfalfa

ISBN 0-88962-668-5 HC   ISBN 0-88962-677-4 PB

I. Title.

PS8555.O5633H65 1998   C813'54   C98-931183-X
PR9199.3.C66H65 1998

Published by MOSAIC PRESS, P.O. Box 1032, Oakville, Ontario, L6J 5E9, Canada. Offices and warehouse at 1252 Speers Road, Units #1&2, Oakville, Ontario, L6L 5N9, Canada and Mosaic Press, 85 River Rock Drive, Suite 202, Buffalo, N.Y., 14207, USA.

Mosaic Press acknowledges the assistance of the Canada Council, the Ontario Arts Council and the Dept. of Canadian Heritage, Government of Canada, for their support of our publishing programme.

Wood engraving by Wesley W. Bates

Printed and bound in Canada
MOSAIC PRESS in the UK and Europe:
DRAKE INTERNATIONAL SERVICES
Market House, Market Place,
Deddington, Oxford. OX15 OSF

MOSAIC PRESS, in Canada: **MOSAIC PRESS**, in the USA:
1252 Speers Road, Units #1&2,   85 River Rock Drive, Suite 202,
Oakville, Ontario, L6L 5N9   Buffalo, N.Y., 14207
Phone / Fax: (905) 825-2130   Phone / Fax: 1-800-387-8992
E-mail: cp507@freenet.toronto.on.ca

for Judy,
Karin, Arn & Meghan
Jeremy,
Justin

...There was, however, one tall, dry-looking old gentleman, with beetling eyebrows, who maintained a grave and rather severe face throughout; now and then folding his arms, inclining his head, and looking down upon the floor, as if turning a doubt over in his mind. He was one of your wary men, who never laugh but upon good grounds-- when they have reason and the law on their side....

The story-teller, who was just putting a glass of wine to his lips, as a refreshment after his toils, paused for a moment....

The cautious old gentleman knit his brows tenfold closer....At length he observed, that all this was very well, but still he thought the story a little on the extravagant--there were one or two points on which he had his doubts.

"Faith, sir," replied the story-teller, "as to that matter, I don't believe one-half of it myself."

-Washington Irving

It is not down in any map; true places never are.

-Herman Melville

CONTENTS

I. Bare Knees Again

II. The Housewife Counts Her Jars

III. The Mailbox's Metal Nose

IV. The Floods are Loose!

I.

Bare Knees Again

Under the dry fence
gooseberries dangled on thin stems,
cottony grass buried the fence-posts, the
grainy dirt trickled with ants.
I smell bare knees again and summer's clouds.

-Margaret Avison

WELCOME TO ALFALFA

It's not likely you will ever have heard of Alfalfa, not many people have. We're just a small town, as you might guess–you're not liable to hear a place with a name like Alfalfa boast, "Home of the world-renowned Alfalfa Philharmonic Orchestra." Nor would you be likely to read in Alfalfa's weekly newspaper, *The Sentinel-Star*, a story that goes, "As a result of a sizable endowment from a local farmer who has long been a patron of the arts, the Art Gallery of Alfalfa made another stunning purchase this past Friday, acquiring a recently discovered painting by Vincent Van Gogh titled *The Milking Parlour*, strengthening the AGA's claim of owning one of the world's largest collections of early modern Dutch art." Not quite.

Some people say the town has always been called Alfalfa, others claim no one in his right mind would give a town such a hick name. No, they say, the town was originally named Alphaville because it was one of the first settlements here in southern Ontario. The story they tell is that back in the 1850s, shortly after Alfalfa became established, Jonas McWhinnie, one of the town fathers, happened to be afflicted with a terrible stutter, and whenever Jonas met a stranger on the sidewalk he would stammer his way through "Good morning," then bid the man "W-w-welcome to Alph-Alpha–" and that's as far as he would get, by then he'd be utterly vanquished and gasping for air, and that's how the town came to be known as Alfalfa. At least, that's what some people say, but as with any story about a small town, it's best to circle this one once or twice, then approach it from the side, downwind and with a good dose of caution. In any case, as far back as anyone can remember, no one has called the town anything other than Alfalfa.

If you happen to be driving into town from the south, you'll run into a sharp bend in the road we Alfalfans call Collie's Curve. It's named that because a number of years ago some high school pranksters celebrating graduation turned the curve's fluorescent yellow and black chevrons the other way and Collie Ferguson, who is known to brag, "I'm Irish, I drink anything that runs downhill," drove home late one night at a good lick of speed from Alfie's Tavern south of town, followed the direction the arrows pointed–as anyone naturally would, sober or otherwise–flew off the road, and careened into Zebrosky's Lawn Ornaments, pulverizing a wide swath through the best selection of ceramic gnomes, fawns, elves, nymphs, swans, turtles, sea horses, lions, flamingoes, dalmatians, and rearing horses this side of the city. But don't worry, if what you've come for is lawn ornaments there's still plenty left.

Once you've negotiated Collie's Curve you'll notice the pavement narrows where a stand of maples forms a leafy canopy over the road, such a low green tunnel that you hunch over the steering wheel as you ease your car through it while you feel as if you might be entering a whole other world, a time warp where anything could happen.

Once you've passed through this portal you'll see four signs. The first is a billboard erected by the Blessed Assurance Gospel Tabernacle that shows the outline of an open Bible and inside it in large letters, PREPARE TO MEET THY GOD. I've always felt the sign's message contains an interesting double meaning: does it suggest that Alfalfa is such a wicked town that those who pass through do so at the peril of their eternal souls– "Abandon Hope All Ye Who Enter Here"?–or does the sign suggest the town is so godly that those who come near had better take off their shoes for they are on the verge of holy ground? I'd like to believe it's the latter but I suspect that, despite their name, Blessed Assurance doesn't. Nor are they the kind of church to delight in any ambiguity.

If the Blessed Assurance people haven't frightened you off, the second sign you'll see is one welcoming you to the six churches in town with the times of their services and listing the names of the ministers: Rev. David Findlater at Calvary Baptist, Rev. Sandra Oppendahl at Grace United, Rev. John DeHeer at First Christian Reformed, and so on, all the ministers' names except for Father Michael Healy's at Sacred Heart Catholic Church. I guess when yours is the establishment that's been around the longest you count on a certain level of brand recognition, and don't have to spend as much time identifying your local reps.

The third sign you'll see is a large one erected by the Chamber of Commerce saying, WELCOME TO ALFALFA, and below it, THE PRIDE OF DAIRY COUNTRY. Two years ago another group of high school students, who are never short of ingenuity apparently, crossed out the word PRIDE and painted in the word ANUS. In a minute you may see why. It took the Chamber a week to notice the students' revision and another week to round up a painter to amend it. The sign also lists the town's service clubs, so if you're the type who enjoys wearing a funny-shaped hat with a little red tassel dangling in your face, take a look.

The last sign is a small blue one with white lettering that says, simply, ALFALFA, and when you see it, you'll know you're here.

If you'd happened to be driving into town a month ago you would have noticed how good the brown and green fields looked–all potential. You'd have seen the first oats and barley coming up, and the alfalfa a most lush and optimistic green. Little spears of corn were just appearing, their symmetrical rows a perfect thirty inches apart following the rolling contour of the land–as any farmer will tell you, this is the most beautiful sight there is on God's green earth.

You may also have noticed that your approach to the town was enhanced by the fragrance of that all-natural fertilizer farmers were spreading onto their fields which is produced in great quantities in any dairy community–a cow's annual production, in fact, is equivalent to your average politician's, namely about 14 tons. This is no exaggeration but hard and fast truth for it was reported in an unimpeachable source, *The Alfalfa Sentinel-Star*. So, given the great number of cows in this area, you know that farmers have quite a lot of it to spread and why they're anxious to get out with their honeywagons as soon as they can get into the fields every spring. I don't want to appear indecorous by discussing this subject at too great a length, but you must realize that in a farming community, this is the smell of money. It was this selfsame aroma, by the way, that was the first thing Dutch farmers recognized when they immigrated to this area shortly after World War II, and was what made them decide to settle here–they tilted their heads upwind, flared their nostrils, and felt right at home.

If the aroma wafting in through your car window wasn't enough to make you turn around and head back to wherever you were coming from, you will see some of the more important business establishments that make Alfalfa the interesting town it is, places like Lucille's Lunch, Melvin's Barber Shop, Hardy Hardware, Art's Mart, and Carr Motors. Establishments such as these are the lifeblood of any small town; without them Alfalfa too would soon shrivel and die. When they are threatened, the town itself is threatened. No wonder the cardinal rule of life in a small town is that you patronize your local merchants.

You can understand the stir, then, that was created last winter by the rumour that one of the big pizza chains was going to open a franchise right here in Alfalfa. Some of the local businessmen who go for coffee in Lucille's Lunch every morning agreed that if a pizza chain was coming then of course McDonald's and Kentucky Fried Chicken and Taco Bell would want to keep up with the competition and set up shop just outside town, then outfits like Rogers Video and Midas Mufflers would move in, followed by Howard Johnson and Canadian Tire, then megastores like Wal-Mart and Costco–and where would they all be? Huh. There'd be dust swirling around the corners of boarded-up buildings, and bleached cow skulls littering Main Street. A mile outside of town would be a commercial strip with garish, blinking neon signs and pink and chartreuse vinyl buildings in art deco style like you see in bedroom communities around the big cities, and pointy-headed, gum-chewing strangers with pencils behind their ears saying "Can I help you?" without even looking at you, and that would be the end of Alfalfa.

Hordes of lawyers would slither into town, and little boys would no longer play street hockey and dream of playing in the NHL because they would all be seduced by the NBA's slick advertising and want to play basketball in the States instead of playing hockey in Canada as they should, and once you start corrupting the hearts of the young it's not just Alfalfa you're tampering with anymore, friend, the very future of the country is at stake.

Other people–they must not be native Alfalfans but people who were astute enough to recognize a land of milk and honey when they drove through and later moved here from the city–said getting a pizza joint was a good thing and that it was about time Alfalfa joined western civilization. They're still lusting after the old fleshpots of Egypt, and haven't lived here long enough yet to appreciate the importance of local establishments.

Like Lucille's Lunch. Situated dabsmack in the middle of downtown, not only is Lucille's the geographical hub of Alfalfa, it's also the social, intellectual, and commercial centre of town. Anything of any importance in Alfalfa is conceived, born, and nurtured here. Standing on the sidewalk outside Lucille's is a large wooden sandwich sign that contains owner Jerry Shivers' thought for the day. Today's is, "A Small Town Is A Place Where There's No Place To Go Where You Shouldn't." Ha. Wishful thinking. You step in through the front door (two sets of doors actually, in deference to winter) but don't feel you should wait to be seated, and don't ask which is the non-smoking section—are you kidding? Lucille's isn't exactly Chez Antoine, after all; people will only turn around to look at you, as if they didn't already know you weren't from here.

On your right you'll see a counter with eight red-leather stools, behind the counter a large white cooler holding milk, pop, and beer, and on top of the cooler a blackboard listing the day's special in red and blue chalk, although regulars here will tell you that more likely than not when they check the board the special seems to be liver and onions. If you're wanted somewhere, and the thought of sitting at the counter with people behind your back makes you nervous, you can choose any of the wooden tables with captain's chairs, or the wooden booths lining two of the walls. Each table is covered with a blue tablecloth, a paper placemat advertising some of the town's main business establishments, a laminated menu, and a small glass vase filled with pink and white carnations and a little splash of fern that look so real most people have to finger them to find out if they are or not.

Once you're seated you will see that on the wall of reclaimed orange brick on your left hang a number of objects of the sort displayed in other restaurants, except these have been hanging in Lucille's long before doing so became a fad, objects that were actually used around here at one time rather than articles the owner bought at some fancy antique auction—a grey bicycle from before the War, an eight foot long crosscut saw, a hand auger, wooden washboards, rusty railroad lanterns, and wrinkled leather ice skates. High on the walls here and there, stained pine shelves contain plants, grey stone butter pots, and squat green bottles—who wouldn't want to *live* here?

At the back of Lucille's is the bar area where the boys go for a beer late at night or during the day if winter drags on and they need a bump before they're ready to face the thought of more weather. There are also wooden booths if this is your fourth night here this week and you prefer some privacy, or you can park on a tall bar stool around a table that's holding a small pail filled with peanuts in the shell.

It doesn't take long before Bonnie Shivers comes by your table to ask what you'd like. You'll see she's friendly even if this might be your first time here. The way she talks to you–"Warm that up for you, honey?" "Put some ice cream on that for ya?"– there are days you'd like to trade in your spouse for one of her at home. Bonnie's been waitressing in Lucille's a long time but she doesn't seem that old–this is dangerous territory here, I know–mid-forties or so. She wears her dark hair in a short bob, nice and easy for work, and blue jeans and a white t-shirt; she doesn't care for those pastel pink or yellow waitress uniforms like they wear in the city. The front of her t-shirt has a large Labatt's Blue logo; the back, in fancy script, says "Lucille's Lunch, Established 1905," and below that "Homestyle Dinning At Its Best." As you can see, we don't go in for proofreading much here in Alfalfa. Bonnie's missing a tooth in the right corner of her mouth. Her husband Jerry would like her to get it fixed but she says, "Why would I want to do that? I already got a husband. Besides, what do you think this is, a lawyer's office? Why should I pay a thousand bucks for a bridge–you think anybody in here would notice and leave a tip?" Regulars at Lucille's know what's coming next. Bonnie's favourite joke: "What's the difference between a Dutchman and a canoe?" Answer: "One of 'em tips."

Jerry's the cook in the back, by the way, can crack two eggs with each hand, four at a time. Wears a stained white apron over the same white t-shirt and jeans and sports a Mark Messier haircut so short he doesn't need a hairnet, as if he'd wear one anyway–that'd be something the regulars here would love to see, Jerry with a hairnet! He'd never hear the end of it. Jerry opens up every morning about five, bakes a couple of dozen fresh blueberry muffins and cinnamon buns, then prepares the potato salad and cole slaw for the day. Bonnie and Rhonda, the other waitress, arrive at six. Sergeant Lofthouse of the Alfalfa police is always one of the first to come in for an early morning coffee, then other customers start drifting in shortly after that, retired dairy farmers who have gotten up at five a.m. without an alarm clock for sixty years and whose internal alarm still wakes them up that early. By eight o'clock it's a steady stream until one-thirty or two in the afternoon. Jerry takes a break then, and comes back again at five for the supper rush. Most nights he and Bonnie don't turn off the lights until close to midnight.

In case you're wondering who Lucille is, that's a bit of a mystery. There may have been a Lucille once, but I'm not sure if anyone knows now who she was. Maybe she went broke waiting for the Dutch people in town to show up. They'll drop in for coffee alright but not for dinner– they're not exactly your eating out types. Besides, it would look a little funny if you sat down in a place like Lucille's and said, "I'll have *boerekool met worst*, please"–Bonnie wouldn't know what it was, and if she did, would wonder why on earth you would want to eat it. Not when you could have the liver and onions.

Maybe now you can see why the merchants having coffee that morning were concerned that the next thing for Alfalfa would be a pizza franchise with red ceramic tiles and orange vinyl seats, serving pizzas shipped by truck from some warehouse in Mississauga. It'd be like eating strawberries from California instead of local ones–they might look like strawberries but they sure don't taste like them.

After you've finished your dinner at Lucille's, one block south you'll see Melvin's Barber Shop, another gathering place for Alfalfa philosophers and one more landmark that would be in danger once the franchise places moved in. Melvin's wouldn't be good enough for people anymore, it would be replaced by some salon in the mall called "Geraldo's Unisex Hair Studio," and some young thing who's gone to community college and gotten a diploma in the science of cosmetology would tilt your head backward into a basin of hot water, blow dry your hair, cut it, then blow dry it some more to fluff it up so you could walk out fifteen minutes later looking like some TV game show host.

Melvin Snyder strikes you as being young, at first, for a barber; he took over the shop from his father Alvin who began it back in 1951. You step in and take a seat on a black leather bench that runs along the wall to your left. As you sit the bench accepts your weight with a grateful little whoosh of air. That's Melvin with his back to you, cutting Irv Pankey's hair and asking Irv how his boy's Little League team is doing. You look around and see a set of cowhorns hanging over the door that goes to the back; in front of the door lies a black and white, long-haired dog, sleeping. It's Melvin's dog Princess, an Australian collie. Beside the dog stands an antique Coke machine. If you look into the bank of mirrors ahead of you, you'll see that hanging above and behind you are team photographs of the Toronto Maple Leafs, going all the way back to the glory years of Horton and Armstrong and Keon and Mahovlich and Bower and Baun. High on the wall above the photographs hangs a 20-pound mounted walleye Melvin caught up north in '73.

Melvin is almost finished with Irv, he's laying a nice warm daub of shaving foam behind Irv's ears which he'll shave with a straight razor. They've gone from Little League to politics now, Irv Pankey muttering how on earth we could have elected the imbeciles we did. "That sweet-deal pension's the first thing that's gotta go," Irv's saying, "ordinary

9

workin' folks like you 'n me, we're the ones payin' for it. Then d'you read where that minister for commerce or transportation or whatever wouldn't declare a conflict of interest over that land deal? I don't know, if you ask me they're all crookeder than a spindle on a spider's ass." Melvin doesn't say much more than "Uh huh" to that. Eighteen years of cutting men's hair and listening to their brilliant ideas is a good lesson in patience and forbearance.

He can't afford to argue with his customers, even when he disagrees with what they're saying, which Melvin will tell you happens now and then. He attends Calvary Baptist Church in town and has his own convictions, but you can't turn your barber shop into a place to proselytize. Before you'd know it you'd be sitting in your chair singing to yourself. Even so, Melvin does leave some literature lying around in the shop for his customers to pick up. Which they do. Even though there are six churches in town, maybe the material Melvin puts out is better than the stuff his customers can get in their own church.

Irv Pankey steps out of the chair, all 6' 3" and 240 pounds of him, and hands a ten to Melvin, who checks his drawer for change, notices he's all out of toonies, and takes out a ten dollar bill. He turns to the dog sleeping on the floor and says, "Here Prin." The dog jumps up from the floor and goes over to Melvin, who folds the ten dollar bill in half and sticks it into Princess's mouth and says, "Give this to Mommy and get some change. That's a good girl." The dog walks calmly through the door to the back with the ten dollar bill in its mouth and comes back just as calmly two minutes later with a small white envelope between its teeth. Melvin takes the envelope, shakes out five toonies, and hands one to Irv Pankey.

"Smartest dog in the world," Melvin says, "I could do ten TV commercials with her." He gives Princess a dog biscuit, which the dog takes over to where she was, lies down, and starts chewing the biscuit. You're not sure you saw what you just saw. Meanwhile, Irv Pankey pockets the toonie, and a man gets up off the bench to your right.

Here you've been sitting on this leather bench for what, fifteen minutes, and it's not until now that you first notice that the man getting up, a grey-haired fellow about fifty, is wearing a ponytail halfway down his back. What on earth is Melvin going to do with that, you wonder. Turns out you've picked an interesting day to drop in. The fellow with the ponytail is Phil Sandy, who moved to Alfalfa in the late sixties to get away from the city, bought a piece of land west of town five years later, built a geodesic dome covered with automobile roofs he cut out of cars in the salvage yard just north of town, and now runs Sandy's Videos on the corner. People still drive by to look at his dome.

"Figured it was time again, eh?" Melvin says as he swings a blue cotton cape over Phil's legs and tucks it in under his chin.

"Well, summer's here and the hair's gettin' to be a bit of a drag. When was I in last, about three years ago?"

"Must be. How much of it you want off? An inch or two?" Melvin turns to you with a grin on his face, and winks.

"The whole thing, Mel. I'm walkin' out of here lookin' like Ross Perot."

Melvin lets out a low whistle. He undoes the green elastic band holding Phil's ponytail, spreads out the hair, and begins combing it out; it falls well over the back of the chair. Melvin takes a strand of it between two of his fingers, then snips it with his scissors. The hair falls to the floor and lies there like a clump of angel hair fallen from a Christmas tree. It contrasts sharply with Irv Pankey's black hair already on the floor. Another snip and a second strand falls to the floor. Fifteen minutes later and you'd hardly recognize Phil. He doesn't look at all like an ex-hippie, more like an insurance salesman, but a respectable one.

In case you're wondering what Melvin does with all the hair on his floor, Murk Foley, who has apple trees back of his house on the west edge of town, drops by the barber shop once a week to pick up the hair to spread around the trees in his orchard. Hair has a strong human scent and it keeps away the deer that like to come in and eat Murk's apples. Nothing beats it.

Speaking of hair, what I was saying earlier about supporting your local merchants I don't want you to take to any extreme. I don't think Melvin would take it ill of me, for instance, if I revealed that Melvin's wife Frances cuts his hair–what's Melvin to do, drive to a neighbouring town and support the barber there? Obviously, if every man in town got his wife to cut his hair Melvin would be in trouble, but if my wife cut my hair the way Melvin's wife cuts his, Melvin might not see me in his shop anymore either. Someone has said–claims Melvin himself told him, so I have no reason to doubt his story–that every time Frances gives Melvin a haircut she takes off her blouse and bra because she doesn't want Melvin's hair sticking to it; she already has to put up with other men's hair Melvin inevitably trails all through the house with his shoes. You can see why Frances cuts Melvin's hair in the kitchen, by the way, rather than in his shop with the big windows in front. He sits in the kitchen chair while his wife circles by him about eye level–I picture Frances having to keep turning Melvin's head straight the way your barber did when you were a little kid. One thing you've got to say about Frances, though, she must have picked up the skill from Melvin pretty well because you can never tell when Melvin's had a cut; he must get one a week, at least. I suppose that, being a barber, Melvin feels he should set a good tonsorial example to the other men in town. But I better let you go now otherwise you'll think I'm one of those long-winded storytellers who doesn't know when to stop.

By the way, if you're looking for that franchise pizza place in town that I mentioned earlier, you won't find it. Turned out not to be a franchise at all but someone from the city who bought Arthur Mooney's gift shop after Arthur died last winter, thought he could make an easy buck here in Alfalfa since we didn't have a pizza place in town.

What happened was, he converted the gift shop into a pizza parlour and takeout, and opened for business. The pizza he made wasn't anything to write home about, but people were so starved for pizza they called in like crazy. Except the guy didn't hit the telephone company for one of those catchy, easily remembered numbers, then on top of that the phone company made a mistake in the yellow pages and reversed the last two digits, which gave the new pizza place the same phone number as Don and Dolores Filice in town. Don and Dolores kept getting phone calls like, "We'll have a medium with Canadian bacon, mushroom, and green peppers on one half, black olives on the other," or, "Send us the deluxe but hold the anchovies." All hours of the night. They answered them politely at first, then later simply hung up. Still people kept calling. Then Don and Dolores got smart. They decided if people wanted pizza that bad and kept calling for it, heck, they were Italian, they made better pizza than that, they'd deliver it themselves. Turned out they made such great pizza the guy from the city didn't have a chance–he folded up and slunk back to the city. Don and Dolores bought the store, and now run DD's Pizza. Do well at it too, you'll have to try their pizza sometime. Especially if you're tired of Lucille's liver and onions.

FOR SALE:
The area's finest selection of ceramic lawn ornaments. Some slightly damaged, at reduced price. Zebrosky's Lawn Ornaments, ¼ mi south of town.

- *ad in* The Alfalfa Sentinel-Star

WILD OATS

Folks in Lucille's Lunch were talking this week about how Miss Evelyn Krikke, an elderly lady in town and a neighbour of Virginia Wiebinga's over on Pearson Place, happened to mention to several other ladies at First Christian Reformed Church after the Sunday morning service that she had seen Albert Zomer steer his green Dodge pickup into Virginia's driveway at quarter to eight the evening before and that she had seen them leave together exactly seven and a half minutes later. It didn't take much longer than that for the rest of the church to know about it.

Albert is a bachelor in his late thirties and runs a chicken farm just north of town. Virginia works in Bob Miller's travel agency across from the Beer Store on Main, and is intelligent, vivacious, and 39. She doesn't consider herself a member of the Last Chance Club at all; she just knows what she wants. Her mother Florence thinks that what she wants can't be found in a town our size, not unless his car happens to break down while he's passing through, and what are the chances of *that* happening with Virginia being within eyeshot just then.

Evelyn Krikke said she could tell Albert was picking up Virginia for a date because of the way he'd dressed up: he was wearing a bright green shirt, its top three rhinestone buttons open to show the eight hairs on his chest, he had pulled the collar of his shirt over his brown sport coat as people do on the western channel on television, and he had slicked down his hair, what he has left of it, with mousse. On his face he had splashed a handful of Brut after-shave whose aroma arrived two minutes before he did, an odour potent enough to fumigate a henhouse.

Someone said that, knowing Albert, he and Virginia probably went Dutch treat. Which is not a very nice thing to say. Think about it: how would you like it if, of all the things your ancestry might give its name to, yours was known for being cheap? But at least Dutch treat doesn't sound bad. You hear the phrase and what it makes you think of is something delicious and decadent, like cream-filled pastry, or like something you'd find in the "Companions" section of the want ads: "Generous male seeks attractive female for afternoon Dutch treat. Discretion assured." So the Dutch don't have it as bad as the Polish, for instance, whose name will forever be linked with sausage. Or the Chinese, who have donated their name to a water torture. You'd almost rather be cheap. No, if your ancestry is going to be remembered at all, you'd like it to be for something a bit more glamorous, even if it might be a tad worldly–like Scotch whisky, say, or French kissing.

But there might be some truth to the reputation the Dutch have for being frugal. Folks were also talking this past week about Oetse Kikkert, one of our retired farmers. Oetse's 79 and put an ad in this week's *Sentinel-Star* advertising a cemetery plot for sale. He'd bought the plot twenty-nine years ago when a salesman came by and made him an offer Oetse couldn't refuse, he'd never run into such a bargain on a piece of real estate. No telling when he'd need it, he thought, might as well be prepared.

Now that he's 79 and still feeling great, though, Oetse figured why pay the taxes on a piece of property he wasn't getting any use out of and wasn't planning on needing for a while. What did it was that he found out what Harvey Buisman, another senior member at First CRC, just paid for *his* cemetery plot, and Oetse decided with that kind of profit he'd be crazy to turn it down. He'd worry about buying another plot when the time came.

Someone who has been in Oetse's place has reported that Oetse keeps a tea bag dangling by its string from a stainless steel pipe above his kitchen sink. He brings his tea mug up to the bag and dunks the tea bag in the mug's hot water until it sports the desired colour. Then he pinches the bag so as not to waste any of the tea. Apparently a bag lasts him a good week; he hangs up a fresh one every Sunday morning.

Oetse may be feeling great but he is old enough to have to wear a hearing aid. Took him several years to admit he needed one, figured he could get along in life alright hearing in only one ear but when he renewed his driver's license last fall he was told he would have to get a hearing aid. He wears it now only when he has to, and even then he makes sure a battery is not only good and dead but beyond hope of resuscitation before he puts in a new one. One Sunday Rev. DeHeer was about halfway through his sermon when Oetse heard his battery give out suddenly and realized he hadn't taken along any extra, and then he felt like one of the five foolish virgins who had left their extra batteries at home.

All of this reminds me of something that happened here in Alfalfa some time ago, shortly after Dutch Reformed folks began to settle this area. I was twelve when it happened, which is just about the age you begin to develop a keen interest in the kind of thing I'm about to tell you. It's a story that people in our community love to tell often, so you know that by now they've had a chance to get it right, with all the exaggerations weeded out, and what remains in the telling of it now is nothing but a clean patch of honest and truthful detail.

There were three farmers in First Christian Reformed: Vander Leek, Lubbers and Klop. They lived quite some distance away from the church, Vander Leek twenty miles north, Lubbers fifteen miles west and Klop eighteen miles east, so they always enjoyed talking together after the service. Especially since farmers standing together tend not to be joined by too many other people, pig or chicken farmers particularly, probably because people figure they're talking shop anyway. Which they are not, because not only do Dutch Reformed people not work on Sunday, they are not even supposed to talk about it. So the farmers discuss their upcoming trip to Florida during the kids' March break, or they chew about the weather, which is still about their work in a way, but if they weren't allowed to complain about the weather what else would there be for a farmer to say?

One Sunday, Vander Leek, Lubbers and Klop were standing together after church and when they'd finished with the weather Lubbers says to Vander Leek, "Congregational meeting Wednesday evening, what do you think of the proposal to give the minister a salary increase next year?"

But Vander Leek doesn't answer right away; you can tell he's got something else on his mind. He thinks a moment, then says, "Tell me something. If it wasn't Sunday today, any idea where I can, uh, obtain the services of a boar?" That's what happens when you do talk about your work on Sunday. You end up talking like that, even if you're a farmer. You can't just talk about that sort of thing on a Sunday in your usual Monday-to-Saturday voice; that would almost be profane, so you launder it up a bit, sort of like when you take on your praying voice: "Lord, as we are about to go on our homeward way now on the evening hour of this day we pray Thee now for travelling mercies. . . ." That's how it is when some people pray: they never just drive home, they go on their homeward way. And they're not satisfied with the Lord's protection, they prefer his travelling mercies. That's like needing to obtain the services of a boar when what you really want is for your sow to be bred.

In any case, Lubbers doesn't miss a beat. He scratches his chin and says, "I didn't know you were going into hogs, Bert. What do you need a boar for?"

The answer doesn't strike Vander Leek as being obvious; he looks deep in thought, in fact, as though there might be hundreds of reasons for wanting a boar. "Well," Vander Leek says, "bought a couple of Yorkshires last month, and now they're in heat. Thought I'd raise some on the side. Maybe butcher 'em when they're ready."

"Doesn't sound like a bad idea," Lubbers allowed.

"You want to take one of them?"

"Ja, sure."

"Funny you fellows should say that," Klop pipes up, "I happened to be talking last week about the exact same thing to my neighbour. His name is Wilbur Leckie. He's Pentecostal, but you wouldn't know lookin' at his pigs. He raises good Yorkshires. He knows I've got a sow or two, said he had a boar he could sell me for a hundred and twenty, but ja, where am I gonna get that kind of money all by myself?"

Then Vander Leek, Lubbers and Klop all had the exact same thought. What if they. . . ? The three of them looked at each other for about as long as it took each of them to divide a hundred and twenty by three, which for a Dutch farmer is not long, only five or six seconds.

"Isn't a hundred and twenty a bit high?" Lubbers says.

"Maybe," Vander Leek says, "but it sounds like we should talk to him. Think you can arrange a time, Len?"

"Ja sure, I'll let you know."

Next Tuesday afternoon Vander Leek, Lubbers and Klop drove to Wilbur Leckie's farm in Klop's old blue Ford pickup. They'd put on suit coats over their work clothes to help them make a good impression.

"You do the talking, Bert," Lubbers said to Vander Leek, "you finished school. But remember, no higher than a hundred and twenty. And see if you can work him down." Vander Leek nodded. They turned into Wilbur Leckie's yard. It lay in hushed, mid-summer calm, as if the very sparrows were listening.

Wilbur Leckie stepped out of his barn to meet them before Klop's pickup had rolled to a stop. "Nice to see you fellows," he said as they stepped out. "Len tells me you're in the market for a boar."

"Maybe we are," Vander Leek said, not wanting to sound too eager, certainly not before they'd seen the animal. He wasn't born in Sarnia.

"Well come on inside and have a look," Leckie said, turning towards the barn.

Inside, they were greeted by the good, familiar smell of pigs. An aisle with cement floor ran down the middle of the barn with wooden stalls on the left and right, each stall holding six sows. Most sows lay on their sides, sleeping; some stood nudging each other, grunting. Wilbur Leckie led them down the aisle to the last stall on the right. "Here's your boar," he said.

Vander Leek, Lubbers and Klop strained to look past each other into the stall. The boar stood directly in front of them, head slightly lowered, its narrow, slit eyes trained directly on them, as if daring them to take one step closer. The animal looked almost lethal, its skin, caked with dirt, like plate armour from which sprang blond hairs as stiff as the bristles of a Dutch broom. Then, as if knowing it was being looked at for breeding, the boar turned to display its credentials, two large round globes bulging from beneath its curled tail, as if to brag: match that.

Vander Leek, Lubbers and Klop stood silent, as if they stood before a shrine.

"My goodness," Klop said finally, voice filled with as close as a Dutch farmer comes to Pentecostal rapture.

"He's no barrow, that's for sure," Vander Leek said.

"How old is he?" Lubbers asked.

"Three, so he's got quite some miles left in him. Notice how long and lean he is? And he's proven himself for me, let me tell ya. In fact, I call him Wild Oats, because he's certainly sown his. He's one boar who always wears his workin' clothes, know what I mean?"

Vander Leek, Lubbers and Klop certainly did.

"So if you're lookin' for a boar to breed several sows, as I understand you fellas are, then Wild Oats is your boy."

Vander Leek felt the weight of Lubbers' and Klop's stares. He knew they were calling for the question. But it didn't seem right to him to just come out with it crassly; he wished he could table the matter until the next meeting.

"He, uh, he–seems to fit our needs all right," Vander Leek began, in English he hoped Leckie could make sense of through his heavy Dutch accent. "How much, uh, what are you asking for him, Wilbur?"

"Well, Len here is a good neighbour of mine, and a fellow Christian to boot, so for you boys I'll let you have him for–" he paused to think, rubbing his nose, "–well he's really worth one-twenty, but I'll let you have him for a hundred and ten."

Vander Leek turned to look at Lubbers and Klop, eyebrows raised as if to say, "Not bad, boys, ten less than we expected. What do you think?"

Klop was nodding vigorous approval. Vander Leek turned to Lubbers. To his surprise, Lubbers seemed uncomfortable, his face screwed up in a grimace as if he'd swallowed a mouthful of dishwater. What was with him?

Then Lubbers turned towards Wilbur Leckie, eyes looking down at the cement floor. "Now Wilbur," he began, "you know we're just Dutch immigrants eh? Can't even speak the language too good yet, ha ha, not that you can tell."

Vander Leek and Klop wondered what on earth Lubbers was up to.

"Just trying to get our farms started," Lubbers went on, "you know what that's like. So, we were wondering, would you consider an offer for ninety?"

Vander Leek and Klop didn't know what to think. Klop looked down at his shoes in embarrassment, shuffling his feet as if he'd just noticed they had collected a contribution from Leckie's barn floor. Vander Leek raised his arm and was about to step in with "Here now, Wilbur, don't pay him any atten–"

But Wilbur Leckie had already begun. "I'll tell ya," he said, his face screwed up as if he'd drunk the same dishwater Lubbers had, "ninety's a bit low." He paused. "It's against my better judgment, but I've always liked your people, and if any of you fellas had a hundred dollar bill in your pocket right now I suppose I wouldn't say no."

"How about five twenties," Lubbers said, reaching into his back pocket. "Comes to the same thing."

Wilbur Leckie shrugged. "Lettuce is lettuce," he said.

Lubbers handed him the money. "Now, we have to get him onto the truck. What do you think, can the four of us lift him?"

"Not unless you want a hernia," Leckie said. "Here, I know my boar. See those two-by-tens there against the wall? One of you fellas take five or six of 'em and lean the ends into the back of your pickup for a ramp." Then he walked to the other wall of the barn, picked up a large galvanized pail, and came back to the stall where Wild Oats stood blithely ignorant of the fact he'd just been traded to a different team.

Wilbur Leckie opened the gate of the stall and pushed the boar into the aisle. Then he took the pail, placed it over Wild Oats' head, and began to push him backwards. "Help me guide him," Leckie said, Wild Oats' grunts amplified under the galvanized pail, then the boar indeed began to walk backwards with stiff heavy steps toward the barn door where Klop's pickup stood waiting. In no time Wild Oats was aboard, ready for transport.

"You let me know if you're not satisfied, Len," Leckie said after they had clambered into the pickup, "but I expect to see the county overrun with little Wild Oats in no time." They waved goodbye and Klop drove slowly out of the yard, glancing through the rear window to see whether Wild Oats stood in need of any travelling mercies. Had the animal, like Balaam's ass, been capable of speech, no doubt it would have asked for mercies of a more stationary kind.

They'd no more than rolled onto the gravel road when Vander Leek and Klop turned to Lubbers. "I thought you said for me to do the talking," Vander Leek said. "And what was this about poor Dutch farmers? Did you really think he'd believe that nonsense?"

Lubbers shrugged his shoulders. "Saved us ten dollars, didn't I?"

"And what made you say ninety?" Klop demanded, his face showing a peculiar mixture of outrage and glee at their good fortune.

"Well, I had to leave him a number in between to come back with."

"Ja but–"

"Besides, I couldn't figure out a hundred and ten divided by three. Ninety seemed a lot easier."

"Ja, and now see what we've got, wise guy! A hundred isn't any easier."

A beatific smile crossed Lubbers' face. "You both owe me $33.33. I'll pay the extra penny."

They turned into Klop's yard. "In any case," Klop said, "what we need now is a *slokkie*, to celebrate."

They were sitting at the kitchen table with a glass of Dutch gin when Vander Leek said, "Now we'll have to decide who gets the boar first. Maybe, Len, since he's here already, why don't you take him first. Dirk, you take him next, I'll take him last." He chuckled. "And see if he's still got anything left. Uh hum, speaking of which, Len," and Vander Leek raised his glass to show it empty.

No sooner had they decided who got Wild Oats when, than they remembered the number of miles between their farms. Vander Leek twenty miles north of church, Lubbers fifteen miles west, and Klop fifteen miles east–it seemed like an awful lot of gasoline just to deliver a boar to the next fellow so he could breed his sows. They thought desperately of ways to get around the problem. After half an hour of spinning their wheels, they came to the sudden realization that there was one place all three of them came to every week, and that place wasn't Lucille's Lunch. But surely they couldn't. . . . Not right in the parking lot.

They did.

Next Sunday morning Lubbers and Klop drove their pickups to the farthest corner of the church's gravel parking lot, Lubbers' truck carrying his sow in heat, Klop's carrying Wild Oats; they'd scrounged together used lumber and built wooden sides onto their pickups out of a sense of decorum. They inched the backs of their pickups towards each other until their bumpers nudged, and dropped their tailgates, one overlapping the other. Then they stepped into the church for worship.

I sat in our usual pew left of the centre aisle that Sunday morning directly behind Len Klop, close enough for me to smell the sour odour coming from the suit coat he had worn in Wilbur Leckie's barn. I strained to look past Klop, as if at an imaginary object far in the distance, listening as I had never listened before, not to the minister's sermon but for any peculiar sounds coming from the parking lot. What I kept thinking about was Wild Oats just outside living up to his name, and how his life was, in the best sense of the phrase, a real Dutch treat.

"Bloopers" of the week

The use of animal power is all that third world countries have to plow their fields. Unlike more advanced farmers here in Alfalfa, they do not own any tractors or concubines.

* * *

In the game of golf there are those it seems like their ball is always being affected by the wind, their ball will go way off to the right or way off to the left, it usually, for some odd reason, keeps going to the left or right no matter which direction they go.

* * *

The rise in the cost of living is rising every year, the rise in the divorce rate, the rise in crime, even the interest rates are rising again–everything in this world seems to be going downhill.

* * *

The weather was so hot this past summer at church camp that every morning me and Carol and Janice got up and went for an early morning swim in the lake to relieve ourselves.

* * *

I knew the girl who had died from Girl Guides.

* * *

- column in The Alfalfa Sentinel-Star, *bloopers provided by teachers at Alfalfa Public High School*

THE GIANT CAULIFLOWER
CHAMPIONSHIP

It's always reassuring when summer finally arrives here in Alfalfa, it's an indication God has not forgotten our town after all even though it might have seemed like it back in February when men walked into Lucille's Lunch with icicles drooping from their mustaches like walrus tusks and women had the smarter sense to stay inside, out of the cold and ice. Finally we get the sunshine and warmth places further south live in all year round, places that grow exotic fruit like guava and mangoes and papaya, tropical places we Alfalfans can only dream about in February. But we're a hardy town, and we've made it through another winter. Now summer has come, even to Alfalfa, and it'll stay another three glorious months when Hilbert TeBrake and Earl Prior take each other on again for the giant cauliflower championship at the Alfalfa Fair. So who needs Jamaica? Where on earth is Aruba? Barbados? What's to rave about pineapples or avocadoes or persimmons when you can eat succulent rutabaga, endive, Brussels sprouts, lima beans. What, us jealous?

Summertime is gardening time here in Alfalfa. After mass at Sacred Heart this past Sunday, Father Michael blessed tractors and people's gardening tools while at Grace United the object lesson of Rev. Sandra Oppendahl's children's message showed bean seeds germinating against the side of a glass jar. The point of her message was going to be God's providential care over his creation so she started by asking the 3 to 5 year olds if they knew what was in the jar and the toddlers, bright little things, said, "Jeeesuuussss." They've learned by now that that is the correct answer to every final question adults ask them in children's messages, and I guess this Sunday they thought they'd cut the preliminaries and just get to the right answer.

All over town the warm weather has brought people outdoors and into their gardens where they're down on their knees, waging the eternal battle against the principalities and powers of darkness, namely weeds. You might not have expected that a town as nearly perfect as Alfalfa would be plagued by such a thing as weeds, but we are. And you'll see that Alfalfans have an interesting variety of ways of keeping them in their place.

Take Ruth Klimowicz who lives on Diefenbaker Drive. She appears to have been deploying a take-no-prisoners approach against weeds earlier this week: neighbours of hers say they saw Ruth down on her hands and knees on Tuesday prying up dandelions out of her lawn with a crowbar. Imagine, a 41 year old woman attacking unarmed dandelions with her husband's crowbar. But as I said, Alfalfa is a hardy town, even the weeds are unusually robust–maybe years of being sprayed with weed killer is slowly turning them into giant mutant killer dandelions that will one day take over western civilization. In any case, it takes more than being threatened with a measly crowbar for them to back down.

Heloise Updegraff, who reports on town events every week in *The Sentinel-Star*, mentioned in her column back in May that right after the weather turned nice and people all over town were spring cleaning their yards, she noticed a lady out on her front lawn with a large ShopVac. She was vacuuming her lawn. Heloise told her neighbour the woman must be Dutch. Heloise's neighbour seemed to think vacuuming the grass was a good idea, however, and has asked to borrow the extension cords to Heloise's husband's electric lawnmower.

Mildred Wilson over on Chretien Crescent, a newer part of town, grows one of the showier perennial gardens you'll find in Alfalfa. She's a widow, still only in her sixties as near as any of us can guess, and since she no longer has her husband Alistair to sap her energy she's able to spend much of the summer in her garden. The arthritis in her knees has been acting up a bit lately, so she doesn't get down on her hands and knees anymore, she uses hoe and rake rather than a trowel now. Her hearing isn't what it used to be either, and it bothered Mildred that she couldn't always hear the phone ringing from outside–she's the kind of woman who's never met a phone she didn't like, she'd pick one up in a phone booth if she happened to be passing by and it was ringing, afraid she might miss some important news. Her children last week bought the perfect gift for her: a cordless phone. Mildred manages to keep it with her now wherever she's working outside.

She'd been battling weeds in her perennial garden along the back fence a good hour or more last Wednesday when Catherine Penney, a close friend of hers in town, dropped by. "How about us two old Presbyterian fossils having a coffee?" Catherine said.

"Have a seat in that lawn chair while I finish weeding these lupins," Mildred told her, "then I'll throw this stuff in the wheelbarrow with the rest of the compost and we'll have coffee out here. It's too nice a day to sit inside."

Mildred was done a minute later and started bringing the hoes and rakes away. Catherine watched her rummaging around in the garden shed when she was startled out of her Presbyterian wits by a loud jangle coming from the pile of weeds in the wheelbarrow right beside her. She almost crashed through the lawn chair on her way down.

"Mildred!" she shrieked, "come here, your compost is ringing!"

~~~~

Besides their gardens, lawns are also important to Alfalfans. Lawns are not merely ground cover, nor a convenient place for your neighbour's rottweiler to leave its calling card; here in Alfalfa lawns are an indication of your moral fibre. Neglect your lawn and next thing you know you'll be cheating on your income tax or sneaking out of town to rent adult movies. Beautiful lawns don't just happen, they take blood, sweat, and bone meal. Aerating, fertilizing, sprinkling, mowing–Alfalfans are expected to do their part. Let your lawn go to pot and townspeople drive by slowly and look sideways at your house as though you've just been charged with embezzling your church's funds.

Hilbert TeBrake went back to Hardy Hardware for several bags of Weed 'n Feed on Monday, thought his lawn was starting to look a little–well, pooped. The weather's been dry, nothing but hot sun for three weeks now–good for growing cauliflower if you water and fertilize them just right, but it also means that plantain and dandelion and creeping jenny have started to show in Hilbert's lawn, and here it was still only early July, the grass already turning brown and just not growing the way Hilbert likes.

Hilbert drives a new 18-horse John Deere riding mower; it's his pride and joy, what a Harley is to a biker. Hilbert finds himself wondering if there'll be grass in heaven–if he could, he'd have his mower shipped in a crate to take along with him when he goes so that he could be the one responsible for mowing the grounds. When he's not been on the mower for two weeks he tends to trade his usual scowl for something even worse, and now it wasn't even the height of summer yet, when he'd be lucky if he got to ride his mower at all. He'd spread a mixture of potassium and nitrogen earlier in the spring, but now it had worn off. What his lawn needed was a little boost.

Hilbert's been feeling as if a little potassium and nitrogen would do him some good as well. Part of it is because of the strain he's been under with Earl Prior winning the giant cauliflower championship the last two years–Hilbert's starting to wonder whether he's losing his touch. Who does Earl Prior think he is–cauliflower is practically the Dutch national vegetable! Let Earl Prior stick to kohlrabi or whatever they grow wherever it is he comes from.

Hilbert's got a row of cauliflower growing out back now, though, that he knows any one of will win him back the title. He's been giving them his own special recipe of fertilizer which nobody knows about, not even the omniscient narrator of this tale, otherwise he would certainly tell you–would anyone stop himself from improving the human condition by holding back the secret of twelve-inch cauliflower heads? Hilbert's been giving extraordinary care to those cauliflower of his, let me tell you; his reputation is at stake here, and no one, not even his grandchildren–especially his grandchildren–come near them.

If worrying about his cauliflower weren't enough, Hilbert's not been sleeping well; he's been waking up three or four times every night feeling as if someone's stabbed his bladder with a barbecue fork, then when he gets up to drain the old radiator all he produces is a *phhhht!* and a trickle that wouldn't keep an Alfalfa dandelion alive. Hilbert's fifty-six, he knows at that age it's his prostate; he's been reading article after article about it lately, it seems, in the newspaper.

So far he hasn't mentioned anything about it to Dorothy. But then, it's not as if he's had to; every time he gets up during the night Dorothy gets another purple bruise on an arm or a leg. She's suggested he go to see the doctor–between Hilbert's leaky bladder and his loud snoring, Dorothy's about ready for a good night's sleep, but Hilbert tells her he should just cut down on the coffee at night.

An hour later, when Hilbert had fertilized about half of his front lawn and was thinking that maybe Dorothy was right about him seeing a doctor, he noticed that the fertilizer in the spreader was disappearing rather rapidly. Usually a bag lasts him until he's completed the front lawn plus the grass on the west side of the house, but now he already noticed the little doohickey swirling the fertilizer in the bottom of the spreader. Then the scowl that is Hilbert's natural expression broke out: he remembered suddenly he'd washed out the spreader with the hose after he used it last, opening it up to flush out the last granules of fertilizer. He'd been so busy thinking about cauliflower and about his prostate blowing a gasket he'd forgotten to reset the spreader at the proper rate of delivery.

Hilbert knew immediately he had done something very, very asinine–and also something very, very visible to the neighbours, including Earl Prior across the street. Hilbert thought for a moment it would be best if he just took two or three sticks of dynamite and blew up the lawn, and himself with it. Instead, he turned on the sprinkler and soaked his lawn a good three hours, hoping the fertilizer would wash away.

A lot of cars have been driving by Hilbert's house on Laurier Lane this past week, at least it seems so to Hilbert. People crane their necks as they drive slowly by, wondering why Hilbert TeBrake would be rototilling his front lawn as if it were a vegetable garden. They especially wonder why on earth he would be rototilling his lawn under cover of darkness, the only light coming from a flashlight he was shining ahead of him. His lawn must have become infested by grubs or something, they figure. It happens, when a fellow neglects his lawn. If they didn't know him better it wouldn't surprise them if he was the kind of guy who voted New Democrat or went around referring to God as our Mother in heaven.

~~~~

Rev. John DeHeer is the pastor at First Christian Reformed. There's no Second Christian Reformed Church here in Alfalfa, which is unusual, because Dutch Reformed people tend to hold their opinions rather vigorously, theological opinions particularly, and it is sometimes said that where you've got six Dutchmen there'll be at least four churches. In any case, back in '52 when First Church was established, its founders had thought the town would more or less be settled and taken over by Dutch folks, so no doubt they wanted to stake their claim to having been there first. Their dream never materialized, and they discovered instead that they would have to get along with Presbyterians and Pentecostals and Baptists and Roman Catholics and other dubious neighbours.

John DeHeer and his wife Dorothy grow one of the larger vegetable gardens you'll find here in Alfalfa. They have to, on the salary First CRC pays their pastor. Besides, they have three older teenagers, hulking guys all three of them, so John and Dorothy count on having to grow enough every summer to feed the five thousand. John figures that whatever they grow they save on their grocery bill–he calculates the saving pays for their vacation at Kilbear every summer. Dorothy's mental picture of their guys, who she feels sometimes act more like neanderthals than human beings, is of them squatting around a fire chomping on a hunk of roasted razorback hog, and she's surprised they'll eat vegetables at all.

It's Dorothy rather than John who does most of the work in their garden; after all, being a minister John does have a lot of evening meetings, even during the summer. But you'd think that when you're already slaving over a kitchen stove in the heat of summer (no central air in this parsonage) blanching corn and beans and cauliflower, someone in the family would say, "Ah no, mom, you already do all the canning and freezing, let us do the hoeing and weeding"– fat chance–but Dorothy actually enjoys this outdoors part of it. It's not easy being a pastor's wife, particularly in a small town, and she enjoys being out in the garden, especially early in the day when the mourning doves are still out. Besides, having to live with four males, it's cheaper than seeing a therapist. And the veggies taste so good.

So it sure was a shame then, a number of weeks later, that John and Dorothy had to fly back to Vancouver for a surprise wedding of Dorothy's youngest sister. She'd held out on marrying until she met Mr. Right, then finally found him while vacationing out west two years ago. Wouldn't you know it, John thought, just when fares are highest. Perhaps he could get a deal from Virginia Wiebinga at the travel agency.

"What are we gonna do with all the stuff in the garden," Dorothy said, "broccoli, cauliflower, cucumber–everything's just getting ready." But what are you going to do when your sister is getting married in Vancouver, tell them to put the wedding on ice for two weeks while you finish freezing your cauliflower and canning your cucumber relish and then you'll be right over? Of course they would fly out.

"That's unfortunate," John said, "here we've worked by the sweat of our brow and now we can't enjoy the fruit of all our labour."

Dorothy looked at him, wondering whether he'd been working with the King James Version lately, but she didn't say anything. Sometimes allowing your husband to feel like a martyr is a bigger victory than winning an argument. But what *were* they going to do with the veggies in the garden? No way their guys were going to pick and freeze them. They'd be lucky to have the parsonage still standing when they got back. They should call someone in their congregation. "It's the Christian thing to do," Dorothy told John. "I know, I'll call Audrey and Walter Nibbelink. They're somewhat new in town, probably haven't had a chance to plant a garden. I'm sure they'd love to have the vegetables."

"Sure is a shame, though," John said, shaking his head. He looked as if he had just chaired a difficult Council meeting.

Turned out Virginia was able to get them a good deal on a flight, a charter that had had a cancellation; the only thing was it left early next morning. John managed on short notice to get his Council's approval for Rev. Adrian Verseput, retired and living in the city, to preach the next two Sundays–no sense travelling all that distance without staying a while. Dorothy tried reaching Audrey Nibbelink all that day between packing and taking care of a thousand other last minute details. Fortunately the Nibbelinks had an answering machine, and Dorothy was able to leave a hasty message: "Audrey, this is Dorothy. We've had to leave for Vancouver rather suddenly. There's lots of vegetables ready to go in our garden, make sure you and Walter help yourselves to as many as you'd like. See you in a couple weeks. Bye."

~~~~

Hilbert's prostate was acting up bad that night, it must have been all the stress of the past week. He got up for a second time to relieve himself about three in the morning, the darkest time of night. Strange things happen at that hour–a man doubts himself without even being awake enough to think about it at three in the morning; he questions the innate goodness of humankind, he even suspects, sometimes, that the whole idea of God is just a hoax and that we have all evolved from the primordial slime and ooze. That's the power of darkness on a man at three in the morning, especially if his bladder's dripping like a leaking faucet.

Hilbert shuffled to the bathroom in the dark, his right hand sliding along the wall to guide him. He doesn't stand up as most of the male species do in the bathroom when he goes, not during the night. For one thing, he could lose his balance in the dark and split his skull open on the bathtub's hard metal edge; for another he might not hit the target, since he's awake enough to feel the call of nature but not awake enough for him to see whether he's watering the right flowerbed, which Dorothy let him know about in no uncertain terms the last several times it happened, so in order to save his marriage he sits down. But it does violate his sense of manhood, therefore it's a good thing he's still only half awake.

That's why Hilbert doesn't turn on any lights when he gets up, they just wake him up so that he has a harder time falling back asleep, and Hilbert doesn't handle sleeplessness very well. There are people who use sleeplessness productively, people who solve problems like whether Thomas Malthus' theory on population was right or not, or who recite to themselves great literary classics like Robert Service's *The Cremation of Sam McGee* while they can't sleep, but Hilbert isn't one of them; he's plagued by demons at night and the less he's awake the less they trouble him.

This particular night he must have been less awake than usual, for on his return trip from pouring the tea, the hallway dark and Hilbert groggy with sleep, he misjudged the proper flight path through the bedroom door by about six inches, which put the left doorpost directly in line with his left eye when they met. He was called back to sudden wakefulness. He spun around with the pain, and was so angry with himself he raised his right fist and struck out at what he thought would be thin air. Instead, he put his fist through a framed photograph of himself and Dorothy that Robert Meyer took eight years ago on the occasion of their twenty-fifth anniversary.

When Dorothy suggested later that morning (after they'd come back from Emergency where Hilbert was given twenty-four stitches) that Hilbert hadn't been his usual self lately and that the two of them should get out for a day together, perhaps a picnic lunch with just the two of them, it seemed such a good idea Hilbert was surprised he hadn't thought of it himself. With all that gauze swathing his hand, he wasn't going to be doing any plumbing anyway. He knew the location Dorothy had in mind.

Hilbert and Dorothy have a special place where they go for picnic lunches. Only about a half hour's drive from where they live Hilbert has discovered a little-travelled county road that crosses a four-lane freeway. Hilbert and Dorothy take their favourite Hardy Hardware yellow lawn chairs, pack a lunch of tuna salad sandwiches and a thermos of coffee, and plunk themselves down at the edge of the road in the middle of the overpass. Dorothy likes the view, the way she can see for miles down the highway in both directions, and Hilbert enjoys it every time a transport truck rumbles by underneath and the whole overpass vibrates. It's their own little spot; no one else knows about it, and they go there whenever they need to regain their sanity. Hilbert must have needed the day out. After an hour on the overpass he took Dorothy for a particularly long drive, then treated her to a fancy supper at a highway truck stop.

~~~~

Walter Nibbelink was the one who had heard the message on the answering machine the previous evening, Audrey had gone to a Toronto Airport Fellowship meeting with a friend and hadn't gotten home until well after midnight. The message from Dorothy was one of three or four on their machine, and Walter was scrupulous to write all of them down–he'd screwed up once or twice before with messages for Audrey, no way he was going to try for three.

"Isn't that nice of Dorothy and Hilbert to offer us their vegetables," Audrey said next morning when Walter told her about the offer, "that's just like them. They're so generous." Dorothy TeBrake had been the first person at First Christian Reformed to invite them over for coffee after the morning service. "We should go there tonight maybe," Audrey said, "do the picking after you come home from work and then see if we can do some freezing tonight already. I wonder why Hilbert and Dorothy had to go to Vancouver so quick, though. I hope it wasn't a death in the family."

"Usually is," Walter said, "when people have to leave so suddenly. Remind us to send a condolence card."

That afternoon they picked up several carton boxes from Art's Mart, filled them with grocery bags to put the vegetables in, and drove to Hilbert and Dorothy's. As expected, there was no car on the driveway and it didn't look as if anyone was home. Just a floor lamp on in the living room to make it look as if the owners weren't away for two weeks. Trust Hilbert to think of that.

Walter and Audrey walked round the house to the garden in the back and were astounded by all the vegetables ready to be picked–beans, broccoli, cucumber, zucchini, enough to keep them freezing veggies a number of evenings. "We shouldn't be hogs, though," Audrey said, "they'll be back in a week or two, so we should pick just the really ripe ones."

"I can't believe these cauliflower," Walter gushed, "I've never seen them so big–they must be twelve inches across!"

They started picking, Audrey attacking the zucchini first and Walter, armed with their kitchen knife, cutting broccoli and cauliflower. They felt as if they'd won a fill-as-much-of-your-grocery-cart-in-sixty-seconds contest, except here it took them a good hour to fill the carton boxes and grocery bags. The sun was still warm with the late afternoon heat, and they stopped every now and then to wipe the sweat out of their eyes.

The vegetables filled the trunk and most of the back seat when they were done. "We should leave them a thank you note," Audrey said.

"I wouldn't," Walter cautioned, "you never know who might see it. They'd know the occupants are away. They could back a truck up to the house and next thing you know Hilbert and Dorothy come home two weeks from now and discover all their furniture's been taken. Nothing left but the walls."

"But Walter, this is Alfalfa. There's people here who go on vacation and don't even lock their doors. That's the kind of town this is."

"I wouldn't be too sure," Walter said, "stranger things have happened."

~~~~

Hilbert and Dorothy had such a good time they didn't come home until just before dark. Hilbert steered their Concord onto the driveway, then stopped and got out to open the garage door. It was a heavy, wooden door–one of these days, Hilbert knew, he was going to give himself a hernia lifting that thing. They were tired, but happy; they'd had a good day together. "You go ahead inside, I'll put the lawn chairs away," Hilbert said, feeling magnanimous while holding the car door open for Dorothy to grab the bulky cooler containing the remains of their picnic lunch. "I'll be there in a minute," he said.

He stood and watched the minty green shoots of the newly sprouted grass of their front lawn. Perhaps life wasn't so bad after all. He would take a quick look yet at the garden out back, then join Dorothy inside. He felt for some reason that tonight his prostate would behave and that he would sleep better than he had in a long, long time.

Are we paying higher gas prices in Alfalfa?

Dear editor,

The Mrs. and me were to eastern Ontario last week and found a wide variation in gasoline prices along the way, as follows; lowest we saw was in Toronto, at 54.9 cents per litre, other towns, even neighbouring ones were at 56.5 to 59.5. Past years prices in Alfalfa have been around the 60.5 mark, and increase even higher on holiday weekends, have you noticed? I wonder about the coincidence!

As you can see, gasoline has averaged about 3 cents more here in Alfalfa. Doing the arithmetic, your car probably holds about the average 60 litres, making the difference $1.80 per tank. Now that does not seem like a lot but over a year it comes to more than $20, and who would not want an extra 20 loonies in their pocket?!

Now, I know that Alfalfa is not the capitol of the universe, but if our local merchants expect us to patronize them, should we be penalized for doing so?

Edward Hopp
R.R. 3

- *letter in* The Alfalfa Sentinel-Star

PEEPING TOM

It didn't take long for folks in town to hear that Betty Murphy saw a peeping Tom Tuesday night in Vern and Nancy Winkel's yard over on Borden Boulevard. The Murphys' house sits back just a bit from Vern and Nancy's, giving them a good view of the Winkels' back yard, and Betty happened to step into her corner bedroom about eleven at night, she said, just about to flip on the lights when she saw someone crouching in the grass of the Winkels' back yard, slowly moving toward the house, then standing up to look right into Vern and Nancy's bedroom.

Needless to say, Nancy's nerves have been a bit on edge since then; after all, no one likes to be spied on in their bedroom in full naked glory, especially when they're thirty-seven and about the same number of pounds overweight, as Nancy is. Other people who heard about it are uneasy as well. A peeping Tom? they say, here in Alfalfa? Vern says that if he ever gets hold of the creep he won't hold himself responsible for what he does to him. Vern drives a cement truck, stands 6' 3", and is a no-nonsense sort of guy.

Next day Vern checks the ground outside the bedroom window with Sergeant Lofthouse of the Alfalfa detachment of the O.P.P., looking for footprints in the flower bed. They find nothing.

"That's strange," Sergeant Lofthouse says, "with this soft soil you'd think you'd at least see some footprints."

"Are you sure Betty saw someone?" Vern asks. He knows she and Fred like to have one or two before hitting the hay and he's not at all sure

Betty might not have had one more than usual and possibly been seeing things. "No reason for her to make up something like that," Sgt. Lofthouse says. Vern doesn't want to press the issue, because generally they and the Murphys get along pretty well.

Better than with Dennis and Millie Cruikshank, who live around the corner. The problem is the Cruikshanks' dog. Dennis and Millie have only a narrow strip of grass for a back yard, so small that it hardly leaves enough room for their dog, an ugly grey terrier, to do its daily squats so that whenever Dennis lets it go out, the mutt insists on crossing onto Vern and Nancy's yard instead, keeping Vern busy flinging the souvenirs back onto the Cruikshanks' yard with a red plastic beach shovel from their daughter Amy's sandbox. If they didn't live here in Alfalfa where nobody bothers with fences Vern would have been tempted to build one.

Another thing: Dennis Cruikshank is a boater. On his driveway sits a sixteen foot white fiberglass runabout powered by a 90-horse jet-black Mercury which he takes out on the small lake just north of here every Sunday afternoon. Every Sunday morning Vern drives by with Nancy and the kids on their way to First CRC and every Sunday morning Vern breaks the commandment not to covet anything that is thy neighbour's. Dennis has invited Vern several times to come with him, and Vern finally gave in to the temptation one Sunday afternoon, thus breaking his church's commandment to keep the Sabbath day holy as well. All day they sat on the water, Dennis Cruikshank pulling in perch and bass, Vern having a hard time catching anything but bullheads. He knew it was because he was fishing on Sunday but he blamed it on the bait: Cruikshank had been too cheap to buy minnows, so they fished all day with scrawny worms. Behind the fancy boat and all, Vern thought, Dennis Cruikshank was nothing more than a small-time, two-bit fisherman. Vern would have to take him up north sometime where he and Nancy rent a cottage, and show Cruikshank some real fishing.

The day after Betty saw the peeping Tom, Vern comes home from work and finds his boys Mark and Kenny stretching a piece of wire knee-high between two maples in the back yard. "Whatcha doin', guys?" he asks them.

"This here's a trap for the peeping Tom," Mark says. "When we spot him we chase him between these trees, see, and he trips over the wire. Then we jump him. We got a rope in the garage to tie him up."

Vern comes close then to breaking the commandment not to take the Lord's name in vain as well. He orders the boys to take down the wire.

38

From the house comes Nancy's voice calling them in for supper.

"Can we hurry?" Amy, who's seven, asks at the table, "I've got play practice at 6:30."

"What do you gotta practise for," Mark says, "all you are is a tree. How can you practise bein' a tree?"

"That's more than I can say for you, chicken. You didn't even dare try out. I'd rather be a tree than a chicken," and she begins to flap her arms as wings and make exaggerated chicken sounds.

"That's enough, kids," Vern says, "eat your cauliflower."

"Hey Dad," Kenny says, "The Cruikshanks' dog had puppies, can we get one? Mr Cruikshank says they only cost twenty dollars."

"Twenty dollars? What does he think they are, thoroughbreds? Besides, that's the last thing we need right now, is a dog."

"Aw Dad, me and Mark read all about training one. Took books out of the library and everything. You wanna know how to train him to pee on the paper?"

"Listen, we're not getting any dog. We're going on holidays in about a month–what are we going to do with him all that time?"

"Danny Stob could keep him while we're gone."

"Well, let Danny get the dog then."

"Besides, Dad, he'd make a good watchdog. That way we wouldn't be bothered by the peeping Tom anymore."

Vern has about heard enough of the peeping Tom. What he won't do if he ever gets his hands on him.

He prowls the house most of that evening, then tries reading the paper, but his mind wanders. He turns on the TV to channel surf a while, but doesn't find anything that interests him. He gets up frequently and walks to windows, peering from a crack in the curtains, which he and Nancy now keep closed evenings. At ten-thirty he suggests to Nancy they go to bed, which is half an hour earlier than usual, and when Nancy goes into the bedroom he tells her to go ahead, he'll be right there. He turns off all the lights in the house so that the only one burning will be the one in their bedroom, then he walks back to the TV room and stares into the back yard from the dark window. He stands there ten minutes, but sees nothing. Finally Nancy, wrapped in her housecoat, peers into the room.

"Are you in here, Vern? What are you doing?"

"Just checking."

They go to bed and Vern lies in the dark wide awake a long time. When he hears Nancy's breathing become louder with sleep he tiptoes to the boys' bedroom, takes the baseball bat out of their closet, and places it in the hallway by the back door. Back in bed, he finally falls into a fitful sleep. In his dreams he sees newspaper headlines announcing the murder of a small-town family of five by a sex maniac.

Of course the peeping Tom is the main topic of conversation that Saturday evening when Vern and Nancy go to Ed and Joan Van Duzen's place for coffee along with two other couples. By the second cup Joan asks who would like a touch of liqueur and whipped cream in their coffee and everyone says that that sounds like a swell idea. The amazing thing they discover soon after is that just about every one of them has had an experience sometime, somewhere, with a peeping Tom.

"Ours happened on our honeymoon," Al Rozema says, looking to his wife Arlene as though asking her permission to tell the story. She nods, wide-eyed, and the look in both their eyes is as if they're experiencing the wonder of their honeymoon all over again. "We were staying in one of those little country motels up north," Al says. "Arlene and I are in the bathroom, I won't say what we were doing at the moment, when all of a sudden I see Arlene's face freeze up and she lets out a scream."

Arlene bows her head into her hands with embarrassment.

"I turn around, and there's a guy's face, right in the window. You know what I did? First reaction I had was to punch him, and that's what I did. Put my fist right through the window! See the scar still, right here along my thumb?" and he holds his hand out for everyone to see. "Funny thing is, the peeping Tom turned out to be the owner's twenty-two year old son. He kept all the bathroom windows open a crack and had an apple crate which he moved from window to window behind the motel."

"What did they do after they caught him?"

"Nothing! His father just gave him a bit of a scolding. He's probably still getting his jollies spying on honeymoon couples at the same motel."

"Bull toot!" Ed Van Duzen says, "the father was probably in on it."

"The worst part," Arlene Rozema says, "is the anger you feel that your privacy's been violated."

"That's just it," Nancy Winkel says, grateful that someone has understood. She brings her hand to her cheek. "Just the thought that you're being looked at," then she shudders her shoulders as if she might be a randy stripper.

Not that Vern Winkel notices. He drains his coffee cup, sets it back down, and says, "Well, if this guy comes around again, I won't be askin' questions first, I tell ya."

"You shouldn't think of it that way," says Ann Plakmeyer, who has been to university and has taken a course in social deviance. "Actually, the last thing peeping Toms are is dangerous. They're more frightened than you are."

"Thanks for the consolation," Vern says. "Wait till you have one, then see what you'd say."

"That's just it, we did," Andy Plakmeyer says, coming to his wife's defence. "Happened while we were still living in Simcoe. This kid stood on the air conditioning unit outside our bathroom window so he could peek over the frosted bottom part. They didn't do anything with him either, because it turned out he was a neighbourhood kid who's got space for rent in his penthouse, know what I mean?"

"Andy, that's not a nice thing to say," his wife says, frowning.

Maybe it's having to relive the unpleasant experience, or maybe it's drinking a second cup of coffee enriched with liqueur, but Nancy Winkel needs a bathroom. She deliberates a moment. She should not have chosen this chair; it's a deep one, and to extricate herself from it will take some effort. Perhaps she can hold the fort a bit longer, she tells herself. She waits several minutes more while Ed Van Duzen tells his peeping Tom story, then she realizes she will have to go, and soon. "Would you excuse me?" she says, and struggles out of her chair. Joan Van Duzen whispers where the bathroom is. Nancy hears her nylons swish against each other as she walks through the room.

She reaches the bathroom and turns the doorknob, but it will not move. She tries again. Still locked. She looks up and down the hall, then places her cheek against the bathroom door. "Who's in there?" she sings softly.

"It's me," a child's voice says, "go away."

Nancy looks back toward the living room, afraid everyone has heard. Now what? She feels a stab in her abdomen, and knows she has only so much time. There has to be another bathroom, somewhere. Upstairs, she tells herself, there must be one upstairs.

Every stair tread creaks as she goes up, which is odd because it's a new house, and she is sure she will hear Joan Van Duzen's voice any moment, asking where she's going. But she makes it to the top, breathing heavily from the climb. Now to find that bathroom.

She walks quickly down the hall, checking each door she thinks might lead into a bathroom, but finding only bedrooms. Who on earth would design a house without an upstairs bathroom? Then she has just one door left to check, which she knows can only be the master bedroom. She's reluctant to peek inside but knows she has to.

It's the master bedroom. Now what?

Then she realizes something. If there's no general bathroom upstairs the Van Duzens have to have an en suite off their master bedroom, but as soon as her mind makes the deduction she knows she can not go in there. Peeking in is one thing, but to actually walk right in and use a couple's private bathroom is something else.

Should she go downstairs and try again there? But what if the child is not finished? She will have to come all the way back upstairs in front of everyone, and that's out of the question.

Perhaps it's the liqueur on an empty stomach that makes her brave or perhaps it's simply need, but Nancy opens the bedroom door and strides right in. With relief she sees the bedroom indeed has an en suite.

She seats herself on the toilet and tries to respect the Van Duzens' privacy by not peeking at their personal things she knows will be on the counter if Ed and Joan are like any other married couple: the hair gel, Joan's makeup, the toothbrushes and crumpled tube of toothpaste, the birth control pills, the jar of Vaseline and who knows what else, yet she cannot overcome the feeling of intruding on the Van Duzens' private space, as if she were a peep–

The realization comes to her with a shock.

She would have gotten up quickly and left the bathroom if it wasn't for what happened next. She's still sitting, thinking that when she flushes the toilet it'll be heard all the way downstairs, then telling herself, well, so be it, when she hears a slight creaking sound to her left, then catches a movement out of the corner of her eye. It's the door of the vanity cabinet right beside her left leg, beginning to open slowly! Nancy sits up straight on the toilet, her breath stuck in her throat. She watches the door slowly open, and she presses her knees together, her right hand slowly moving toward her panties stretched taut as a drum between her knees. Her heart is doing a beat double time inside her chest. Her hand stops at her knees, paralysed. The cabinet door opens another inch, then stops.

Moving from behind the vanity door is a huge cat. Pure black it is, stepping smoothly and oh so slowly over the floor's ceramic white tiles, until it reaches the closed bathroom door and sits. It looks at Nancy with large green eyes, waiting for her to open the door.

Nancy returns its stare, as if to make sure it's looking only into her face and nowhere else. When the cat finally turns its stare away from her she reaches down, pulls up her panties while bending forward as much as possible, and stands. She brushes the front of her dress, all the while looking at the cat. It sits looking up at the door handle. Nancy peeks into the vanity and on the floor inside lies a rumpled pink bathrobe, covered with black cat hair. She walks over and gives the cat a soft caress between its ears, the cat raising itself to rub its head against her hand. Then Nancy opens the door and the cat scoots out.

Later, on the drive home from the Van Duzens', Vern is surprised to hear Nancy say, "You know, I think Ann Plakmeyer may be right; peeping Toms probably aren't dangerous at all. Anyway, in my heart I've forgiven him." Vern glances at her and sees a look spread softly across her face, one he has never seen on her before, peaceful and mysterious.

They've been in bed maybe fifteen minutes after coming home that night, Vern's snoring already in fifth gear, when the phone rings, and both of them sit up with a start. They look at each other, Nancy irritated that Vern still hasn't turned down the volume of the phone right beside their bed, Vern wondering who might be calling at this hour–this late at night it's sure to be bad news.

He picks up the phone.

"It's him," he hears a woman's voice hiss, "Vern, it's him again!" then he recognizes Betty Murphy's voice from next door: "It's him again on your back lawn!"

Vern flings back the blanket and pulls on his jeans and shoes by the bed. "Stay here," he whispers to Nancy. He runs to the hallway by the back door, grabs the baseball bat, and runs to the front door.

He'll have the best chance to surprise the peeping Tom by going around the front of the house, he thinks, then jumping him from around the corner. He circles the house, tiptoeing through the grass, reaches the far corner, and peers around.

He sees someone crouched low in the grass about fifteen feet from their bedroom window, only his back visible. Vern creeps a few steps forward, hands gripping the handle of the baseball bat. He feels a strange sense of power over the figure bent in the grass and for a few seconds waits, like a cat letting a bird momentarily escape. When he's five feet away and just about to pounce, however, the peeping Tom makes a sudden motion as though he has heard Vern and is scrambling to get away.

Something–it could only have been grace–prevents Vern from swinging the bat. Or perhaps it's the flashlight the peeping Tom shines down into the grass, which Vern had not expected, or the tin can sitting in the grass illuminated by the beam of the flashlight. Or perhaps it's something familiar about whoever it is squatting in the moonlight that makes Vern hesitate, for he thinks suddenly that he recognizes the silhouette.

"Dennis, is that you?" he asks.

"Huh!" the figure exclaims in fright, then turns. "Vern? You scared the bejabbers outa me!" He holds his hand to his chest.

"Dennis, what are you doing?"

Dennis Cruikshank takes a second to catch his breath. "Well, thought I'd do some fishing tomorrow, and I figured you wouldn't mind if I, uh, borrowed some of your dew worms. With the rain we had earlier today you should see how many there are." He pauses. "Hope you don't mind."

Vern holds the bat behind his back, hoping Dennis will not notice it in the dark. "Shoot, no, help yourself."

They stand silent a moment then, two neighbours on a moon-lit lawn at 12:30 in the morning with nothing to do but talk, but unable to do so because each feels flooded by a wave of relief, one because he has been frightened close to a heart attack by what turned out to be not a monster of the night but only a neighbour, the other because he has just come within a hairbreadth of breaking the commandment not to kill and has been miraculously spared.

Finally Dennis says, "Feel like coming fishing tomorrow, Vern?"

"Na, tomorrow's Sunday, Dennis. You know us."

"That's right, I forgot. Well, maybe next Saturday then."

"Sure, that would be nice. Give me a call." He turns toward the house. "Anyway, good fishing. Hope you land a big one."

"Thanks. If I do I'll bring you some."

Vern walks back toward the house and thinks of his kids sleeping safely inside. He looks up and sees a spangle of stars in the vastness of space high overhead and through the thin branches of the willow a full moon that drenches the roof of his house and lawn with a sheen of silvery light, and then he is struck by his own smallness. He thinks how strange it is that other people are rarely as evil as we think them, while a good person like himself is capable even of murder, and then he asks a prayer of forgiveness. He looks toward the house and sees a bright sliver of light shining from the crack between the curtains of the bedroom where Nancy lies in a warm bed, waiting for him.

The word on the street

"I don't know, I wouldn't feel comfortable with my wife doing it. I think certain things are just better left to the imagination."

-Frank Atherton, 32

* * *

"I'm all in favour of it, why not, I'm a bachelor. Grin and bare it is my motto."

-Leo Papple, 63

* * *

"I think it's terrible. Legalized abortion, government sponsored gambling, now this. What's this country coming to?"

-Ann Van Berkel, 48

* * *

"Hey, I backpacked in Europe last summer and there's nothing I haven't seen. Why not here? I had a great time."

-Joey Shurtleff, 21

* * *

"Do we really want our children to be exposed to this right in our own streets?"

-Julia O'Keefe, 59

-person on the street responses to the question, "What is your opinion of the new law allowing women to go topless in public?" in The Alfalfa Sentinel-Star

TAKE MY SILVER AND MY GOLD

If you were to drop in at Melvin's Barber Shop where some of Melvin's regular customers form a think tank now and then to work at solving the world's big problems, like what to do about international terrorists (dropping the atom bomb on 'em would be a start), and if you were to ask them which people here in Alfalfa they would consider rich–not just comfortable, or fairly well-to-do, but out-and-out filthy rich–well, make sure you're not a stranger, first; they'd give you a look that would send you scuttling back to wherever it was you came from pretty quick. People here don't exactly appreciate strangers coming around and asking such a question. They'll figure you're a kidnapper looking for prey. That, or a lawyer.

You could be here casing the town to set up competition for Howard McDivitt, who practises law in town and serves as mayor. Even though Howard's a lawyer people don't think of him as slimy, otherwise they wouldn't keep re-electing him mayor. But they wouldn't consider him well-heeled either, not when he could move to the city and join the corporate and criminal lawyers there with their 30-foot cabin cruisers and 40-foot RVs and 50-foot heated indoor swimming pools–you don't exactly hit the gravy train drawing up wills or notarizing passport applications in a small town. While Howard does have one of the statelier old homes in town, it's not what people would call opulent.

Other people might name Doc Summerall maybe, but he's a doctor; doctors are supposed to be well off. It's a compensation they deserve for spending their days treating people's backaches, bunions, and boils.

Besides, when kidney stones have you doubled over and screaming with pain, would you want advice from some plumber in coveralls carrying a hacksaw? After all, we're not talking copper pipes here–doctors deal with our bodies, so we prefer them to look prosperous. Their wealth ensures our health. So we're willing to put up with doctors who look suntanned and can smile in January when the rest of us feel grouchy and look as pasty as bread flour. Doc Summerall's place out in the country may be professionally landscaped and may have a long curving drive made of interlocking red brick, but it's not as if his property has a stone wall and wrought iron gates guarded by Doberman pinschers or anything.

Still, there are several Alfalfans whose recent experience gives them reason to look forward to a modicum of affluence.

~~~~

Casper Blokkedoos felt flattered some months ago that he was among a small group of men approached about a once-in-a-lifetime investment opportunity when there were shrewd people around with *real* money. Casper is retired now; for thirty-two years he ran a Dutch import store in the city, then moved to Alfalfa several years ago to get away from everything: traffic and smelly air, the threat of burglaries and muggings. He sees the smash and grab robberies on television programs like *COPS*, and reads about gas station and convenience store holdups in the papers–he figured he'd been lucky he hadn't been hit, some young punk in spike haircut and studded leather jacket brandishing a pistol and screaming, "You! Fatso! Give me all those silver spoons behind the glass! And I want those gold necklaces in that display case. Now put all your King peppermints in this bag–MOVE, or I'll blow your brains out!" and all Casper could say was, "Here, take the silver and gold, just don't shoot."

So when an offer to buy his store came along several years ago, Casper decided he'd sell even though he was just 60; that way he and Nell could still enjoy their retirement. His store had done rather well. Dutch people do like their Delft blue plates and pewter vases and fine delicacies such as horsemeat or smoked eel, so Casper is somewhat familiar with the complicated world of international trade. A man has to know what he's doing or he could lose a bundle. Still, while Casper got a bit of money when he sold the business, it wasn't nearly as much as he'd hoped given the lousy state of the economy, and he worries whether it's enough to pay for the charitable causes he'd like to support–that and the travelling he and Nell have planned.

Casper wonders what it would be like to win big in the lottery, which he wouldn't be so foolish as to play even if his church didn't frown on gambling, but he dreams of winning five million and then giving much of it to charities: he'd give a hundred thousand to cancer research (Nell's brother in Palmerston has just come down with lung cancer), he'd give two hundred thousand to his denomination's World Relief Committee what with the floods and droughts and earthquakes happening everywhere these days, he'd donate half a million towards a new sanctuary for First Christian Reformed, the church was built back in the early fifties and shows it, he'd give a couple hundred thou to each of his four children, and, and . . . . He and Nell would keep only a hundred thousand, maybe two, of the winnings, that's all they would need for the travelling they have planned.

Casper and Nell have been back to Holland, of course, four or five times in addition to the business trips Casper used to take there every other year or so, and they enjoy it whenever they go, but things there have changed–either that or he and Nell have. What strikes Casper is that his brothers who stayed in Holland have lost their *zip* or whatever: they live in comfortable state-owned apartments, receive nice pensions from the state, enjoy a state medical plan that pays their hospital bills, and can even die comfortably, if need be, through the state's enlightened euthanasia program. Just a little injection in the arm, and it's like falling asleep. What his brothers have lost, Casper feels, is their sense of enterprise, their personal initiative. They sit on their little cement balconies smoking their cigars and sipping their afternoon sherry–I don't know, Casper tells himself, there's got to be more to retirement than that, maybe I've become too North American.

He and Nell have visited other places in Europe, like Italy and Spain, and Nell would like to go to Greece, and France, which are OK with Casper–maybe they could start there, he thinks–but he has his mind set on slightly more unusual places that will satisfy his need for adventure–for risk, even, if you come right down to it. Places he reads about with glossy photographs in the *National Geographic*s that come to their house, exotic places where people wear strange costumes and practise strange rituals. Places like Nepal. Like Thailand, or Zambia. Now *there* would be places to visit.

~~~~

Bernie Biggs' good fortune started more recently, last week in fact. On Tuesday he stopped in at the lumber yard to pick up some pieces of pine for his wood carving hobby, then he dropped by the post office when he found a letter in his box with his name and address written on it in red ink. Bernie's not much of a letter writer; in fact, he and Denise don't even mail out Christmas cards with most of their family living right here in Alfalfa, so they tend not to get a lot of mail in return. About the only people kind enough to write them on a regular basis are the hydro and telephone and gas companies.

Driving home, Bernie is intrigued by the red ink on the envelope. There's no name of a sender anywhere, but he can tell by the smooth handwriting that it's done by a woman, and he's kind of leaning forward in the saddle at the thought of a woman writing him a letter in red ink. He wonders whether he should show the letter to Denise. Maybe later.

As soon as Denise leaves for Caroline Strick's surprise baby shower that evening Bernie sends their three kids outside to play, goes to the bathroom, locks it, sits down on the toilet lid, and opens the letter. "Dear Bernie," the letter begins. Bernie reads further:

> *My name is Angela Savelli, and I'm writting you this letter from my chaise lounge beside the swimming pool my husband and I bought from the earnings of Tony Bright's amazing money-making program which I am about to pass onto you. But first, let me tell you that every detail in this letter is absolutely true! Twelve months ago I received a letter just like the one you are reading right now. It seemed TOO GOOD TO BE TRUE! But, I decided I had nothing to loose, and followed the instructions. Twelve months later, my husband and I have paid off our mortgage, bought a cottage, plus the swimming pool I'm lounging beside at this moment. AND STILL THE MONEY KEEPS COMING IN! A few more years, and my husband and I hope to be financially independent.*

Bernie stops reading. He wonders what it would be like, at the age of 32, to be financially independent. The phrase has an almost magical ring to it: financially independent. Bernie asks himself what he would do with his time. Well, he could keep himself busy with his wood carving. He could carve his plaques and animals during the winter, then spend his summers going to country fairs and trade shows. He could carve himself a nice display sign in varnished pine: "BERNIE BIGGS ~ WOOD CARVINGS."

Then Bernie stops himself. There has to be a catch. Making so much money has to be more complicated than that–either that or the whole thing is illegal. That must be it. He imagines himself falling for the scheme and then being sent off to jail, leaving Denise and the kids to deal with the newspaper headlines and whatever else. I may not be a rocket scientist, he tells himself, but old Bernie wasn't born yesterday either. Still, he's curious to see what the rest of the letter has to say.

~~~~

Frankly, there are times Casper wonders whether he retired too early at the age of 60. He misses the hurly-burly of business, the adrenaline rush brought on by risk: at that price, can I sell fifteen dozen of those almond cookies before they go stale, or only ten dozen? If I place those Christmas candles on the front counter by the cash register, I bet I could sell half again as many. Maybe I should get a new supplier for soya sauce; with that dumb packaging on the brand I get, no wonder it's not moving. Important decisions like that, the sense of adventure they give, are what Casper misses.

So when he got a phone call last Monday from Vic Cargill, an old business acquaintance of his from the city, inviting him to a special meeting over lunch next day at the Silver Pines Golf and Country Club just south of the city to discuss a unique business opportunity Vic thought Casper might be interested in, Casper said he'd come. He felt the old entrepreneurial juices start flowing again; this sounded like the very kind of thing he had been missing, a little something on the side to make him excited about getting up in the morning again, something a bit more adventuresome than seeing his bonds and money market funds drop another seven or eight hundredths of a point.

He wondered what the opportunity was that Vic had for him. An inside tip on a stock, maybe. A can't-miss product about to hit the market but looking for someone to provide a little start-up capital, perhaps. In any case, what reassured him was that he has known Vic Cargill a long time; Vic belonged to Cedarvale Bible Church in the city, and served with Casper on the local board of the Christian Businessmen's Association. If there was one man on earth Casper could tell, "Here's $100,000, it's my life savings; I want you to invest it for me however you think best," Vic Cargill would be the man.

~~~~

Bernie's heart begins pounding harder in the bathroom the further he gets in the letter–all he has to do is send twenty dollars to the person whose name is at the top of the list (Angela Savelli), type his name on the line at the bottom, and wait for people to start sending him money. The more letters he sends out, of course, the more money he will receive. And the beautiful part of it, Angela says, is that it's all perfectly LEGAL! Well, that makes the whole thing quite different now, doesn't it, Bernie thinks. And what Bernie rather likes, not being much of a writer, is that Angela has even included a copy of the letter he can photocopy and send. Then Angela goes on to give testimonies of people from all over North America who were as skeptical as he undoubtedly is at this moment, but who nevertheless followed the instructions and are now reaping the rewards. He reads the first one:

If your like me, no doubt you are thinking that this must be a hare-brained idea, and your about to throw this letter into the garbage. But STOP! This letter, if you follow up on it, will change your life, as it did mine. I was unemployed, depressed, and ready to end it all when I recieved the letter that changed my life. Now, three years later, I own a brand-new Corvette, a state-of-the-art McIntosh computer, and a 48" television and home entertainment centre. Tony Bright's system worked for me, it can for you too–if you choose to sieze the moment.
<div style="text-align:right">Wendy Smith - Moose Jaw, Sask.</div>

Bernie reads the next letter:

Hi, my name is Cameron, and for years I've been looking for a means of suplementing my income. I was employed in lawn maintenance; and somehow I was always short of money. Then I received a letter introducing me to Tony Bright's system. Let me tell you what happened with me. Being skeptical, my initial mailing consisted of only five hundred letters. So you can imagine my surprise when it brought a return of $5000! My income this past year from Tony Bright's system was $75,000. Needless to say, I've given up my job in lawn maintenance. You can too!

Cameron Philips - Flagstaff, AZ

~~~~

Casper walked toward the clubhouse of the Silver Pines Golf and Country Club. There was not a cloud in the whole sky; birds chirped, happy to get away from the office and spend the day on the golf course. Despite the weather, however, Casper felt sad, and realized it was because the heart had gone out of summer. Grass had turned brown weeks ago with the heat of August but now, Casper knew, summer was dying. The leaves on a few trees had already begun to turn yellow. A few more weeks and they'd be covering the tomatoes against frost.

Seeing the clubhouse of Silver Pines, though, cheered him up. Coming here felt like old times to Casper; he'd had a membership here for years, felt it was important for immigrants such as himself to mingle. Cost him a bundle every year, but it was worth it.

Golfers walked by dressed in brightly coloured golfing togs–canary yellow and cardinal red; their golf cleats clicked on the cement walk. Old friends greeted him: "Hey there, Cas, good to see ya again." "Long time no see, Casper, how's the missus?" Casper loved the camaraderie. Not bad for a D.P. who stepped off the boat at 22 and started a successful business.

When he walked into the clubhouse the carpeting cushioned his shoes. He looked around through the dim light of the dining room and saw Vic Cargill waving to him from a table in the corner. A gentleman he had not seen before sat with Vic.

"Casper, good to see you again! I'd like you to meet a good friend of mine–Jay Leach. Jay here has been in sales, to put it mildly, his whole life, and also happens to be a member at Cedarvale Bible, where you know Janice and I belong."

Casper shook Jay's hand. Jay Leach appeared to be in his late forties. He had smooth, well-tanned skin; a gold chain hung around his neck–Casper could see he was very successful. They sat down in red leather chairs.

"Jay's been involved in pretty high-level international trade for a number of years," Vic went on. "Some months ago he approached me with an investment opportunity that sounded interesting. I looked at it pretty closely, and decided to come on board. Later Jay and I talked about fellow Christians who might want to take advantage of the same opportunity, and of course your name immediately came to mind. But

I'll let Jay himself tell you about, uh, what this involves."

Casper noticed a well-worn Bible lying on the table beside Jay's silverware.

"Vic tells me you've just sold a very successful import retail business in the city," Jay said.

Casper shrugged. "Pretty small potatoes, actually."

"You don't have to be modest," Jay smiled. "Besides, you and I know it's the Lord who gives the increase, right?"

Casper nodded.

"Well, let me get right to it. As Vic says, I've been a player on the international import scene for some time, and over the years I've managed to make some–strategic connections. One of these is a business partner I have in Manila, a gentleman named Edward Cox. You'll see his name here," and Jay pointed to the bottom of a letter indeed signed, as nearly as Casper could tell from the handwriting, by Edward Cox. He looked at the letterhead at the top of the page; it read, in gold embossed script, The Manila Hotel.

"Vic tells me you were born in Holland, is that right?"

Casper nodded.

"Well, as a Hollander involved in importing, no doubt you've had business dealings with the far east, places like Indonesia, maybe even the Philippines, right?"

Casper nodded; he sure had. Where would his store have been without nasi goreng and bami noodles and sambal oelek? He'd been to Djakarta, in fact, on more than one occasion.

"Now," and here Jay's voice dropped, so that Casper had to lean over to hear, "I'm sure you remember Ferdinand Marcos of the Philippines. Died back in 1989?"

Casper nodded.

"As you know, Marcos amassed a rather sizeable personal fortune. Remember Imelda's shoe collection? Whatever else you think of the man and how he obtained his wealth, the fact is, as you know, that while some of his assets have been seized and appropriated, much of it is still missing and unaccounted for."

Yes, Casper had read about that.

"Now, we come to the part I need you to keep confidential, if you don't mind. You can understand why. Edward Cox, my business associate that I mentioned earlier, in Manila," and Jay pointed again to the letter, "has reliable contacts that are involved in the process of recovering a large quantity of gold bars Marcos stashed away in secret

56

locations throughout the Philippines." Jay glanced at two golfers sitting down at the table next to theirs, then looked directly into Casper's eyes. "Now, what my partner and I are looking for is some capital to help finance this extremely promising venture. Vic here, as he said, has committed himself to a certain amount, but my associate and I are open to others, particularly fellow Christians, benefitting from this endeavour. As a businessman yourself I don't need to tell you any venture has a certain amount of risk involved, but overall the prospects are extremely favourable here. Favourable enough, in fact, that you could be looking at double or even triple return on your investment. How does that sound?"

Casper said it sounded rather interesting alright.

"You should know the results within three or four weeks," Jay said.

Casper thought hard. He needed to know how large a financial commitment Jay Leach had in mind. "Vic," he said, "would you mind me asking how much you've invested in this?"

"Fair question," Vic said. "I'm in for forty thou."

Casper gave a mental whistle. Whoo, Vic was going for a bundle. At triple return, it would set him up handsomely.

~~~~

Bernie is a little disappointed with what happens when he calls information in Moose Jaw, Saskatchewan and asks for the number of Wendy Smith there. First, a tape recorded voice asks him to give the name, then for a while there's nothing but silence so that he almost hangs up, finally an operator comes on and tells him, "I'm sorry, we have no Wendy Smith listed in Moose Jaw. Would you like to try another initial?" Bernie figured he'd give Wendy a call to make sure all this is on the up and up, but if she doesn't live in Moose Jaw, Saskatchewan as she says she does, now he's not so sure.

Then he realizes something—of course! Wendy Smith is married and her number will be listed under her husband's first name. The letter makes reference to her husband, doesn't it, so there you are. Suddenly Bernie feels a lot better. But how is he to know which Smith to ask for? A town as big as Moose Jaw has to have at least a dozen Smiths. Bernie decides maybe he should call Cameron Philips instead.

But when he calls Flagstaff, Arizona and asks for the number of Cameron Philips he is told there is no such listing there either. Maybe this whole Tony Bright thing wasn't all it appeared to be.

When he thinks about it further, though, Bernie tells himself, Bernie, if you were Wendy Smith or Cameron Philips and you had sent out hundreds and hundreds of letters all over North America, just suppose each person you sent one to ended up doing what you just did and called you to find out if this program was kosher; wouldn't you end up taking an unlisted number? When he realizes that, he feels quite a bit better again.

He thinks perhaps he will not tell Denise about Tony Bright's program; it will be a nice revelation, a year from now, to show her a surprise bank account with thousands and thousands of dollars in it. But it'll probably be best not to be too greedy; he'll start slowly and see if the whole thing works.

Still, Stanley Ott, the postmaster here in Alfalfa, raises his eyebrows and looks at Bernie over the top of his gold-framed reading glasses next day when Bernie asks him for five hundred stamps.

"Did you say–five hundred?" Stanley says.

"Uh huh," Bernie says, trying to appear nonchalant by looking not at Stanley but around the post office, as if he might have been sent here to estimate how much longer the paint on the walls will last before the room will have to be redone.

Stanley looks at him. "Stamps are not like light bulbs, you know, that you can buy in bulk in case the price goes up next week. Six months from now when the cost of sending a letter goes up you'll be in asking me for 490 five-centers."

"That's OK, I'll take five hundred," Bernie says. "Got a lot of letters I need to send." He thinks he'll wait a week or two before asking Stanley for a post office box; it'll take at least that long, the mail being as slow as it is, before return letters start coming in and he and Denise are on their way to financial independence.

~~~~

Casper Blokkedoos is a careful man, not one to rush into anything. But if 32 years of running a successful business has taught him anything it is that there are moments you have to seize or they pass you by. Any investment good enough for Vic Cargill was good enough for Casper. Fortunately, Jay Leach was a fellow Christian he could trust.

Casper stepped into the Alfalfa Royal Bank next day, cashed in some of his investments drawing no more than a measly four and a half percent, and wrote out a cheque for $30,000. Franklin Gilchrist, the manager, certified it for him.

"That's a goodly sum," Franklin said, curious to know just who this Morningstar Corporation was that Casper was writing a cheque for $30,000 to, but also curious to know the source of Casper's inside information. But Franklin Gilchrist did not rise to the position of bank manager without knowing how to respect his clients' personal financial matters. Nor did Casper tell him.

~~~~

After Bernie has dropped off the two cartons full of letters at the post office, he stops in at Melvin's Barber Shop for a haircut; he figures that if he's going to come into as much money as it appears he's going to, he'll have to look a bit more successful. He can't go around looking like some yahoo. Maybe he should buy himself a new shirt at Michael's Men's Wear, the kind with rhinestone buttons. And a tie to go with it, one of those nice black string ties with a turquoise stone set in silver.

When he steps into the barber shop he's lucky there's no wait, Melvin is alone in the shop sweeping the floor. Melvin puts away the broom, says "How's tricks?" and wraps the blue cotton cape around Bernie's neck after Bernie sits down in the leather chair.

Five minutes later, Peewee Melnyk steps in, then Earl Prior and Bob Tonkin. After hellos all around, Peewee and Earl pick up sections of the city newspaper Melvin subscribes to so his customers can keep abreast of important events happening beyond Alfalfa.

"I see the Jays lost again," Bob Tonkin says. "Worst thing they ever done is letting Alomar go. Now there's a player for ya."

"You said it," Earl Prior says, stoking up his pipe. "Next thing you know even the Tigers will catch 'em."

"Hey," Peewee Melnyk shouts suddenly. "You guys read the first section?"

Nobody has.

"Well, listen to this," and Peewee starts reading. "'Prominent city businessman Jay Leach was charged with fraud and theft over $1000 in court yesterday after he convinced several persons from this area to invest large sums of money in a fantastic scheme to recover a secret cache of gold in the Philippines.

"'Among those Leach is accused of bilking are Vic Cargill, local businessman who invested $40,000, and former city store owner Casper Blokkedoos, who wrote Leach a cheque for $30,000.'"

"Casper!" Bernie shouts from the chair. "He lives here in Alfalfa! Moved here–what, two or three years ago. He asked me to carve a plaque for him, with him and his wife's name on it. The reason I remember is I recall thinking–Blokkedoos, what kind of a name is that? Couldn't hardly fit it onto the plaque."

"You don't say," Melvin says, stopping the steady clipping of his scissors.

"Well, he's $30,000 lighter now than he was then," Earl Prior says.

"You guys should read this," Peewee Melnyk informs them. "Apparently this Leach guy transferred the seventy grand to his own bank account, then bought a $40,000 cabin cruiser two days later, which he was planning to sail down to the Caribbean where he owns some property."

"I'll bet he was," Bob Tonkin says.

"You'd think anybody with that kind of money would be too smart to fall for something like that," Bernie says.

"I'll say," Bob Tonkin agrees. "It's about as dumb as these pyramid letters going around. Any you guys receive one of those?"

"You got one too, eh?" Earl Prior says, without looking up from the sports section. "I received one last week–craziest scheme I ever heard."

"What letters?" Bernie says. Melvin has stopping his cutting.

"What they do is ask you to mail the sender twenty dollars, if you can believe it," Bob Tonkin says, "and then you're supposed to watch the money roll in."

Peewee Melnyk lets out a roar of laughter. "What a crock!"

Bernie's hands jump involuntarily beneath the blue cape, sending a shower of hair falling to the floor. He looks wildly out the window. Around his ears Melvin's scissors resume their steady clip, clip, clip.

II.
The Housewife Counts Her Jars

Suddenly now the ragged oak
And maple overnight are fire,
The green sluice falters in the elm,
The ribs and roots of storage fail...

The buzzsaw shines and birch and fir
Are corded near the kitchen door.
Around the roof the farmer trims
The eaves; the housewife counts her jars.

-Ralph Gustafson

THE RAGWEED BLUES

The weather this September has been no great shakes here in Alfalfa. We broke the monthly record for rainfall that has stood since 1933, which is a long while considering that time moves only half as fast here as it does anywhere else. The month we usually get the rain is April, when you raise your umbrella (unless you're a Dutchman, and the neighbours may be watching) and endure the rain while you tell yourself the farmers probably need it, which they don't, at least not in April. They'd rather have it spread out evenly over the summer, about an inch every week (and at night, thank you). But when the weather is so wet it's as if you've been taking a month-long cold shower and your skin stays permanently wrinkled like leftover corn flakes that have sat in milk since yesterday morning, you feel like stopping in at Melvin's Barber Shop to see whether folks running the weather there know what on earth they're doing.

Perhaps October will be better; with the fall colours it's usually the most beautiful time of year. October is pictured every year by a glossy colour photograph invariably called "Autumn Splendour" or "Russet Grandeur" in Andy Stokes' Texaco station calendar which shows maple trees such a bright scarlet that by the end of the month you wish you could hang around in October a while longer instead of having to move on to November and watch the leaves fall. The trouble with November is it always reminds you of your mortality, especially once you're past 39. November and February are similar, in a way: they're everybody's two least favourite months, but at least the Lord arranged for February to have only 28 days in order to help everybody get through it a bit faster. The end of February it's like everybody gets let out a few days early for good behaviour and before you know it, it's March. But in November we all have to serve the full sentence without a chance of early parole.

So far this September we have not yet had our first frost, which the cauliflower and tomato growers here in Alfalfa sure have appreciated, but is unmercifully late for people suffering from allergies. For weeks they've looked out their bedroom windows first thing in the morning to see if it has frosted overnight, then see it's sopping wet outside again. The roadsides around Alfalfa grow enough ragweed to supply the rest of Canada, and every September it bombards the noses of defenceless Alfalfans with pollen. The problem is so serious, someone in town once said, every year just before Labour Day a big truck backs up to the delivery door behind Stanley McCormick's Drug Pharmacy and strange men in orange uniforms unload boxes of Seldane and Claritin by the cartful, but surely that's the hallucination of a brain come unhinged by an overdose of antihistamine.

If anyone knows the misery caused by allergies, Hannes Tazelaar does. The edges of the roads around his dairy farm south of town are overgrown with ragweed, and every year about Labour Day Hannes is reduced to a sniffling, sneezing, eye-rubbing tatter of a man. Had the Psalmist been able to see Hannes in early September he might have changed his mind about man being made a little lower than the angels.

A town like Alfalfa isn't large enough to have an allergist, so Hannes has to drive all the way to the city to see his, a Dr. Jewell. Hannes has been seeing him for about four years and has been through the whole routine with him, including the scratch and win test on the insides of his arms which indicated he's allergic to ragweed and essence of dog. It's not something Hannes talks about readily, especially to the other boys in the sale barn, because he knows they'll think he's imagining things, but let me tell you about it.

Every summer Dr. Jewell gives Hannes a series of injections to protect him from ragweed that fall. He starts with a mild dose in June, working up to full strength gradually till the end of August. Hannes' wife Fanny isn't sure whether the shots do any good; she's skeptical about the way doctors prescribe drugs, and would prefer that Hannes see someone who takes a more holistic approach. Fanny has a sister in Bowmanville who sells homeopathic products. But Hannes isn't too sure about all this "holistic" and "homeopathy" stuff; he's not sure just what they mean, they're not exactly words he and the other boys in the sale barn would use.

Last summer Hannes and Fanny went to Holland to visit a cousin Hannes hadn't seen in thirty years. He took along the ragweed serum, which had to be kept refrigerated during the flight. His cousin directed him to a small medical clinic in the village, where a nurse administered the injections. They had a nice time in Holland, then came a day when Hannes and his cousin went to the beach on the North Sea, which happened to be a topless beach, as most are in Holland, which was why Fanny wasn't too keen on going and thus stayed home. Hannes had taken along a book containing tables of the history of Holstein milk production in the province of Friesland in case he got bored, but he didn't so much as take a peek at it–in fact he ended up staying at the beach so long he came home with a severe case of sunburn.

The morning of their flight back to Canada, Hannes went in for his final allergy shot; by then he was up to .5 cc's. The nurse held up the vial, drew the yellow serum into the hypodermic needle, then said in the most impeccable Dutch Hannes had ever heard that there was not enough in the vial for an injection of 5 cc's, there were only 4 cc's left. She was a different nurse than before, a beautiful blonde woman in a white uniform which hugged her figure. Hannes had never seen any woman so beautiful, and besides that she was very friendly, and when he wondered if she ever went swimming at the beach--well, just thinking about it made his hands tremble as he rolled up his left sleeve.

Hannes didn't figure how he could be through the serum so soon already, nevertheless he shrugged his shoulders. "Just give me what's there then," he said, "it'll hold me till I get back to Canada." At that moment, for all Hannes cared, she could have injected him with amaramadiophiobarbitol, the serum used to execute murderers, and at the hands of this nurse Hannes would willingly have gone to his death. She gave him the injection of 4 cc's.

A strong and unexpected reaction hit Hannes less than an hour into their flight later that day. It began with a headache, then came sniffles that he could not control, his sinuses dripping like the faucet in the milk parlour Hannes had been telling himself to fix but which he hadn't gotten around to yet. Then came sneezing, loud uncontrolled explosions his soaked handkerchief did not manage to muffle. At one point on the flight he broke his all-time record: seventeen sneezes in thirty-nine seconds. Afterward he sat in his seat dizzy from the effort; the only thing he saw was gold objects shaped like asterisks swimming in a blue-green haze inside his head. It took a full minute before he saw that passengers all around were looking at him. The elderly lady smelling of eau de cologne sitting beside him got up from her seat and scuttled off like a frightened crab; he did not see her the rest of the flight. He wondered where she'd ended up; airplanes weren't exactly like buses, where you could get off every two blocks. It wasn't until he was home the next day and remembered the nurse's exact words that he realized what had happened. What Hannes did not know was that poetry apparently wasn't the only thing that got lost in translation, sometimes it was scientific accuracy as well. His sinuses did not stop dripping until after Labour Day.

As for Hannes's sensitivity to dogs, they have a large mongrel named Trip who is a soul-mate to Hannes and is about as intelligent as a tree stump but is good with the kids–what's a farm without a dog? Dr. Jewell told Hannes he was faced with a choice: get rid of the dog, or keep his runny nose and itchy eyes. Hannes asked for confirmation, could he have the scratch test one more time? Within five minutes he had his answer. He drove back to Alfalfa with a heavy heart and an angry red swelling on his arm.

He'd been through a lot with Trip, twelve years' worth. Everywhere that Hannes went the dog was sure to go. He thought back to just after Amanda had been born and Trip would walk around the house with the baby soother in his mouth. And there was the time Fanny had baked a week's supply of bran muffins, which she eats for breakfast every morning because they enable her to treat a bodily problem in holistic fashion. She'd set the muffins on the kitchen table to cool, then went to the family room to watch TV while she did some ironing. When she came back half an hour later all that was left of the muffins was a dozen chewed up paper muffin cups and a scattering of crumbs on the vinyl kitchen floor; underneath the dining room table lay Trip with a guilty smile on his face that said, "I *know* I shouldn't have, but whatever's going to happen, it was worth it."

It wasn't. It's hard to understand why an intelligent dog like Trip would do that–maybe he felt sympathetic vibes with Hannes' runny nose. In any case, Trip didn't go wherever Hannes went the next several days; he asked if he could be excused and trotted off to the barn to endure the wages of sin in dignity and solitude. You have to admire a dog with character like that. Hannes didn't see how in the world he could let him go.

Not even after what happened in the swimming pool. Hannes and Fanny had decided that living out in the country as they did, away from the facilities in town, they would have to provide certain diversions for their children themselves, it was either that or drive them into town every

66

day. They'd put in an in-ground swimming pool six years ago. Turned out Trip was terrified of water, had been ever since a snapping turtle had clamped onto a foreleg of his in a muddy pond when he was a pup. Trip wouldn't jump into the pool if his life depended on it, not even to fetch the tennis ball you could get him to retrieve for hours until his tongue dragged on the ground. Hannes thought all Trip needed was to find out it wasn't so bad, you watch, he'd end up loving the water, and threw him in. I don't know if dogs have heart attacks, but poor Trip came close. He spent the next three days hiding under Hannes and Fanny's bed.

The following summer Hannes had bought a solar blanket for the pool, which cost him a bundle but prevented the water from evaporating in the heat. Hannes had just installed the blanket, and stood a long while admiring the way it shimmered on top of the water. Trip was meandering around the pool helping out by shooing crickets and chasing away flies, when he saw Hannes on the other side of the pool turn to head back to the house, which was his signal to follow. Now Trip, being an intelligent dog, didn't have to go to obedience school to learn that the shortest distance between two points is a straight line, he'd figured that out long ago by himself, so that's what he did, smart dog, and walked onto what looked to him like a nice piece of carpet where the pool used to be.

The result was–memorable. It took Trip less than a step to realize his feet were no longer treading on terra firma but that he was sinking rapidly in dreaded water. He had no intention of following Conrad's dictum in the destructive element to immerse, he just wanted to get the blazes out of there, and that right early. Hannes's screaming he did not at all find helpful either; he didn't need Hannes's cheerleading, he was doing his best as it was. His feet splayed out like a swaybacked nag, he scratched and clawed, then swam, and managed finally to make his way back to solid earth.

He shook the water off his body, and was so relieved at his deliverance he ran up to Hannes to lick his face, which was made easier because for some reason Trip did not understand, Hannes was down on all fours pounding the grass with his fists. It was a while before Trip saw that funny carpet covering the pool again. He knew better than to go near it this time.

It's not a story Hannes has shared with the boys in the sale barn. As for his allergies, the shots did not appear to be helping, for even in January, when ragweed lay buried under six feet of snow, Hannes's sinuses were so congested he could hardly breathe. There had to be some other cause.

67

Hannes was enjoying a glass of cold milk with a slice of buttered cranberry bread one evening when Fanny came home from her Calvinettes meeting at First CRC and said she had important news. Calvinettes, for those not in the know, is an organization designed to instill in young girls Christian character, although with a name like Calvinettes it's surprising any girl would want to go. Have you ever heard of Mennonettes, or Lutherettes? No wonder the name is being changed to Gems. In any case, Fanny said she was talking with Judy Mantel and Claire Van Sickle, two of the other Calvinette counsellors; both of them had gone to see a doctor in the city and had experienced amazing results!

"His name is Dr. Wolfe and he treats food sensitivities," Fanny said, eyes wide with excitement. "You should hear what happened to Judy Mantel–you remember how she had these terrible migraines? Her own doctor asked her how old she was, then when she told him she was 53 he said 'Mmmm, I see,' and said it was something brought on by menopause. Then he told her, 'Here, this is a prescription for Valium.' Can you imagine! She went to this Dr. Wolfe and he tested her and found out she's sensitive to certain foods. She cut them out of her diet and her migraines have disappeared.

"Claire Van Sickle says her sinuses were always plugged, she had constant headaches, then she went to this doctor, he took her off certain foods, and *her* symptoms have disappeared. Says she's never felt as much energy as now. Her sinuses have cleared, and besides that, she's lost twenty pounds in six months!"

Then Fanny leaned towards Hannes and lowered her voice as if she were about to divulge some information the kids doing homework in their bedrooms should not hear: "She also says her and Oscar's love life has never been better." Fanny paused, then placed her hand over Hannes's. "You know how you're always tired, Hannes, especially at night? I mean, it makes sense, your body spends so much of its energy fighting the poison in your system, you don't have any stamina for, you know, other things. Do you think maybe *you* should go and see Dr. Wolfe, Hannes?"

Poor Hannes–his wife had just revealed dark thoughts he had no idea she was thinking. He felt sick to his stomach–now he not only had his allergy problem to worry about, but the very props of his manhood had just been kicked away from under him, no way he was in any frame of mind to think about seeing a doctor specializing in *food* allergies. For all he knew the man would probably tell him to cut out coffee or stop eating cauliflower.

But as Hannes thought about it, the more it struck him that if Judy Mantel and Claire Van Sickle had been helped by this Dr. Wolfe, wouldn't he be crazy not to at least give him a try? What harm could there be in that? Didn't Naaman the leper think the prophet Elisha was crazy when he told him to do nothing more complicated than jump into the Jordan seven times? He must have asked himself, why seven? Wouldn't three, or maybe even two times do? For all Hannes knew, his own faith was being tested here.

Three weeks later he drove to the city for his appointment with Dr. Wolfe, whose office was located on the second floor of a large brick mansion shaded by huge trees in an older, ritzier section of town. When Hannes looked at Dr. Wolfe's nameplate he noticed his name was not followed by "M.D." but by a scramble of letters that might have come from an oculist's eyechart. Hannes had no idea what they meant. Well, *if* this Wolfe was a quack, he was certainly a well-heeled one. Hannes stepped into the office, registered with the receptionist, took off his Sokota Feed cap, and sat down.

Two other people sat in the waiting room, a man who might have been Hannes's age although it was hard to tell with the bushy brown toupee he was wearing that curled up high in the man's neck, and a woman at least fifty dressed in an egg-yellow pantsuit and wearing a perfume so ardent it made Hannes's eyes water. Both of them were reading magazines and paying no mind to a television monitor high in a corner of the room showing a video explaining the ins and outs of acupuncture. Hannes felt a sudden sense of alarm–clogged sinuses was one thing, next thing his wife was questioning his manhood, and now he was about to get stabbed with Chinese knitting needles.

A young woman called in the fellow with the toupee, then the woman in the yellow pantsuit. Fifteen minutes later she called Hannes and ushered him into a small room containing a chair, a stool, and a brown naugahyde couch raised at one end. Hannes sat down in the chair. Five feet away a human skeleton dangled from a stand–something drastic and sudden had happened either to Monsieur Toupee or to Madame Egg Yolk–Hannes could not tell from the skeleton which of the two it was. And was that Transylvanian organ music coming softly through the ceiling loudspeakers? Hannes wondered whether he could still make a run for it.

Too late. A man stepped into the room; Hannes looked him over quickly–if anything bizarre was going to happen to him at the hands of this Dr. Wolfe he wanted to be able to give the authorities a clear physical description. Hannes was less than encouraged by the man's appearance: he seemed about 40, wore a chequered white and black shirt with western-style buttons, black denim pants, and black leather boots. This guy was a doctor? He seemed all decked out to do some calf-roping, or line-dancing. But Dr. Wolfe sat down on the stool and lifted a boot to rest on the top rung as if he had just sidled into a bar. "What can I do for you?" he asked.

It wasn't the question Hannes had expected, it sounded too much like something a department store salesclerk would ask. What you can do for me is heal me, Hannes wanted to say, I just want to feel my old self again, but that didn't strike him as a helpful thing to say, he'd have to start at the beginning, so what he did say was that there were these two women at their church, see, First CRC in Alfalfa, the women's names were Judy and Claire, and happened to be Calvinette counsellors along with his wife Fanny and. . . .

Next thing he knew, Dr. Wolfe had asked him to lie back on the naugahyde couch; its surface felt cold through his clothes. "I'm going to test you for some food sensitivities," Dr. Wolfe said. "I want you to touch your left thumb and index finger to your clavicle, like this, and I'm going to be handing you a series of vials, alright? Hold the vials to your chest with your other hand here. Then I want you to raise your left leg about twelve inches every time I hand you a new vial and you try to hold your leg in the air while I try to press it down. Got that?" Hannes got it all right, he just wasn't sure what it all had to do with the price of wheat. He could imagine himself telling the boys at the sale barn–"He had me hold these little vials, see. What? Vials–don't you know what vials are? Then I had to lift my left leg and–hey, what're you guys laughing at?"

"He had you *what?*"

"Lift your left leg, did you say?"

"Was that beside a fire hydrant, Hannes?"

Aaaah, shaddup. At least it was better than being stabbed with needles.

Hannes lost count, but it must have been 50 or 60 vials Dr. Wolfe handed him to hold over his chest. And it was amazing, Hannes had no difficulty keeping his leg in the air for most of them, but six or seven times his leg muscles turned to jelly against the pressure Dr. Wolfe applied and his leg came down despite his efforts, almost as if it had a will of its own. Finally he was allowed to sit up.

"What I've had you do," Dr. Wolfe explained, "is hold a number of vials containing a selected series of food concentrates over your esophagus. That's the tube that food passes through to your stomach. Whether or not you can keep your leg elevated is a kinesiological method of testing to see which substances you may have either an allergic or hypersensitive reaction to. Don't ask me to explain *how* it works, all I know is *that* it works. Did you notice there were times you were unable to resist my pressure?"

Hannes nodded.

"It appears you may have a sensitivity to the following substances; there are seven of them: cheese, chocolate, coffee, corn, cow's milk, wheat flour, and white sugar. Five c's and two w's for easy memorization, but I'll give you a chart in a moment."

Then Dr. Wolfe went on to explain that health food stores sold cookbooks containing recipes that avoid certain foods. Hannes was to avoid as much as possible the seven substances identified by the test, some follow-up appointments would be necessary, the first of which Hannes should make for a month from now with Yolanda the receptionist, who would be happy to accept payment for today's consultation by cash or cheque.

The more Hannes thought about it as he drove home the more he knew there was no way he could do without some of the foods he was supposed to avoid. How could he get through a day without coffee? Until he had his first cup in the morning he was nothing more than semi-human, his mouth drooling and reeking lizard breath, even good old Trip knew enough to stay out of his way. And cow's milk–that was his livelihood, for pete's sake, how could he avoid drinking the stuff? And what were the others again–sugar, and chocolate, and wheat, and cheese? Why, he'd have to revolutionize his lifestyle–he'd end up like one of them health freaks from the '60s eating nothing but rice cakes and raisin granola and goat-milk yogurt and alfalfa sprouts the rest of his life!

Aaah, there wasn't anything to it, he knew all along this Dr. Wolfe was nothing but a quack. He'd gone just to please Fanny, otherwise he'd never hear the end of it. Still, though, what *about* Judy Mantel and Claire Van Sickle, he couldn't argue against that now, could he?

Life sure was complicated sometimes. Perhaps someday he could make more sense of it. Maybe what would help him sort it all out was talking about it with Trip; after all, he was such a smart dog.

FOR SALE:
Large 3 BR ranch on 2.4 acres ½ mi west of
town. Workshop + barn. Good for chicks.
384-1993.

   -ad in The Alfalfa Sentinel-Star

IN WHICH VIRGINIA WIEBINGA
FINDS TRUE LOVE

Virginia Wiebinga came home from her latest date with Albert Zomer one night and saw the red light of her answering machine flashing. Albert had taken her to the Alfalfa Fair, where they had gone on a ride called The Salt and Pepper Shaker. She and Albert had been strapped into one of two metal cages which twirled vertically round and round, end over end. Thirty seconds into the ride Virginia had lost hold of her purse, which tumbled around in the metal cage, disgorging its contents. By the time the ride had ended, some kindhearted souls had collected the purse's bounty which had rained down to the ground below. Virginia and Albert stepped out of the metal cage in front of a wildly cheering crowd. On the ground the objects in her purse had been gathered into a neat little pile: among other things, there were her lipstick and compact (the mirror shattered), her driver's license and credit cards, a photograph of herself taken when she was in high school, a package of kleenex, two dollars and seventy-eight cents in change, and two tampons. Albert was helpful in suggesting to her she was very fortunate to get it all back.

Virginia pushed the play button on her answering machine; it was her mother, Florence. "Virginia dear, your father and I were wondering if you're not doing anything whether you'd like to come over for coffee next Saturday evening."

Virginia called her mother next day. "What's the occasion?" she asked.

"Oh, no particular reason," Florence said, but Virginia knows that whenever her mother says "your father and I" when she invites her over for coffee for no reason it's because she has a *very* specific purpose in mind, and that's to discuss what she calls Virginia's "prospects," or lack of same. Virginia is 39 and still single, which happens to a beautiful woman with a graduate degree in English and who knows what she wants. So far Virginia hasn't found it, at least not here in Alfalfa.

But don't get the impression her life is dull. Au contraire. There are always the affections of Albert Zomer, of course; other than that, she works in Bob Miller's Travel Agency in town, and as with any business she has to know the product, and she's acquainted herself with it plenty. She's travelled the world over: snorkled in Cozumel, paraglided in New Zealand, hiked the rain forests of Costa Rica, skied in Switzerland–not bad for a chick from Alfalfa. Hey, who needs a man? However, *should* love hit her over the head, well, she *is* a woman. But just because she's 39 doesn't mean she has to compromise her principles. Would you? Life's too short to spend fifty long years of it with some turkey is what Virginia believes.

It seems to Virginia, though, that turkeys are exactly what she's had to put up with. Before Albert Zomer, Virginia had been blessed with the amorous attentions of Sam Tinklenberg, a trucker whose business motto on the side of his truck reads, "Need A Haul? Give Sam a Call. He Carries a Lot of Weight." The first time Sam took Virginia out was to the stock car races, the second was to a drive-in movie called *Nightmare on the 13th Floor*, when a ferocious thunderstorm–the kind you see on canvas backdrops used by cheap department store photographers–came along and got so violent it ripped huge sheets of plywood off the drive-in screen and sent them flying, so Sam and Virginia spent the rest of the evening at Sam's playing gin rummy when she could have been curled up in a chair at home reading a good mystery novel. After surviving the thunderstorm with her Sam must have figured he'd established a relationship with Virginia: no doubt she'd want him to keep in touch and phone her on his cross-country hauls from wherever he happened to be stopped for the night.

The last one did him in.

"Virginia? It's Sam. I'm here in Craigellachie stayin' over for the night and–

"Craigellachie. In B.C. Dropped off a load of tractor trannies in Calgary yesterday and now I'm on my way to Vancouver to pick up a load of furniture and here I am sittin' by the side of the Trans-Canada under a full moon with everything so quiet and peaceful I played my mouth organ a while and then I got to thinkin' about you and–

"What? Can't hear you too good, it's those trucks that come rumbling by.

"1:00 a.m.? It is? Oh yeah, forgot about those different time zones, I guess. Sorry. Anyway, I've been thinking–

"Virginia, are you still there? Virginia?"

Every time Virginia turns down another prospect her mother says to her, "Oh, Virginia." She says it in that tone she has you'd think she'd suffered the calamities that afflicted Job–Florence, not Virginia. "Oh, mother," Virginia replies. What doesn't help is that Virginia's three younger sisters have all gotten married already, Valerie and Veronica a good thirteen years ago now, and even Vivienne, nine years younger than Virginia, married five years ago.

Virginia feels her mother's notions of love have been clouded a bit by the books she buys at Velma's Book Exchange in town. Her mother's favourite novels have covers that show blond, long-haired hunks with chests hard as steel hovering over ravishing, nubile young women whose diaphanous bodices defy gravity while clinging to the southern slopes of their heaving, ample bosoms–oh, it's enough to arouse in even a hack of a storyteller the most luminous prose. But what Florence reads is not exactly the kind of literature you will find in the library of First Christian Reformed Church of Alfalfa. Deep down Virginia is almost sure she owes her name to the heroine of whatever pulp novel her mother happened to be reading just before Virginia was born. Still, perhaps she should be thankful–her mother could have been reading a book about some babe named Vashti, or Verbena, or Vedette.

Looking back on it now, Virginia will never know what possessed her to agree to it, but her mother said that if she had no intention of marrying anyone, as appeared to be the case since she was close to pushing 40, then perhaps she should respond to some "Personal" ads–not the kind in the city newspaper, those were from a bunch of sex perverts, but if you knew where to look you could sometimes find very nice ones, like the ads in a Christian magazine Florence subscribed to. After hints about as subtle and insistent as Chinese water torture, her mother pushing her with "Promise me you'll write to *one*, then I'll let you decide from there," Virginia had concluded there was only one way to get her mother off her back.

Next time she was at her mother's and Florence had raised the point she'd sighed and said alright, she would look at the ads. "Oh, Virginia," Florence said.

"Oh, mother," Virginia said.

She read the first ad:

> Christian young man, 36, although Mother
> says I look no more than 26, independent,
> artistic type (I sing tenor in church choir),
> almost handsome, even more so with lights
> dimmed low (ha ha), seeks Christian woman
> with intelligence, and humorous. Beauty not
> necessary of course (I Peter 3:3-5), but would
> be appreciated all the same. Write Box 777.

No. She'd rather put up with her mother's Chinese water torture. Perhaps the next one:

> Father of four, divorced, self-employed,
> would like to meet financially independent
> Christian lady in her thirties looking for
> fulfilment. I am 42 and don't have time to
> read much but do enjoy euchre, bowling, and
> the Red Green Show. Traditional woman
> only please, must be good with children, no
> smokers, druggies, or bar flys. Please send
> recent photo. Box 519.

No thanks. She already had a job. There was one more:

> Oh, to be in love now that September is here.
> Widely assumed to be in my 30s (but actually
> a block further up the street, although not
> lacking *joie de vivre*), this moth still desires
> the star. I'm no Antonio Banderas, but
> neither do you have to be Melanie Griffith.
> Instead, you are spiritual, brainy, *soignée*,
> and droll (3 out of 4 would do). No
> photograph, please; let's retain the element
> of surprise. Box 845.

Well, if she'd promised her mother to write to one it might as well be to a human being rather than to an alien or a troglodyte. Anyone who read Browning, knew French, and used words like *soignée* had to have something going for him.

She wrote a letter and two weeks later received a reply:

Dear Virginia,

What a beautiful name you have! And how fortunate (dare I say even providential?) we both live in southern Ontario, no more than 40 kilometres from each other, so we can meet in person rather than having to correspond. Let me tell you a bit about myself. I'm an accountant (specialize in income tax), was saved at a Billy Graham crusade when I was 16 (the sermon was on Ephesians 3:14-19 (since then my special personal Scripture), & wear glasses (too much staring at figures I suppose). My hobbies include reading (although not mystery novels, which you say you read. Tolkien's my all-time fave followed by James Herriot & the poetry of Rod McKuen, although I've read Cyrano de Bergerac at least five times (no, I do not have a preternaturally large nose)). I also enjoy listening to music (Tchaikovsky, Chopin, Zamfir—as you can see, I'm nothing, if not eclectic); and I enjoy crossword puzzles (the tougher the better (absolutely loved the full-page one in the Globe & Mail several years ago (took me the better part of two months to solve))).

But what really turns my crank, if you'll pardon the vernacular, is insects (would you believe?), collecting them in particular. I think I must have one of the better moth collections east of the Mississippi (sorry about the American reference— should I say the Red, then? (you know, the one that flows south from Lake Winnipeg and flooded this spring, which, no doubt, you know)). I'd love for you to see my collection—in fact, what I'd really like to do is to take you out some night sugaring (for moths, that is) in the woods back of my house (yes, I own my own—the house, not the woods). If you don't mind, it would be best if we came to my place, where I have all my stuff and where I know my way around. We could get to know each other a bit, then as soon as it's good and dark, head into the woods together—how does that sound?

Yours Truly,
Myron Q. Fowles

It sounded nothing if not kinky, Virginia thought, it had a definite sense of mystery even, straight out of Stephen King. Was that what made the letter intriguing to her? Was it the perverse need to be able to say I-told-you-so to her mother afterwards while looking positively droll? Or was it plain old curiosity that drove her, the desire to see what the man behind the letter looked like, this Myron Q. (Quentin? Quincy? Quimby!) Fowles who did not have a preternaturally large nose? But there were some things that didn't fit. Could one like Chopin *and* Zamfir? And the ad quoted Browning but the letter said he read McKuen–another odd combination. Whatever. More mystery. She decided, despite a little voice inside that warned her, "Virginia, you're gonna regret this," that she would go ahead.

She met Myron Q. Fowles that Friday night–if she was going to get murdered in the woods by an axe killer she might as well get on with it. Myron had given her directions over the phone, his voice precise, friendly: about the way she would expect the voice of an insect-loving accountant to sound.

The evening she drove to meet Myron was warm, very warm still for September. If she weren't on her way to meet a man she had never met she might have thought it was the weather that gave her a sense of foreboding, as if something were brewing in the air. She almost turned back five times in fact, after she imagined headlines that screamed "Woman's Body Found Hacked in Woods," then she contented herself with stopping the car, taking a slip of paper from her purse and writing on it, "Myron Q. Fowles did it," and hiding the paper in a corner of her glove compartment in case he ransacked her car. She told herself she'd read too many Agatha Christies, she was out of her tree, how could she have allowed her mother to talk her into going ahead with this? She wondered whether the red dress she'd put on was the right thing to wear for traipsing through woods. Then, after a thirty minute drive, she stopped in front of a house, an unpretentious yellow brick bungalow on the edge of town. She'd never liked yellow brick. On the front lawn stood a white sign with black letters that read "Myron Q. Fowles," then below that, "Accounting Services." And yes, there were indeed woods behind the house. So far, at least, things checked out.

No doubt you prefer not to be taxed with the details of their introduction: their polite handshake, the surprise each felt that the other looked remarkably human (despite the thick-lensed glasses Myron wore), their cordial but understandably awkward conversation over coffee, then Myron's showing Virginia the best private collection of moths east of the Red River, the most brilliantly coloured moths Virginia had ever seen (they *were* impressive), pinned in beautiful display cases made of mahogany laid in with glass–we will not dwell on any of this, interesting though it may be, when what you really want to find out is what happened in those woods behind Myron Q. Fowles's house. So let us proceed.

After they'd conducted the preliminaries, Myron came up from the basement carrying a white plastic pail, a flashlight, and a canvas bag slung over his shoulder. Virginia smelled something syrupy and sweet–could it be Myron's deodorant, she wondered.

"Ready?" Myron said.

They stepped outside, the air still hot despite onsetting dusk, and as Virginia followed Myron towards the woods behind his house in the gathering dark, she felt the air hang heavy as before a storm. She looked up and saw large banks of clouds had gathered overhead. As she walked through tall grass towards the woods she felt little creatures, crickets or grasshoppers she concluded, leaping against her bare legs. She *should* have worn slacks. When they reached the woods darkness had almost completely fallen. Virginia, she thought, you are *crazy*, gal, how do you get yourself into these things?

"I'm going to smear this molasses on some trees," Myron explained, "then we'll wait half an hour and go back and see, OK?" His eyes seemed unnaturally large behind the thick lenses of his glasses.

Virginia nodded. Well, it did have the air of mystery. She followed Myron and watched him daub the sticky mixture on trees and stumps. Tree trunks and leaves flickered in the beam of his flashlight. She began to perspire in the warm, humid air; all around her she heard the steady, rhythmic croaking of frogs and other strange denizens of fen and bog.

"Come on, let's sit down," Myron said, pointing his flashlight to a fallen tree, then from the canvas bag slung over his shoulder he took a bottle of wine and two plastic glasses. "Care for some?"

"OK." She seated herself on the tree trunk. Well wasn't Myron just the romantic, she thought, your basic candlelight and wine in the woods–her mother would love it. Maybe Myron would read to her some Browning. Or McKuen. Then, from somewhere far off she heard a faint rumble of thunder. They sat in silence a moment.

"Where did you learn French," Virginia asked, "university?"

Myron looked puzzled. "French? I don't speak French," he said.

Virginia looked at him. "But your ad," she said.

Myron did not say anything for a moment; finally, "Oh." Another pause. "Well, to be truthful, I had a little help with that ad."

Virginia looked but could not make out his face, only his vague outline in the dark. "A little help?"

"A friend, a guy I know who writes copy for an advertising agency in Toronto, he helped me with it."

"I see. Sort of a. . .Cyrano de Bergerac thing."

"Huh? Oh." Myron chuckled. "Very good. Yeah, I suppose."

"Does he do your dating for you too?" She tried not to sound too biting.

"Why don't we go and see what's happened," Myron said, rising. He pulled the canvas bag back over his shoulder, glass clinking from inside.

The woods were black with night now as they followed the route of trees Myron had sugared. Virginia was amazed by the variety of insects swarming around each tree. At one, a large moth, light brown with huge blue eyes on its wings, sat feeding on the molasses now dripping towards the ground. The moth was absolutely luminous in the beam of the flashlight, its colours much more brilliant than in daylight.

"Myron, look at it," Virginia said. "It's beautiful! What kind is it?"

"A polyphemus, named after the giant in Greek mythology." Myron crept up to the tree, held a jar beneath the moth, and after a moment the polyphemus fell into the jar. On another tree sat a smaller moth, two small black eyes peering from its yellow wings, and when Myron held the jar beneath it, it too fell in. "Male io," he said.

Virginia felt uneasy. "Why can't you do what birdwatchers do?"

"You mean just look at them?"

"Yes!"

Myron laughed. "But why, when you can collect them?" He kept moving from tree to tree, one moth after another, brown and yellow and green, falling into the jar.

"Myron, what's in the jar?"

"Chloroform. This just stuns them. Later I put them into a cyanide jar to kill them, otherwise their wings will stiffen up now already. Here, want to smell it?" and he held the jar out towards her. She turned her head away from the pungent smell of chloroform.

Then she heard the wind in the trees suddenly, and saw a flash of lightning. The thunder clap followed almost immediately. Virginia imagined the headline that appeared next day: "Woman and Accountant Felled By Lightning in Woods." What would the folks in Alfalfa think?

"Myron, shouldn't we be heading back?"

"Yeah, just another tree or so."

Virginia was forced to stay by his flashlight, following him.

Suddenly the rain began to pelt the trees overhead while thunder crashed and the woods were white with light for a split second all around them. "Myron!" Virginia screamed. She did not wait for him but dashed through the woods as fast as she could in the dark. Wet underbrush clawed at her legs; rain soaked her hair, her shoulders. She ran towards where she thought Myron's house would be, afraid she had completely lost her sense of direction, then when she reached the edge of the treeline she saw the lights of Myron's house a hundred yards off to her left. She slogged though tall wet grass as if she were running though water a foot deep; once she fell, striking her shoulder sharply on a rock. By the time she reached the house she was drenched.

She did not bother waiting for Myron but ran for her car parked on the road, unlocked the door, and threw herself in. She sat breathing heavily, water from her hair streaming down her face. She turned the ignition key, her car whined and whined, and finally caught. She turned on the headlights and wipers, rain pelting the windshield, the hood, the roof, then she wheeled into Myron's driveway to turn around–and caught his figure in her headlights.

He was shouting "Virginia, wait!" then he was beside her knocking on her window. She locked the door, put the car in reverse and backed out. As she peeled away she looked into her rear view mirror and saw the silhouette of Myron's figure standing on the road, both arms waving.

She drove as fast as she dared with the rain splashing in gouts against her windshield, so hard her wipers barely managed to clear the water away. Ahead of her she saw the rain bounce off the highway in her headlights, little explosions of water leaping up off the pavement. It drummed against the roof over her head.

Then, when she had been driving no more than ten minutes away from Myron's house, her car sputtered once, sputtered again, then Virginia heard the engine die. She turned the ignition key and pumped her gas pedal in a desperate attempt to revive the engine. Nothing. Come on baby, she pleaded, but felt the car lose its speed until it barely crawled and she had no choice but to steer it onto the highway's gravel shoulder, where the car rolled slowly to a stop.

She buried her face in her hands a moment, rubbed her eyes, and pulled back her soaked hair. She tried starting the car again, but it did not respond. When she looked around she saw no house or farm lights anywhere. Well, gal, what are your choices, she asked herself. You could stay here and–what? Sleep in the car overnight, drenched? Or start walking for help? Where? Ahead? But how far to the nearest town? Back? To Myron's town? She didn't like either option. She could flag down a passing car, she supposed, but who knew what kind of kook she might run into?

She had pretty well decided she had no choice but to start hoofing it, what the heck, she was already soaked–maybe she'd see some farm lights soon–when a car came from behind her, put on its high beam, then slowed and stopped on the shoulder ahead of her. Through the rain she saw a tall figure step out of the car.

~~~~~

What with events transpiring as they had over the weekend, Virginia remembered she would have to call her mother. That Tuesday evening she picked up the phone.

"Hello, mother? Thought I'd better get back to you. You remember that coffee date we made for Saturday night? I'm afraid I won't be able to make it."

"How so, dear? Something happen?"

"Well, yes. I have another date, actually. I mean, an actual date."

"Oh Virginia, with that nice young man you visited Friday–what was his name, Maynard Flowers or something."

"No, mother, not him. You're not going to believe this, but you remember that thunderstorm we had Friday night? Well, coming back from Myron's–what a creep, by the way–my car stalled on the highway, right in the middle of nowhere with rain coming down in buckets. Finally a car stops and this man steps out and I'm wondering if I can trust him but he looks rather harmless soaking wet so I roll down my window and he asks me whether I need any help. I tell him my car's stalled, can't start it no matter how much I threaten it, and he says with the rain my ignition system probably got damp, and if I want, he could take a look under my hood. Now, it's been a while since a man asked me that, mother, but like I said, he had a kind face so I tell him, I'd appreciate it if you would, I mean what choice do I have, right? So he goes to his car for a rag and he lifts up my hood and wipes the wires dry in the distributor cap or whatever it's called, I don't know beans about these things, but anyway, the short of it is that fifteen minutes later he's got my car running again."

"And?"

"What do you mean, and?"

"Then what happened?"

"Well, what do you want to know? He's a photographer–no mother, he wasn't taking photographs of covered bridges, we don't have any around here. He's a freelancer and he was out taking photographs of the thunderstorm. Well anyway, so we got to talking and one thing led to another and–"

"In the *car?*"

"Oh, mother. I went out with him yesterday and had a wonderful time, he's a very nice man; in fact, he's invited me to go out with him again on Saturday, which is why I can't make that coffee at your place."

"That's alright. Which church does he go to, dear?"

"He's Baptist, actually."

Now, Virginia could not see her mother raise her hand to her mouth at that news, of course, but whether Florence did so because she was feeling uncontainable joy at her daughter's new prospect or shock at his being Baptist, who knows?

"Mother, are you there?" Virginia said.

"What's his name?" Florence said, finally. "Valiant? I've always wanted a son named Valiant. If I had a son I'd name him Valiant. Or Valdemar. Or Vittorio. Oh, Virginia."

"Oh, mother," Virginia said.

Police report

This past week was a busy one for law enforcement in our area. Police report several break-ins.

The Medical Centre located at 432 Main Street was broken into sometime between 9:00 pm Friday and 10:00 am Saturday. A number of syringes were stolen. Also taken were vials of xycaine and testosterone. Anyone knowing anything about this break-in or noticing any peculiar behaviour is urged to contact police.

Sometime between 9:00 pm Saturday and 10:00 am Sunday, persons unknown entered the Drug Pharmacy on Main through the roof.

Once they were inside the building the thieves smashed all the video surveillance equipment. Police are still trying to ascertain exactly which goods were stolen, although it is suspected the crooks were primarily after drugs and\or cigarettes.

One oddity: police say they found a gold hoop earring with blood on it on the floor back of the store. While police surmise the suspects may have come from out of town, nevertheless citizens are urged to be on the lookout for anyone missing a gold hoop ring and possibly showing a torn earlobe.

-news story in The Alfalfa Sentinel-Star

SOME ASSEMBLY REQUIRED

There are moments in a man's life when he realizes something with such sudden, startling clarity he wonders why he hadn't seen it earlier, as if he had pillow stuffing for brains; what he feels then, after he's given his forehead a good clap if he's Dutch, is an irresistible urge to talk to friends or neighbours wherever they might be gathered, at home or church or Lucille's Lunch, to tell them his discovery. Unless circumstances dictate it must be kept a secret, of course.

Deep philosophical musing such as the above doesn't come often to Hilbert TeBrake–he's no Spinoza, after all–but these very thoughts (except not quite so eloquent, perhaps) came to Hilbert's mind one Saturday morning in October as he stood in a swirling cloud of dust raised by his sweeping the leaves out of his garage for the hundred and thirty-seventh time that fall. He's normally a patient sort of fellow Hilbert likes to think, and not at all given to wild exaggeration, but every man has his limit, and this leaf problem had exceeded his last fall already. Or was it the year before?

Somehow all the leaves not only from Hilbert's own trees but also from those of his neighbours, especially Earl Prior's row of pin oaks across the street, keep finding their way into Hilbert's garage, as if their car, a thirteen year old Concord, were a huge magnet and the neighbourhood's leaves so many iron filings.

The problem is, their garage door, a homemade jobbie, is unusually heavy. Dorothy always comes into the house wheezing after breaking her back trying to heave it open, then having to hang from the door in order to pull it shut–it's become as good as any television sitcom for the neighbours across the street to see a 5'2", 147-pound woman doing a clean-and-jerk as she leaves the house, then leaping up and dangling from the top of the garage door when she arrives back home.

As for Hilbert, he never closes the door any sooner than he has to–what's the use, Dorothy will be running out to Art's Mart or somewhere in half an hour anyway, so why bother risking a hernia? A man's got to protect his equipment. In the meantime, in blows another four or five bushel baskets' worth of Earl Prior's leaves for Hilbert to sweep away. What's more, with the door open all the time, mice have begun nesting in the pile of firewood Hilbert keeps inside the garage, and from there they somehow find their way into the rest of the house. When Hilbert watches the Leafs on TV he's sure he keeps seeing dark little shapes flitting across the floor.

What Hilbert realized suddenly (the dust may have been clogging his nasal passages, but the ducts in his brain were still clear) was that an automatic garage opener was the simple solution to the problem–how come he hadn't seen it earlier? Open the door, drive out, close the door. Open the door, drive in, close the door, all by just pushing a button. No more leaves inside. The longer he thought about it the more Hilbert liked the idea. Come to think of it, a week from Wednesday was Dorothy's birthday. He'd been racking his brain trying to think of a gift for her, and a garage opener would make a great present. Hilbert still remembered how thankful she'd been her last birthday when he'd bought her a handy little Dirt Devil so she could vacuum the inside of the Concord without having to lug the heavy upright outside.

As I said, insight doesn't come readily to Hilbert, but he knows enough that when it does he has to act on it, otherwise it'll evaporate faster than an election promise. He'd have to see what kind of a deal he could get in town from George Hardy. While he was there, maybe he'd stop in at the doctor's office to make an appointment for that checkup Doc Summerall had been nagging him to get–"You're what, fifty-six, Hilbert?" he says, his mouth pursing, his nose sniffing twice, and his eyes blinking the way he does every five seconds. "You should be getting your ticker and the old prostate examined every year. Automatic. You have Andy Stokes check your antifreeze and your spark plugs every fall, right? It's the same thing. Your body's a precision instrument, Hilbert, you've got to take care of it–" sniff sniff, blink blink.

Ah, Doc Summerall was probably right, Hilbert knew, his prostate *had* been acting up all summer. He would make the appointment by phone except then Dorothy would overhear and get all worried, needlessly, about his health. Other than that wobbly prostate of his, he was fine.

He came back home an hour later with an automatic garage opener and an appointment for the following Tuesday at Doc Summerall's. It was a good thing he balanced the books rather than Dorothy, this way she'd never notice the cheque made out for a good two hundred something to Hardy Hardware. He knew Dorothy would never feel right about him spending that much on her. And it *was* more than he was used to spending, but this birthday she was turning fifty-five; she deserved something special.

He hid the garage opener under a piece of canvas tarp inside the tool shed in the back yard. Now, could he manage to get the thing installed without Dorothy knowing about it so it would come as a surprise? Tuesday evening she'd be at church for Martha Society, Thursday evening was choir practice–an evening or two would do it, it was just a garage opener, an old mechanical pro like him, he'd have it up in no time. Dorothy wouldn't even notice the rail and the opener in the garage ceiling, the way she walked leaning forward and looking down at the ground.

Nothing stirs a man, nothing gives him as much sense of purpose as an altruistic mission for his wife–maybe it's a subconscious act of penance for being a jerk the rest of the time. But Hilbert was more than stirred: he felt absolutely inspired. No sooner had Dorothy left the house later that day than Hilbert rushed to the tool shed to get a sneak preview of the installation instructions, might as well plan it out ahead of time.

He opened the carton and was dismayed to discover not the two or three pages of instructions he expected, but a thick, 48-page manual. He riffled through it. He was just installing a garage opener, for goodness sake, what did they think he was doing, performing a brain transplant? The manual contained diagram after diagram, one showing sectional door installation and another demonstrating one-piece door installation (that was him), diagrams explaining how to install the chain and sprocket cover and diagrams illustrating how to assemble the T-rail and cable pulley bracket. There were even diagrams showing large white exclamation marks and jagged lightning bolts inside black triangles, with words in large bold-face saying, "WARNING! TO REDUCE THE RISK OF SEVERE INJURY OR DEATH TO PERSONS, READ AND FOLLOW ALL INSTRUCTIONS!"

Hilbert snorted. It would take more than that to scare him off. But it might be three evenings' work instead of two.

He quit work an hour early the following Tuesday for his appointment with Doc Summerall; he'd made it for late afternoon so he could arrive home the usual time without Dorothy knowing where he'd been. He stepped into the waiting room and muttered to himself when he saw that seven or eight people would be ahead of him. When Hilbert told a customer a plumbing job would be done by a certain time that's when he'd have it done; why doctors couldn't keep to schedules like everyone else he'd never know. Especially with the money they made. Then Hilbert noticed others had taken the few *Reader's Digest*s available and now all that was left for him were ancient issues of the *Presbyterian Record* and dog-eared copies of *Christian Woman*, and somehow neither of these inspired Hilbert to face the moment when Doc Summerall would strap on his plastic gloves, release them with a *snap!*, dip his finger in Vaseline, and ask him to lie down on his side on the examining table.

For a while Hilbert contented himself, if you will pardon the expression as being apropos to Hilbert, with guessing the ailments of the people around him. The gal to his left was obviously pregnant, except that wasn't an ailment, women were used to it, but the way that that sour-looking fella across the room with the hairs sprouting out of his nose sat scrunched forward, for instance, Hilbert figured he must be here for a tapeworm—which reminded him of the one about the guy with the tapeworm and the cookie and the hammer, and then he couldn't stop himself from laughing, so that several people looked at him. Now if he'd only had a *Reader's Digest* people would have thought he was reading "Life's Like That" instead of laughing at them, or, even worse, laughing for no reason. You shouldn't be laughing in a doctor's office, Hilbert always feels, it's like a church that way, both are serious places. You know the gospel says "Jesus wept," but you've never read a text that says "And Jesus split a gut," now did you? Sounds almost sacrilegious, doesn't it. So there you are. Such profound thoughts come often to Hilbert, and he doesn't always know where they come from. But it doesn't surprise him. The way he sees it, women sense things more, but men have *ideas*.

Then, after he had figured out what was wrong with each of the others in the room and was in the middle of calculating what Doc Summerall must make if he managed to see clients at the rate they were being called in, say one every five minutes, eight minutes at the outside, and the government paid him, what, fifty bucks a shot, multiply that by 300 working days and, holy cow, that sure beat plumbing!–when suddenly he heard the nurse call his name: "Mr Hilbert *Te*Brake." She didn't stress the second syllable of his last name the way she was supposed to, but the first, as if she were making a fine distinction: not a coffee break, but a *tea* break. Right in front of seventy-five people.

The nurse led him down a narrow hall, stopped, and raised her arm. "The pink room today, Mr. *Te*Brake. Doctor will be with you shortly." Sure, Hilbert thought, and I'm Catholic. Besides that, he hated pink.

He sat down and noticed that the end of the examining table across from him had metal stirrups, as if *he* was here for a pregnancy checkup instead of the woman sitting beside him, then his glance moved up and he saw a Herman cartoon taped to the ceiling above the examining table; it showed a pair of huge, furry ape hands clinging to a man standing in front of a Maternity Ward sign, and Hilbert got up to read the punch line, heard a soft knock, and scrambled back to his seat. Doc Summerall stepped in.

"Hilbert, glad you could come in." Doc sniffed and blinked. The white coat he was wearing reminded Hilbert of the technician in a muffler commercial he had seen on TV. Doc glanced inside a file folder. "It's been four years since you've been in, I see." He laid the folder down. "Well, might as well go right to it. If you'll remove your clothes, you can hang them on that other chair." Hilbert turned and started unbuttoning his shirt and heard behind him the *squeeeek-snap!* of Doc Summerall putting on rubber gloves. He draped his clothes over the chair, hesitated a moment whether or not to remove his boxer shorts, then decided he would keep them on.

"Now, just sit on the edge of the table here, if you would, Hilbert." The white paper crinkled like wax paper and was cold on the inside of Hilbert's thighs. His feet dangled six inches above the floor and he felt uncomfortably like a child sitting in a tall chair. He glanced up and saw that the punch line to the Herman cartoon read, "Nurse, are you absolutely certain this one's mine?" Then Doc Summerall ran through the routine Hilbert remembered from before: the *pssh pssh* of the blood pressure pump, the popsicle stick down his throat while he gurgled "Aaaah," Doc Summerall's gloved hand below decks, tickling him so that he almost laughed instead of coughed as Doc Summerall asked him to. Hilbert wished he could see what Doc was writing then inside the file folder. "Patient seemed–sagging. Possible iron deficiency. Appeared overly sensitive to touch. Gangrene? Removal of testicle may be necessary."

He was expecting next to be asked to lie down on his side, but Doc Summerall began placing his stethoscope here and there on his chest, the metal clammy and colder than a dog's snoot against his skin. Then

Doc placed his hand on the left side of his chest and pressed down, his fingers probing back and forth.

"How long have you had this lump here?" Doc asked, blinking, and Hilbert brought his hand to his chest. Lump? He'd never felt any *lump*; he wasn't exactly in the habit of fondling himself. But sure enough, there it was, a rubbery little blob just bigger than a half-inch ball bearing, right beneath his left nipple. He raised his eyebrows. "I hadn't noticed that little critter there before."

"Hmmm." Doc Summerall ran his hand down his face, hard, hard enough to flatten his nose. That bad? Hilbert thought, with panic. His sister-in-law in Blyth, brother Clarence's wife Janet, had had a lump removed last year, malignant it turned out to be, and she had to go in for a–what was it called again, it wasn't a mysterectomy, but something like that.

"Well, we've got several options, Hilbert," Doc Summerall was saying. "We can leave it there a couple months, see if it grows, or becomes more jagged, then if it does we can remove it. Or we can decide not to take any chances, and just take the darn thing out. Thursday's my day at the hospital, it'll take just a local, half an hour later you'll be on the street. How about we do that?" Sniff sniff, blink blink.

Somewhat numb, Hilbert agreed. This had all happened rather suddenly; a reflective fella as Hilbert is, he likes to think about something like this a while.

That evening Dorothy must have thought Hilbert was unusually quiet at supper. Granted, he was not exactly a conversationalist even at the best of times. For Hilbert eating time is for eating, but he didn't schmeck the way he usually did. The meal did have meat and potatoes, so it couldn't be that. And the new lawn had grown back in nicely after Hilbert had over-fertilized it last summer. He even seemed to have gotten over Earle Prior beating him for the giant cauliflower championship by default. In any case, she thought he'd been rather quiet lately, even–dared she think it?–secretive. Did men show symptoms of menopause? she wondered. Maybe he was thinking of winter just around the corner. Winter was never a good time for Hilbert, that was probably it.

As soon as Hilbert saw the old Concord turn the corner that evening he went out back to fetch the garage opener. Dorothy didn't usually come home from Martha Society until after ten, so that would give him a good two hours, enough to make a good dent on it. He studied the diagrams a while to get the lay of things and was surprised at the number of parts involved: clevis pins, carriage bolts, header brackets; hex screws, rail braces, and safety reversing sensors–he wondered suddenly whether he'd given himself enough time to get the thing installed by Dorothy's birthday. One thing, though: it cost a bit more, but he'd been sure to buy an opener with the safety beam at the bottom. He'd read in the paper about a garage door without one that had come down on a kid in Calgary and smothered him, no way he was going to have Dorothy strangled by a runaway killer of a garage door.

He followed instructions and assembled the T-rail, then attached the cable pulley bracket. He looked at his watch and saw it was 8:30 already. Then he remembered: sure was a strange thing about that lump in his chest–was it his chest, or breast? Naw, men didn't have breasts, they had chests. Just like they had nipples alright except you shouldn't call them nipples with men. At least he got a good report on his prostate. "Just slightly enlarged," Doc Summerall had said, "normal for geezers your age." Then doc explained they were treated with microwaves now, of all things, killed off the excess tissue that way. Bodies sure were intricate, though, it was amazing how many things could go wrong. Doc sure had it right when he called them precision instruments.

He got only as far as fastening the T-rail to the opener that night before he had to put things away or else Dorothy would come home. He'd decided he wouldn't mention anything about his small operation next day–ah, it wasn't even worth calling an operation, it was just a little snip and stitch job. No sense worrying Dorothy needlessly. Tomorrow night he would keep on his t-shirt going to bed and she wouldn't notice a thing.

Still, he was a little nervous walking into Alfalfa General next day. He hated the way hospitals smelled of Lysol or formaldehyde or whatever it was. There *was* always a chance too that his lump was malignant–then what was he going to tell Dorothy? He was sure he'd round a corner and meet Evelyn Krikke, in which case Dorothy would know about it within half an hour, or he'd run into someone else from church and then he'd have to think fast. "Yeah, one of my ah, customers is in, from out of town you know, he's got uh–cancer. Cancer of the uh, you know, down there with men. Yes. Has only so much time, I'm afraid. *Had* to take off time from work to see him."

But he met no one, and found the right ward okay and was lying down on a soft leather table before he knew it, Doc Summerall swabbing his chest with something wet and very cold. Maybe it *was* formaldehyde. Then Doc spread a green cloth with a six-inch square

95

hole in it over his, well, left nipple. Hilbert wasn't sure whether he should pray for a successful surgery or not since it wasn't a big deal, same as he was never sure he should pray before eating a salad, which wasn't really a meal. His Uncle Gerald had always said, if it costs less than five dollars you don't have to pray for it, but that was twenty years ago so he should probably up it to six or seven dollars by now.

Then Doc Summerall injected the needle into the left side of his chest, a sharp, piercing little pain, and the rest Hilbert couldn't even feel. Now and then he felt Doc Summerall tugging slightly against something in his chest while they talked about what the Leafs' chances were this year, maybe the boys would have a big season, and it wasn't fifteen minutes later that Doc Summerall said, "That's it. Want to see it?" and Hilbert thought a moment and said, "Sure." Then Doc raised a forceps that held a bloody little white blob that looked like a piece of fat from one of Dorothy's roasts before she put it in the oven, and Hilbert said, "I'll be darned."

"I'll just put in a couple stitches here, they're the dissolving kind so you won't need to come back in, then I'll give you some bandages for you to change every day, and you'll be on your way. Soon as I get the biopsy result I'll give you a call. Take the rest of the day off, Hilbert, I don't want you to strain anything."

That evening Hilbert wondered whether maybe he shouldn't work inside the garage either, he wouldn't want to rip open any stitches. Ah, he wouldn't be doing anything heavy. And he was still only in the assembly phase, he hadn't even gotten to the installation part yet–he'd better stay with it, otherwise he wouldn't get the thing up before Dorothy's birthday next Wednesday.

He had to admit waiting for the biopsy result was a bit tense, maybe he'd taken this whole thing too lightly. Trouble was, a lump was one of those women's affairs, they knew more about these things; he would rather have dealt with matters *he* was familiar with, simple things like skinned knuckles and blisters when he burned himself with hot lead– you didn't need a biopsy for those. Especially if you were a Calvinist. A Calvinist like Hilbert knows about slivers and split fingernails; he knows we live in a world of suffering and pain, he's not like those New Agers who listen to tape recordings of ocean waves and whale sounds and construct wind chimes from pieces of coloured glass and eat barley greens.

Hilbert looked at all the nuts and bolts and metal bars strewn across the garage floor. Somehow he'd have to find a place for each one of them–it would be a miracle if he managed, he thought, especially after he glanced at the next instructions in the manual: "With the trolley against the screwdriver, dispense the cable around the pulley. Proceed back around the opener sprocket, as in figure 2. Be sure sprocket teeth engage the chain, then continue forward to the trolley threaded shaft." Hilbert had to read the words three times before they made any sense, it was as tough as reading the book of Revelation. It was a good thing he loved Dorothy, or he would have bought her something that didn't require assembly, like an electric can opener, or a Weed Eater so Dorothy wouldn't have to get down on her hands and knees with the clippers to trim the edges of the lawn after he had roared by on his John Deere.

He lifted the assembled T-rail and slipped a twelve-inch piece of two-by-four under it to keep it from staining the garage floor. He thought again of his lump and knew suddenly it would be malignant. Half his chest would have to be removed, nothing left but a gaping hole, then he'd have to endure chemotherapy treatments for the next six months and all his hair would fall out and leave him as bald as Yul Brynner except not quite as handsome, and then chances are he would die anyway. At least Dorothy wouldn't have to heave the garage door any more, he wouldn't want her to croak too because of a heart attack.

He paced the house all that weekend, couldn't even watch the Leafs for stretches longer than ten minutes before getting up to grab another coffee, then the following Tuesday afternoon when he happened to be at the house picking up some pieces of copper pipe and Dorothy hadn't gotten home yet from work the call from Doc Summerall finally came. "Well Hilbert," Doc said, "looks like what you had was a lipoma after all."

"A lip–?" He paused a moment, filled with alarm. "Is–is that good or bad, Doc."

"A lipoma? Just some fatty tissue, as I told you."

Hilbert couldn't remember Doc Summerall saying anything like that. "Now what, Doc?"

"Nothing. You're a healthy man. How's that incision healing?"

Hilbert knew he'd get that dad-blamed opener installed, it was nothing for an old pro like him. He'd finished it the last minute while Dorothy was still at work on her birthday, and he'd even found a place for every part, not so much as a screw or a bolt left over. He and Dorothy were just turning into their street after he'd taken Dorothy out for a birthday dinner at his favourite truck stop restaurant where they make a great hot chicken sandwich that swims in nice thick gravy the way Hilbert likes, when Hilbert stopped the Concord on the shoulder of the road a block from their house. He'd worked this all out in his mind.

He walked around to Dorothy's side, opened her door, and said, "You drive."

She looked at him as if he might have had a screw loose–I mean, Hilbert just did not *ever* ask Dorothy to drive with him in the car, but being the Christian wife she is she got out, walked to the other side, and climbed behind the wheel.

Hilbert made a motion with his hand as if he might be shooing away a fly. "Go," he said, "go."

When she was within twenty yards of their house Hilbert asked her to pull over. Dorothy stopped the car, nonplussed. Maybe thoughts of oncoming winter *were* making Hilbert come unhinged.

"Well," Hilbert said, "are you ready for your birthday present?" Dorothy was curious; she thought maybe Hilbert had forgotten, for normally he had presented his gift to her by now. He obviously hadn't forgotten her birthday, though, because he'd taken her out for dinner, which he wouldn't have done in the middle of the week for no reason. She felt good he'd remembered after all. Especially after what he'd bought her last year, a Dirt Devil of all things.

Then Hilbert handed her an object that looked like the remote control of their television, except it didn't have all the numbered little black buttons. "Press here," Hilbert said, pointing to a grey spot.

Dorothy wasn't sure she could do that *and* steer, but managed it without running the Concord into the ditch. She glanced over at Hilbert but he sat there looking at their house with eyes open wide and sort of a smile on his face, a look she hadn't seen on him since the time the Leafs won the Stanley Cup, but that had been so long ago Dorothy was surprised she remembered it. She pressed the remote control or whatever the thing was, not sure what to expect. For all she knew she might be setting off a bomb.

"Now what?" Dorothy asked.

Hilbert's smile had turned into a frown. He grabbed the gizmo from her. "Here," he said, "you're not doing it right." He pressed the gizmo again and again with a jabbing motion now as Dorothy started the car forward, turned into their drive, and stopped in front of the garage door. She thought Hilbert would be a gentleman and lift the garage door for her–after all, it *was* her birthday–but he ran up the steps, unlocked the front door, and stepped inside so urgently you'd think he'd heard the phone ringing.

She found him inside the garage pressing a similar remote control gizmo mounted against the wall, which she had noticed earlier today, then she'd seen the contraption in the ceiling of the garage and realized Hilbert had finally gotten tired of having to lift the heavy garage door and had decided to buy himself an automatic garage opener. Oh, so *that* was what the little thing was–but why had he asked *her* to open it? And it wasn't like Hilbert to spend that much money on something so frivolous and unnecessary as a garage opener, he was usually more tight-fisted than that.

She saw Hilbert hadn't calmed down any and was still stewing about the garage door not opening. He kept pressing the switch mounted on the wall, but nothing happened. Then he started fuming about George Hardy, sell *him* an inferior product, would he, right here in Alfalfa? Just wait until he got his hands on *him!*

Dorothy looked here and there trying to find why the thing wasn't working, but she'd never understand a precision instrument like a garage opener, she would have to leave that to people like Hilbert who understood these things.

Looking at the garage opener in the ceiling she remembered the story she'd read in the paper not long ago about a garage door that had come down on a small boy in Calgary–or was it Lethbridge?–anyway, it had been an opener that didn't have one of those safety beams near the floor that would have stopped the garage door, the paper said, otherwise the boy would not have been crushed, but here she noticed Hilbert had been smart enough to buy one with the safety bea–

Then she noticed something.

She walked to the garage door and said, "Hilbert, I think it would work if you moved this," and she lifted a little piece of two-by-four leaning against the frame of the garage door so that it blocked the beam of the safety sensor, right where Hilbert must have left it standing as he was cleaning things up.

She was surprised at the look on Hilbert's face, which for some reason wasn't at all as happy as she thought it might have been, especially since the garage door went open like a charm when Hilbert tried it.

Then she remembered.

"Hilbert," she said, "what was it you were saying about a birthday present?"

Around town with Heloise

What gorgeous weather this Thanksgiving weekend, for a change. Trees have changed into their fall attire. Truly much to be thankful for.

At Grace United Pastor Sandra Oppendahl gave each of the children a bright coloured leaf with the message that the seasons may change, but God remains the same. Seasons may come and go but the time to say thanks is always. Rodeo great Jimmy Don Roberts gave a talk about finding reasons for thanks, even in the perilous fortunes of a bull rider. Melody Shepherd gave a reading of Helen Steiner Rice's "A Thankful Heart."

Ed and Gladys Gillespie were among many Alfalfans who spent the weekend with family. They left Friday morning for Brantford to spend Thanksgiving with their daughter and son-in-law Bill and Amanda Bruce.

Unusually busy weekend for some reason for our volunteer firefighters. Friday evening they were called to the scene of an accident, reported by the person calling to be quite serious. When firefighters arrived they discovered the accident was not severe, just a car in the ditch, all that was needed was a towtruck. Next day a passerby called to report a fire at the home of John and Betty Seeley. Turned out to be a false alarm.

The caller mistook meat smoking procedures for a fire.

That same night firefighters were called to the home of Bruce McCarthy with reports of a vehicle on fire. Firefighters put out a blaze under the hood of a pickup which stood perilously close to the house. Cause of the fire has not been identified, but Bruce McCarthy said the truck had just returned from the auto body shop for repairs.

Give thanks this season for our committed and capable volunteer firefighters.

Have you noticed the days are getting shorter? Just in case you missed it.

That's all for now.

-column in The Alfalfa Sentinel-Star

THE RAPTURE OF
CHARLIE WIMMER

Had *The Sentinel-Star* not run an article about Charlie Wimmer quitting his job last Friday in the produce department at Art's Mart because he expected the rapture to happen today, folks in Lucille's Lunch would have had little else but the wet weather to talk about. So it was a good thing Charlie gave them something to take their minds off the fact that October has been a complete write-off because of all the rain and now here they would soon have to go through November, an even worse prospect.

Apparently Charlie has been listening to a radio program called "The Prophecy Hour" broadcast by somebody named Harley Mizell all the way from down in Virginia. Charlie left First Christian Reformed Church in town six years ago and joined the Blessed Assurance Tabernacle, where he can raise his hands and shout hallelujah and amen without other members of the congregation turning and glaring at him. St. Paul might well instruct believers to lift holy hands in prayer, even in the very same chapter where he states women should be silent in church, but there are some folks at First Christian Reformed who consider the first command to be puzzling if not outright questionable because raising hands seems to them to be excessive emotionalism, but they will become extremely emotional should you question Paul's injunction about women.

From his stool at the front counter of Lucille's Lunch this morning, Peewee Melnyk is showing everybody his hot-off-the-press copy of *The*

Sentinel-Star with its front page photograph of Charlie Wimmer, prematurely bald, along with a three-column story of how Charlie said today would be the day of the rapture. That gets everyone's attention pretty fast, and Peewee begins reading the *Sentinel-Star* story with dramatic voice:

"'Today is the day Charles Wimmer believes he will disappear. He is also convinced all non-believers will discover they have been left behind when millions of other Christians all over the world suddenly disappear. Skeptics, however, claim Harley Mizell is just one more deluded prophet who has mistakenly predicted such'"–Peewee halts, then stumbles over the speed bump at the end of the sentence–"'cat–cataclysmic events as the end of the world.'

"'October 24 is the day,'" Peewee reads, regaining momentum, "'that all true believers will experience the rapture, according to Harley Mizell, who is a shoe salesman and radio preacher from Virginia. He says it will happen this afternoon, eastern time, between 1:00 and 4:00 o'clock.'"

There's a low commotion as people look at their watches. "Hey Peewee," Ben Locke hollers when the hubbub has subsided, "you've got three hours to get your life in order!"

"Not to worry," Peewee offers with a broad smile, "my wife's already seen to that!" and all the regulars at Lucille's break out in guffaws.

Peewee raises his hand to restore order, then reads about how Harley Mizell says the rapture signals the beginning of the Great Tribulation, a time of horrible tumult and persecution. The sun will be totally darkened, the stars fall from the sky, and the moon turn to blood. The only way for people to be saved, Mizell says, will be through martyrdom.

"Peewee will do fine, then," a voice hollers, "he's used to martyrdom."

Yeah," Bob Tonkin says, "his wife's seen to that as well. Ha ha!"

Peewee ignores the jibe. "'Wimmer has been handing out tracts around town this past week,'" he reads, "'warning people of the great event about to–'"

"I'll say he has," Earl Prior says between puffs on his pipe, "between Hardy Hardware, the Art's Mart, and Lucille's, he got me three times. He's as bad as them army cadets."

"Except with the cadets at least you get an apple," Ben Locke says.

"Don't say that," Earl grimaces, "that's how all the trouble got started the first time!"

Peewee resumes reading. "'When asked whether he was sure about the prediction, Wimmer replied, "You bet I am. I don't plan on being here after today." And his wife? Wimmer admits wife Marva is not at all as sure as he about the rapture being today.'" Then Peewee reads about how Charlie Wimmer explained that Harley Mizell's prediction was the result of 1500 hours spent studying passages throughout the Bible.

The Sentinel-Star then quotes the Reverend John DeHeer, pastor of First Christian Reformed Church of Alfalfa, who is asked his opinion of Harley Mizell's prediction. Rev. DeHeer states that "as we approach the end of the millenium it's no wonder predictions for the end of the world would increase." He agrees there are signs pointing to the imminent end of time, but disagrees with Mizell's identifying a specific date. "Reformed eschatology," he says, "has never endorsed a pre-millenial dispensationalist rapture," but the story does not go any further into that.

The Sentinel-Star does go on to tell about how Charles Wimmer took a drive yesterday, stopping at a number of places here in Alfalfa for a last look, about how he went to see the wading pool in the park where he had swum as a lad, the grocery store where he had his first job as a carry-out boy, and some of the spots in the country where he had courted his wife. He would not reveal which.

Then Peewee reads the story's final paragraph: "'Asked how he intended to spend the day of the rapture, Wimmer said that he would probably take care of some last minute chores around his house. "Leave things in good order you know," he chuckled. When pressed about what would happen if the rapture weren't today, Wimmer said he would simply return to his old job–if they would have him. But he remains absolutely convinced the rapture will happen today.'"

There is a moment's silence; then, from a back booth of Lucille's Lunch a stentorian voice begins counting down: "Ten. Nine. Eight. . . ."

The matter of Charlie taking care of chores around the house as reported by *The Sentinel-Star* had come about four days earlier that week as Charlie sat in his living room reading one of Harley Mizell's tracts about wars and rumours of wars, when Marva came up to him. "Come here once," she says in a voice that seventeen years of being married to Marva tells Charlie she isn't going to say it twice. "I've got something to show you," she says and marches to the dining room.

Charlie follows, shoulders drooping like a puppy about to be scolded for having watered the flowers in the carpet. "See there," she says, "look what it's doing."

Uncertain just who "it" might be, Charlie does indeed see a water stain darkening the pink dining room carpet, spreading in an oval shape directly beside the turquoise wall. He looks at it, but is unable to arrive at any explanation for its being there, since their dog Cleo, a miniature collie who must have grown bored with life here in Alfalfa, ran off mysteriously only a week ago and was probably living it up at this moment with some floozy of a poodle in Grand Bend, smart dog.

Charlie looks at the stain on the floor, mystified. "Where do you suppose it came from?" he asks.

His quandary is broken by a large drop of water falling with a loud plop onto the carpet, and Charlie glances upward. There on the ceiling is an even larger water stain, its serrated edge rusty brown; its shape, Charlie thinks, resembles Lake Superior. The ceiling's smooth plaster surface is pocked with moisture; the white paint has started to peel. Even as Charlie looks he already sees the slow, inexorable forming of the next drop about to fall.

"The gutters," Marva explains, "they're plugged. With all the rain we've been having the water's seeping through. You'll have to clean them."

Until Marva pointed it out to him, however, Charlie has not noticed the leak. That happened four days ago, so today, rapture day, Charlie will clean the gutters. It seems to him an appropriate last thing to do, like getting his house in order.

It's a good thing Marva has her feet on the ground, a balance to his own personality. He hates to think what shape the house would be in if it were not for Marva's practical bent. Well, lay not up for yourselves treasures on earth, he reminds himself. Even so, it had taken him several months before he'd gotten around to replacing the washer in the dripping kitchen faucet. Smart it was of Marva to turn off the water in the basement as a way of finally getting him to fix it. He'd turned on the tap to fill the kettle with water for tea, and had watched, dumbfounded, as no water came out.

After inhabiting this planet a number of years you expect certain causes to lead to certain effects. Throw a stone into the air and it'll come back down–usually sooner and closer than you think. Hit your thumb with a hammer and a unique sensation follows, that and astonishing your children with vocabulary they knew but didn't know you knew. So when you turn on the tap, water's supposed to come out. Charlie had

106

turned it on, heard it hiss a mocking *phhhhht*, and–nothing. Droughtsville. He'd turned around to see Marva leaning against the door frame, arms folded, eyebrows raised, fingers doing a paradiddle against her cheekbone and an I-was-wondering-how-long-it-would-take-you look on her face.

He wonders now which of them their daughter will take after. Marva, probably. Deborah already shows her mother's attention to detail, and will no doubt eventually become– Oh yes, he thinks, remembering.

Well, to get at it then. He will need work gloves, to prevent blisters and cuts. And a trowel, to scoop out the crud. He wonders how he would look, entering the Kingdom clutching a trowel. Well, he could do worse; there's something appropriate about it. He will also need something to pick up the mess from the ground: a rake and shovel. He knows there is something else, what is it? Oh yes, a ladder. He will need an extension ladder, which he doesn't have. On sale at Hardy Hardware, he has noticed in this week's *Sentinel-Star*, for $129.99, which he also doesn't have. He figured he wouldn't need one, and now, of all times, his gutters decide to plug. Perhaps Irv Pankey next door will indulge him one last time. Irv's a good sort, active in local Chamber of Commerce activities, umpire of Little league games in town, 6'3" and considerably overweight, so that in his umpire's padded blue uniform he looms behind home plate as large and solid as a Brink's truck. More important, though, from what Charlie can see, he's also about as aware of spiritual values as a Brink's truck.

Irv waddles into his garage where the ladder hangs against a wall. "Quite a story in the paper about you today," he says. "So you figure this is it, eh?" and he spreads his hands as if he were calling a runner safe.

"Certain of it. You won't see me after today," Charlie says. He pauses. "And what about you, Irv? Where will you be tonight?"

Irv smiles beatifically. "Me? I'm gonna pour myself a cold one and watch the third game of the Series tonight, Charlie. As for eternity, I'll worry about that later."

Charlie reaches into his shirt pocket for one of Harley Mizell's tracts. "Read this, Irv."

He watches his neighbour turn the tract over as if he has never seen one before. Charlie hoists the ladder to his shoulder. "Thanks again, Irv. I'll return it soon's I'm done. But if I'm gone like I said, you'll find it against the house. And, uh, promise me you'll read that one, Irv."

"Sure, Charlie. Maybe between innings."

Charlie carries the ladder back to his house, shoulder and arm between the middle rungs, the ladder heavier than he thought. He looks at his watch and sees it's five after one. He is just easing the tip of the ladder against the house, softly so as not to scratch the paint, when Marva opens the kitchen window. "Charlie, would you mind getting a package of hamburger from the freezer for supper tonight? There's a one pound package, get that one would you?"

Without thinking Charlie walks over to the garage where the freezer stands, an old chest model. He rummages among packages of frozen meats and vegetables, pizza and ice cream, finds the hamburger, and shuts the lid of the freezer.

He's halfway out of the garage, walking between the car and the studded wall where the garden hose hangs, when he realizes what he's doing. Is it a test of his faith? It takes him less than a second to make up his mind. He places the hamburger back in the freezer, reaches around, and pulls the freezer's electric cord from the wall socket. That will show whether he has faith or not. He walks out of the garage, picks up his rubber work gloves, and puts them on, ready for battle. He looks up the length of the ladder stretching high towards the sky, then glances at his watch. It says 1:18. Trowel in hand, he ascends the ladder rung by rung.

The little trowel works well, enabling him to scoop the leaves and mud from the gutters without having to use his hands. At first he works from the ladder, then he gets tired of having to climb down to move it constantly, and clambers onto the roof itself. Soon the driveway beside the house lies splotched with sodden little black piles. He sees a car drive by slowly, its passengers, an old couple, pointing at his house. All day cars have crawled by, he has noticed. Must be the *Sentinel-Star* article. Strange, what attracts people.

From where he is high on his roof he notices he can look into the Pankeys' bedroom window. A bright red spread covers their bed. (He just knew their loo must be blue). Irv and Gail invited him and Marva once long ago for an evening of cards. He'd never had time for cards, and played badly. Irv and Gail have not invited them again.

Down the opposite side of the street he can see far past Donna Melanchuk's Cut 'n Curl all the way to Carr Motors on the highway. A Scripture verse comes into his mind suddenly: "Let him who is on the housetop not go down to get the things that are in the house." He has always wondered what that verse meant, but he shivers now as he thinks of it coming to fulfilment.

Climbing the ladder earlier he noted with chagrin that the paint on the house was starting to crack and peel. And he painted it only two summers ago. Andy Hardy at the hardware store told him it was moisture coming through the walls from the inside that does that. Perhaps next spring he could–oh yes, and he catches himself again.

Below him a screen door slams and he sees Deborah enter the garage; from his vantage point high on the roof she seems no taller than a midget. He wonders if she is doing her homework. He arranged for her to come home from school at lunchtime today but for her to be given assignments to be done at home. "Oh Daddy," she complained after reading the article in *The Sentinel-Star* this morning, "you come off looking like such a–*dweeb!*" Charlie did not need to ask her what the word meant. She'd been offended by him, worried about what all her friends would think of her.

The interview at *The Sentinel-Star* had gone well, he felt, he'd never talked to a reporter before. And the story was fair too, except maybe for the line about Marva, he wishes that hadn't been put in. Makes it sound almost like internal dissension. But the story will awaken many people; Harley Mizell will be proud.

He looks at his watch again and sees it's 2:35. He notices the sun has disappeared overhead. A cold breeze has started up. Down below, Deborah walks back out of the garage with the package of hamburger.

At the Art's Mart, Ronnie Sparks will be taking care of produce. Typical of what you'd expect from a young kid these days: smart, with a good head on his shoulders, but no sense for what's truly important. The others were skeptical too. Polite, but non-committal–all but Art Evans himself. Of course. He's the one who has to worry about staffing. "You sure you want to do this now, Charlie?" he said. "What am I gonna do for the week you're gone?" Short-sighted, that's what he is, and Art even an elder at St. Andrews Presbyterian.

Charlie begins to feel his knees from scraping against the coarse roof shingles. He's been working a long time, finally reaching the east side of the house. The wind has begun to pick up now, and over the trees to the west the sky has turned rather dark. He has not talked with anyone a long time.

He has almost reached the end of the last gutter when Marva's voice calls to him urgently from below. "Charlie! Charlie, come down! Channel 11 just called, they're waiting for you uptown to do a live, on-the-spot interview. You're to meet them as soon you can in front of the bank!"

He looks at his watch, then at the ten feet of gutter still to be cleaned. It would have been nice to have gotten done. But he feels no hesitation.

It seems appropriate, a last opportunity to witness to others. He climbs down to meet Marva standing at the bottom of the ladder, talking before he has even reached the ground.

"Hurry, Charlie. Oh, but look at you, look at your pants."

It's true, his pants are splotched with crud. Well, this is no time for social niceties. Did John the Baptist wear a suit?

He pulls off his work gloves and within minutes is in his car, driving toward town. It's too bad Marva and Deborah will not be able to see him interviewed on television. He has not allowed a set in the house; most programming, he feels, is too secular, if not outright demonic. He has his suspicions, however, that Deborah often goes to a friend's house two doors over.

He parks behind Lucille's Lunch across from the bank, and tells himself to be calm. There will be reporters, cameras, thick black cables coiled on the ground, spectators milling about. He must speak clearly.

He rounds the corner across from the bank, then notices a strange thing. There are no reporters at the intersection, no television cameras. Have they gone inside one of the buildings?

He crosses the street, looks up and down the block, but sees nothing. He glances at his watch. He's surprised to see it says 3:57, he did not know it was this late. Then, when he realizes the time, he is flooded with panic, unsure whether he can wait even a moment longer. He turns and heads back toward his car, desperate to go home and be with Marva and Deborah. He runs awkwardly against a red light across the intersection, too impatient to wait for the television crew he knows will never come, his mind too filled with impending dread for him to see the crowd of faces bunched in the window of Lucille's Lunch, laughing as at a colossal joke.

DOG   MISSING in the vicinity of Abe
Fettke's farm on Concession 6, a 3 year old
black lab,neutered, answers to the name of
Lucky. Call 383-5769

-ad in The Alfalfa Sentinel-Star

PUTTING UP THE STORMS

A ndy Plakmeyer is sipping his first cup of coffee of the day in the kitchen breakfast nook with his wife Ann, who's in her white terry bathrobe with her eyes still pinched shut and her hair not combed out, looking as if she's put on a Phyllis Diller mask for Halloween. Andy knows she'll go back for another hour or two of sleep the moment the kids are out of the house while he's out slopping joint compound on the sheets of drywall he hung yesterday in Les Maslowski's new insurance office in town. It strikes Andy he's not exactly decked out for a Hugo Boss *GQ* advertisement himself with the white splotches of goop covering his white shirt and white workpants. Then, when he's in the middle of thinking that if it weren't for the grace of God you'd wonder what on earth it is that keeps two human beings together their whole lives, an awfully sober thought to have before the sun is even up on the first day of November, he's interrupted by the phone ringing above his left ear.

Andy looks across the table at Ann, whose eyes are suddenly open with the ringing of the phone, then he looks at the kitchen clock above the fridge. It's only 7:05, the kids barely up after going to bed late the evening before with Halloween.

"Some guy who wants it done yesterday, you watch," Andy says, grabbing the phone to stop the ringing in his ears. He knows at seven in the morning it's not going to be the town library telling him the kids' books are overdue.

Andy doesn't even have time to say hello.

"Yeah, Andy? It's Milt. Milt Coombs, just past the fairgrounds? Got me an emergency situation here, Andy. Water mattress sprung a leak upstairs during the night and my living room ceiling's hangin' like a water-filled balloon."

"What were you doin', Milt, makin' love to a porcupine? Or sleepin' with a screwdriver in your back pocket? Hee hee. Sorry, Milt, couldn't help that."

"I tell ya, the dang thing sprang a leak."

"How much of the mattress emptied?"

"Pert near the whole thing."

"Yeah, well, no wonder your ceiling's falling then. Tell ya what Milt, I'll see if I can stop by later today to have a look, OK?"

Andy figures he'll drive out to Milt's place on his way home either today or tomorrow, which is the earliest he'll have Les Maslowski's office done. Then he's got to start thinking about Roger Latham's house over on Clark Court, where the plumbers and electricians finished a week ago and Roger's been giving him a hard time about when he can come to drywall the house so they can move in before the snow starts flying.

~~~~

Milt Coombs is in his henhouse later that morning catching chickens. He'll slaughter ten or twelve of them today and pop them in the freezer to help get him through winter. The chickens, however, aren't cooperating, the dumb clucks, as if they've noticed their number is decidedly dwindling and that this may have some logical connection with the chopping block and the freshly sharpened axe resting in the grass thirty feet away. The birds mill together furtively in a corner of the henhouse so that none of them will stand out, skittering away from Milt with a sharp-eyed look that says "Murderer! Don't think we don't know what you're up to!" Milt sneaks up on one minding its own business in a corner, then lunges when he's within two feet of it. The chicken squawks and leaps straight up as Milt dives for its legs and grabs nothing but air. His dentures come flying out of his mouth as he lands with a whomp, feathers and dust swirling into his face. "Thuck me down the thewer," Milt mutters, picking up his teeth out of the sour-smelling dust.

After he's put himself back together again he catches a chicken, one that bears a surprising resemblance to himself, a scrawny-looking bird with the feathers pecked off the top of its bald red head. Milt steps out

of the henhouse with the chicken dangling from his hand and walks
through the cold November air towards the chopping block resting in
the grass near the house. Beside the block sprawl the bodies of six
decapitated white chickens, their heads with bright red wattles and
milky blue eyelids lying off to the side in a little pile.

Milt takes the chicken by the legs, places its body on the bloodied
wooden block with his left hand, and picks up the axe with his right. The
axe is too big, he knows, he should be using a smaller hatchet, and as
he raises it the chicken suddenly sees its life pass before its eyes and
begins to squawk in Milt's left hand. He shortens up on the axe handle
and raises it, and just as he's about to bring it down onto the block the
chicken, in a desperate last attempt to let Milt know she'd prefer death
by lethal injection, flaps its wings so that only the bottom tip of the axe
catches its neck, blood spurting onto the white feathers but the neck not
completely severed and the bird still alive enough to think that, on the
whole, she'd rather be in Philadelphia. Milt has to raise the heavy axe
and bring it down again before the chicken stops writhing in his hand.
He lays the bird, its legs still twitching, beside the others, then tosses its
head onto the little pile. Blood from the severed heads stains the grass.

Before heading back to the henhouse Milt glances down the road
leading to town to see if Andy Plakmeyer is on his way yet. All he can
think of is his ceiling inside the house dripping water into the pails he's
placed all over his living room floor. He's not sure how he can explain
what happened when Andy comes by to fix the ceiling, but he'll think
of something. Maybe if he's lucky Andy will mind his own business and
not ask so that he won't have to tell him about how it all started with the
eggs thrown against his house two nights ago and how everything went
downhill from there.

The problem was, he'd been late this fall putting up his storm
windows. Normally he'd have them up before the end of September
already just after he'd picked the last of the tomatoes and the first frost
hit, but this year he didn't get the windows up until just before
Halloween. It was the weather, the wet October they'd had, that
prevented him. He'd pictured himself trying to put up the windows in
a driving, cold fall rain, his foot sliding off a slippery wooden rung and
him falling all the way to the ground from the top of the ladder and
breaking both his ankles or cracking his skull open on the cement walk.
He had to wait for dry weather.

Be thankful you don't live in Calgary, he told himself, he'd read in the paper they'd had their first snow there a month ago already, ten inches of it, snapping tree branches with the leaves still on them. If he didn't get his storm windows up soon next thing he knew the snow would hit Alfalfa too, and there he'd sit all winter with the summer screens still on for anyone driving by to see. "Wonder what's wrong with Milt," people would be saying, heads shaking, "does it seem to you he's slowing down?" Then would come that shrewd look that crosses the faces of people who have life all figured out. "Happens often, you know, a man's wife dies and he goes to pieces. Usually doesn't take long."

The day he put up the storms the wind had come blowing out of the northwest. He'd started with the second storey windows, might as well get the tough ones out of the way first, he'd told himself.

He started up the wooden ladder carrying the storm window that went with the empty bedroom on the protected side of the house, and managed to get it into place. His second time up was to do the dormer window of his own bedroom in the southwest corner of the house by the tall sugar maple, bare of leaves now. On a limb that stretched over the roof of the house Milt could see a squirrel twitch its tail, then run off and down the tree as Milt approached. The reason he remembered it was because it was pitch-black, not like the usual brown squirrels he saw around town. He'd have to trim that branch over the roof sooner or later, just clogging up the gutter with leaves every fall. Besides, one winter storm with the leaves still on the tree as in Calgary and the branch could break and put a hole in the roof. Except Milt liked the leaves near the bedroom window in the summer, for shade.

He wondered whether he should have gotten a high school student to put up the storms for him this year, then chastised himself for even considering it. Give in on the first step and next thing you knew he'd be sitting in the Sunset Lodge along with all the other old buzzards, hands quivering and his toothless mouth drooling into his oatmeal. What he *should* have done, old fool, is listen to Hallie when she'd told him years ago to buy aluminum storms and screens so he wouldn't have to go to all this trouble every fall.

He managed to carry the window all the way up, then took off the gloves he was wearing and blew into his hands to warm them; the gloves were thin cotton ones for gardening and were no match against the cold wind that whipped his trousers against his skinny legs like a flag furled around a flagpole. The ladder underneath him shook in the wind.

He put his gloves back on, lifted his right foot over the eavestrough and onto the shingles of the roof, and was raising the storm window to hook it into place when the wind picked up out of the northwest. Watch it now, Milt, he told himself, struggling to maintain his balance atop the ladder. Suddenly a strong gust whipped around the corner of the house, whistled through the bare branches of the sugar maple, and blew against the storm window raised above his head. The gust took hold of it, and had Milt not had the wits to let go of the thing he would have been blown off the roof and gone flying through the air still holding the storm window. Just like those fools on television who jumped off cliffs holding on to big bright sails and glided in the air for miles. He might not have hit earth until he'd reached town, people watching an old man sail through the air like a kite, clutching his storm window. As it was he'd just managed to grab hold of the ladder with one hand and the eavestrough with the other while the storm window sailed into the air without him, flew across the lawn, and came crashing down in a million shards of glass onto the gravel driveway down below.

"Holy shit!" Milt hollered, and just managed to pop his dentures back into his mouth. He clung to the top of the ladder, scared spitless, afraid the wind would pick him up as an afterthought. It took him five minutes, legs shaking, to return to earth. And now here he is, the weather cold enough to pickle your liver and him short a storm window until he gets George Hardy at the hardware store to make him another.

He walks back to the henhouse, craning his neck to see whether Andy Plakmeyer's white van is coming up the road from town. Once he's finished butchering the chickens there are the other things he still has to look to: the cord of apple wood to chop, the car to be brought in to Andy Stokes to be winterized, the blade to attach to the Massey-Ferguson so he can clear the driveway of snow, bales of straw to place around the bottom of the house. He realizes again how lethal Canadian winters are–a person could get *killed* out there. He thinks of all the rituals he has to go through every November to protect himself, just like the animals–no wonder Canadian women don't shave their legs during winter, Milt thinks, just like raccoons grow extra thick fur. He'd grow an extra layer of protection too on his skinny bald legs, if he could. It would be easier than having to wash longjohns every week.

Nuh, fall's a miserable time, Milt thinks. Has been ever since Hallie died and left him fourteen years ago. The later the fall the more miserable Milt feels, as if he's been stranded in a bus station in a strange city late at night with the last bus for home gone. It's the barrenness, the sense of absence everywhere that gets to him, not just Hallie's absence from the house, nor the absence of their five children who have all moved away from Alfalfa, but everything else that has fled: the birds all gone, who seem to have had the good sense to board the last bus south before winter; no boys playing football anymore in the vacant lots in town, the sun pale and weak now falling behind the slate-grey barn by four in the afternoon already, the grass that has lost its greenness and is now a drab greyish-brown. The leaves stripped from all the trees everywhere scuttle across the earth in the stiff early November wind.

The neighbours' kids have all grown into gawky-looking teenagers with outlandish haircuts, and only a few children Milt is unable to recognize come trooping to his door now on Halloween, dressed up as pirates or witches or cats, their parents standing by their cars on the road and bundled up in heavy coats. A week ago Milt thought he'd better buy some candy for the few children who did come by, and walked out of Art's Mart with a bag of fruit lollipops, but this year, after what happened on Devil's Night, Milt turned off all the lights on Halloween and sat inside his garage as if no one were home so that no cars had stopped and he'd ended up eating the candy himself since he'd lost his teeth anyway, a 67 year old man with a bubble in his cheek and a white plastic lollipop handle sticking out of his mouth as he washed the dishes or sat watching television.

Actually, Milt surprised himself by buying candy at all–he did it for the little tykes, not for the older punks who have been tormenting him. If it were up to Milt he'd do away with Halloween altogether. Nothing but an invitation for juvenile delinquents, and that clown Sergeant Lofthouse in town not doing a thing about it. It had started again this year on Devil's Night the day before Halloween with eggs thrown against the storm windows he'd washed and put up only a day earlier, so that he'd had to go back out there and clean the windows again, except the cold weather had frozen the egg splattered against the glass so that even brushing with detergent and hot water hardly got the smears off.

He'd known they were coming for him of course–they always did. One year they'd smashed a load of pumpkins against his front porch and strung a dead farm cat from a branch of the sugar maple out front, another year they'd tilted a plastic pail half filled with water and cow shit up against his front door, then knocked and run. When he opened the door the liquid splashed against his stockinged feet and spread across the carpet in a dark brown stain. He saw them on the road in the dark, howling with laughter. Last year they'd put rocks through every one of the windows in his garage. He still hadn't replaced the glass–why give the punks an invitation to do it again?

So he should have known they were coming, yet they'd caught him off guard this year by coming the night before Halloween. He'd been sitting in his living room with the lights on so anyone and his canary out there could have seen him plain as day. They could have been five feet away from the house in the dark and he would have had to press his face against the window, hands cupped around his eyes to block the light, and he still wouldn't have seen them. A sitting duck is what he'd been.

He'd spent the day putting up the rest of the storm windows after his scare of the day before took away any thoughts of going back up the ladder, and now his legs were tired from climbing up and down all day. He sat down in his chair with his nightly nip to see what was on TV before heading off to bed.

When the first egg crashed against the front window he knew immediately it was them. He grabbed the broom handle from the pantry and ran out to give them a royal tanning, he'd teach the little bastards a thing or two, but by the time he reached the front of the house they were already fifty yards down the road, five or six of them laughing and running off towards town. No chance to catch them, not at his age.

So last night, Halloween, he was ready for them. He'd loaded his shotgun with #7 shot–not lethal past thirty feet but still plenty inducement, in the butt, to skedaddle–and sneaked to his upstairs bedroom where he could get a good view from the dormer. With no storm window in the way he could fire where he wished.

Sure enough, it wasn't half an hour later and they'd come back. He could see the car a ways up the road through the bare branches of the sugar maple outside the window and he could tell, the way they were driving slowly, it was them. He pumped the shotgun once to put a shell in the chamber and opened the window.

But instead of stopping at the house, the car drove by slowly, as if its occupants were unsure whether to attack or not. Milt couldn't see how many of them were inside. Thirty yards past the house the driver gunned the engine and the car sped off. Had they seen the barrel of the shotgun in the open window? Not bloody likely. Ah, he knew what they were up to, the little peckers. They'd decided to come back later when he'd gone to bed so they could get away with whatever they were going to pull this year. Well if that was the way they wanted it, he'd oblige. Did he have a surprise for them–he'd scare the little twits into the middle of next week. If they were coming later, he could wait. One shot into their backsides and they'd run off with their tails between their legs. He knew where he'd do it from, too, a place where they wouldn't be looking for him. But he'd need some fortification out there in the cold.

He looked at his watch. 10:15. Past the time he usually took his snort. A guy his age didn't stay as healthy as he was without a little tonic. He went downstairs, grabbed the bottle, and turned off all the house lights. He put on his winter parka and the cap with the ear flaps and walked out to the garage with his shotgun crooked in his left arm, the bottle under his right. Inside the garage he grabbed a wooden crate to sit on and had taken a spot by the open window quicker than you could say Jack Daniels.

Hoo, the first slug went down sweet and hot. He sat back. The moon was full, he noticed. Good. He could see better, that way.

He wondered if his neighbours were being vandalized too, or if he was the only one. What was there about him that made them pick on him? Like one of those chickens in the barn all the others took it out on. Pecked right to death, some of them–there'd been ones that hadn't made it he'd had to dig under. Hot dang, that grog tasted good.

Things hadn't been the same since Hallie died. Maybe that was it. She'd been their strength, no doubt about it, not a person in town who disliked her or would do the things to her they were pulling on him. Hours she'd spend every fall making gauze-wrapped little packets of candy for the kids who came trick or treating at the door. After she up and died on him he'd given candy grudgingly at the door, nothing but dad-blamed foolishness, bad for the teeth at that. Strange, he always thought he'd be the first to croak and now Hallie had gone and left him on his own.

He set the shotgun against the wall and took another swig.

He'd changed, it was true, since Hallie died, in ways she would have been surprised to see. How clean he kept the house, for one thing, which had been her domain. 'Course, there was also a magazine or two downstairs she'd be surprised at now, that she would. Not to mention the liquor, Hallie being the good Presbyterian she was. And the waterbed which he wouldn't have thought of buying if Hallie were still alive–who ever heard of a 67-year old widowed Scot with a waterbed. Milt chuckled at the thought–hee hee, Hallie'd have had conniptions at that alright. Strange, the things a man did after his wife passed on. And at his age, sly dog.

He thought he saw some movement in the sugar maple by his bedroom window. He grabbed the shotgun and brought the muzzle to the open window. Something was moving, alright, in the branches. He strained to make it out in the moonlight. Well, if it was an animal he had no truck with it. It was human varmints he was after.

He looked at his watch. Eleven, and they still hadn't returned. Now he wasn't sure just what to do; it was long past the time he usually hit the sack, but if he went to bed they'd come back sure as shootin' and no telling then what pell there'd be to hay. He stuck his head through the open window frame for a look-see outside and glanced up and down the road in both directions. Nothing. Things out there stiller 'n a witch's snoot. As cold, too. Probably better to go to bed after all, whatever was going to happen would happen.

He straightened up and almost lost his balance in the dark, then felt a searing pain against his cheek. *Leapin' lizards!* His hand flew to his cheek, feeling for the blood he knew would be there. Jumpin' Jehosaphat, the pain! He knew immediately what he'd done–gashed his cheek on the nail he'd pounded into a wall stud to hang the winter tires on. He steadied himself against the garage wall. The devil, he'd downed a glass or two more than usual, he had. The garage swirled around him in the dark. Now he was *good* and pissed off! Where had he put the shotgun? Somewhere by the window. He groped around for it, eyes still closed with the pain in his cheek, then felt the jagged glass in the frame of the garage window slice into his hand. Judas priest! He fumbled again for the shotgun and felt its cold barrel against his hand. He'd take it upstairs with him and keep it by the bed in case those birdbrains came back and the fur began to fly. But first he'd have to put something on his cheek. And take care of his hand.

He walked in the moonlight toward the house. He could feel frost stiffening the grass. He was sick of the cold, already sick of his pain. It would be good to be back in the house, warm with his longjohns under a layer of blankets. Another Halloween would be gone, with just the eggs against his window this time. And a gash in his cheek.

He hadn't been back in the house five minutes, and was just reaching into the medicine cabinet for the Mercurochrome to clean out the cuts on his face and hand, when he heard the noise. He stopped dead in his tracks.

Something upstairs. He stood still, not moving a muscle, and listened.

Someone was up there alright. He knew he heard just the faintest noise, as if someone were creeping across the floor. His bedroom, dammit, his and Hallie's *bed*room!

He grabbed the shotgun and walked stealthily toward the staircase. How had the little buggers made it inside? Of course! He'd left the back door open and they'd come in while he, like a schmuck, had been out watching the front of the house from the garage.

He took one slow step at a time, inching his way up the stairs, sure whoever was up there could hear the steps creaking. He twitched his head, trying to shake out the cobwebs brought on by the booze. His hands gripping the shotgun still felt stiff from the cold of the garage.

He was six feet away from the door of his bedroom, which stood open. Milt felt a draft of cold air–had they opened the window? His mind raced. Had they tried to make a getaway? But how, from a second storey window? Then he remembered–dang! He'd left the dormer window open himself when he was up here earlier.

He took the last several steps toward the open door not worrying about whether he might be heard, stepped into the doorway, and levelled the barrel of the shotgun at the middle of the room.

Empty. No one there.

Then Milt was sure he saw something move suddenly at the foot of the bed, startling him, and before he knew it the shotgun jumped in his hand, its roar shattering the bedroom's silence. He thought he saw something scamper off the bed and leap through the open window. He scuttled after it across the wood floor that was suddenly awash with water soaking his stockinged feet, and ran to the window.

He pointed the barrel of the shotgun through the open window but all he saw was an empty branch of the sugar maple swaying, swaying softly in the cold moonlight.

~~~~

Andy Plakmeyer is loading the last of his tools and pails of joint compound into the white van. He's finally finished with Les Maslowski's office, tomorrow he'll start on Roger Latham's place. Doggone, back out into the cold, he'll have to take an extra thermos of coffee. Which reminds him–he still has to stop in a minute at the Five and Ten to pick up the balloons Ann asked him to get for Stacey's birthday party day after tomorrow. She's probably sitting at home this very minute convinced he's going to forget. Aha. Not this dude.

Walking over, though, he knows there's something else he has to do. Something for Stacey's birthday? Party horns? Plastic forks? Paper plates? Nope, just balloons.

Then he remembers. Balloons. Milt Coombs' ceiling. He didn't manage to stop there yesterday, Milt calling him again, and if he doesn't stop in soon Milt will be having a bird. He'll go there first thing in the morning. If Milt can call him at seven he should be able to drop in on Milt just before eight.

When he drives onto Milt's driveway early next morning he notices shards of glass illuminated by his headlights, and steers his van around them. Milt must have hit something, he thinks. Ten seconds later he doesn't need to knock on the door, Milt's waiting for him before he's stepped out of his van. Andy sees Milt is sporting a mean red streak across the left side of his face, and when he comes closer he can see it's a deep gash. His left hand is wrapped in white gauze. Milt's face looks haggard, as if he hasn't slept.

"Have an accident on your driveway, Milt?" Andy says, "I noticed the glass." Milt only grunts something inaudible.

"Looks to me like you may need stitches there. What d'ja do to yourself?"

"Come on in the house," Milt mutters, starting to walk towards the back door.

Inside the house the living room ceiling is sagging, the drywall threatening to come crashing down. Andy can see a good volume of water has seeped down from upstairs. The whole ceiling will have to come down and be redone. Dark water spots still stain the living room carpet.

"When can you get at it?" Milt says, looking at Andy sharply out of the corner of his eyes, his head ducked down into his neck like a wary bird. A two-days' stubble of white beard stands out on his chin. The tan on his face stops an inch or two above his eyes, the top of his bald head a creamy white.

"How'd you lose *all* the water from the bed, Milt?"

"I tell ya, it just sprang a leak and I couldn't stop it."

Sure, and the Pope's my sister, Andy is thinking. "Were you home, Milt?"

"Sure I was home." His piercing eyes look straight through Andy.

"Well didn't you notice the leak?"

"Nuh, came down too fast. How soon can you get at it?"

Somethin' here's not adding up, Andy tells himself. I may be nothin' but a dumb drywaller, but I know a cock and bull story when I hear it.

"Maybe I should have a look upstairs," he says.

"No," Milt shouts, jumping like a startled chicken and moving between Andy and the stairway. "I mean, just tell me, what's it gonna cost me to get it fixed?"

"Can't tell ya that unless I see what the, uh, structural damage is to the ceiling joists and so on, Milt. I'd hate to go to all the trouble of putting up new drywall only to find out later you've got, you know, some other problem up there. Gotta check it out," and he steps by Milt toward the stairway. There's something he's hiding up there, Andy's sure. A body,

123

for all he knows.

"Just a quick look then," Milt says leading him up the stairs.

"That's right Milt, just a quick look."

He follows Milt Coombs into the bedroom at the top of the stairs, glancing around quickly for anything unusual. "Weeell, let's have a look here," he says, walking around the bed. He sees the rubber liner of the waterbed has been scrunched up into a ball. Nothing unusual there.

Then something familiar strikes him, an odour he knows well. He sniffs his nose lightly so Milt won't notice, sniffs again, then he's sure. The unmistakable smell of sulphur and charcoal that comes from only one thing. He's smelled the same odour every fall, duck hunting with the guys.

A shotgun's been fired in the room the last day or so, then. Now why would Milt do that? And why fire it into the waterbed? Andy reaches for the balled up rubber liner to have a look at it, to check underneath it, but Milt steps in and grabs his arm. "You wanted to have a quick look at the floor," Milt says, "so go on and do it."

"Sure, Milt," Andy says, getting down on his hands and knees, "just a quick look at the floor."

He peers under the waterbed, then sticks his head in all the way to look at the underside of the bed. A glance is all he needs.

Just as he thought.

He gets up from his hands and knees. "Well, Milt, doesn't look like any serious damage here. We'll just have to rip off the old drywall downstairs and put up some new. Shouldn't take me more than a couple half-days."

"When can you get at it?"

"The earliest would be, oh, about a week."

The same sharp look from Milt's crazy, blinking eyes above the red gash on his cheek. "No earlier, huh? Well, I guess that's what it'll have to be then." He places his hand in Andy's back and gives him a soft shove to usher him out of the bedroom.

Andy's mind meanwhile is racing, trying to piece together the details. Glass on the driveway. A man with a gash in his cheek, his hand all bandaged up. Fires a shotgun into his waterbed. But no sign of blood anywhere. Till Andy sees blood, Milt's just a crazy coot who fired a shotgun into his waterbed, nothing criminal about that. Idiotic, maybe, but not criminal. He'll have to ask Ann, maybe she can figure it out, she reads Agatha Christies all the time.

Andy heads back down the stairs, glancing everywhere, not

wanting to miss anything. Milt shows him out the back door. The sun is up now, rising in the east, but still the morning is cold. Then, as Andy is walking back to his truck something in the grass to his left catches his attention in the early morning light, no way he can miss it, and when he looks at it carefully he can see it's blood, splotches of it on the grass. Jiminy crickets, Andy thinks, what's been going on here then, a bloody massacre? There's no mistake about it, it's blood alright.

Andy steps into his truck and inches it forward slowly, then as he eases it onto the road he turns his head and sees Milt standing in the cold without a coat, standing on the grey-brown grass and fading into the early morning mist as insubstantial as a ghost, as if nothing has happened, nothing at all.

III.
The Mailbox's Metal Nose

The earth is frozen
The beautiful trees are frozen
even the mailbox's metal nose is cold
and I'm getting a little chilly myself

-Al Purdy

ELECTRIC BLANKET

A day after the rapture was supposed to have taken place back in October as Charlie Wimmer had said it would, the only ones missing from Alfalfa were George and Hillie Droge (who had not gone to be with the Lord in the air but to visit Hillie's mother in Owen Sound)–them and Abe Fettke's dog Lucky, who, I presume, doesn't count. It would have been interesting to read the headline in the newspapers next day: "RAPTURE OCCURS ON DATE ALFALFA MAN PREDICTED. FARM DOG ONLY ONE IN TOWN TAKEN." Wouldn't *that* have surprised a few souls in town?

No, if God had acted in the spirit of modern ecumenism at all you'd expect him to at least have taken a representative sample from each of the churches about town: twenty Pentecostals, let's say, from Blessed Assurance; fifty Anglicans from St. Paul's (they're more reserved, you'd need more of them); about the same number of Catholics–*if* (the Presbyterians at St. Andrews would tell you) you could find that many at Sacred Heart who didn't worship Mary. Of course, no members at all from First Christian Reformed would have been taken, since they don't believe in the rapture in the first place, being amillenialists, and therefore were going about their usual business of putting in an honest day's work in this vale of tears and checking the city paper to see how their RRSPs had done since yesterday.

It's early December now and life here in Alfalfa has been going on pretty much as normal since the rapture didn't happen after all. Folks in Lucille's Lunch were handing it to Charlie Wimmer afterward, though, for not feeling too humiliated to take back his job in the produce department at Art's Mart. Think about it: one day you're telling folks all over town you're going to be leaving them for higher things and a day later you're back at the same old job instead, wearing a cute little bow tie and a white apron with dirt smudges all over it while you're spraying water on the cauliflower to keep them looking nice and fresh. Talk about a major paradigm shift.

So there was Charlie last week back in the produce section at Art's Mart putting the finishing touches on building a two-foot high pyramid of Ontario Golden Delicious just in from Crandall's Orchards west of town. Charlie may not be a whiz in the prophecy line but he's the champion architect of artistic fruit displays of McWhinnie Township: whether it's oranges, which are comparatively easy, or apples, which are bloody difficult, ask any produce clerk, because they're not round and not all the same size (the apples, not the produce clerks). It doesn't matter, once Charlie constructs a fruit pyramid it's a paragon of symmetry and form. Now, most customers, adults anyway, have the sense to take their apples from the top of one of Charlie's pyramids, and even so it's a sacrilege for them to start dismantling one.

Then Ibbe Rozema walked into the store with two of his grandchildren.

I don't mean to suggest that all Frisians are dimwitted, not at all, nor that all grandparents are unmindful–at least, with grandparents you know they're just out of practice being around youngsters because one of the advantages of being a grandparent is being able to hightail it back home to avoid having to put up with a tired, screeching child or to deal with a diaper full of matter the colour and consistency of canned spinach. It's one of the rewards of a long, godly life mentioned in the book of Leviticus. So you can't blame Ibbe for what happened. Besides, he's had a rough weekend.

He'd come into Art's Mart with his two grandchildren, Al and Arlene Rozema's kids Alexa and Zachary–where do people *find* such names, Ibbe wondered, whatever happened to the good old tradition of naming kids after their grandparents? Al and Arlene had decided they needed to spend some time together, so they asked Al's folks Ibbe and Tetty to take care of their two kids and their dog Ernie (which is another story), and drove to Niagara Falls on a hotel get-away package Al saw advertised in the city newspaper. Tetty wanted to treat the grandchildren to chili for supper and had asked Ibbe to run out and pick up two jars of V-8 juice, which Tetty says is the clue to great chili, and

Ibbe, who's retired from farming and still can't stay away from anything green, strolled into the produce section to check out the vegetables. It happens every time he steps into a grocery store–it's as if the floor is leaning steeply towards the produce corner and Ibbe inevitably rolls that way like a marble in a tilted pinball machine. He thought he'd buy some cauliflower, which, with a Yukon Gold potato or two and a pork chop, Ibbe feels, is better than chili any day, especially at his age–funny things happen to a guy's exhaust system after he turns fifty, and Ibbe's behaves best, he's discovered, when he runs on lower octane fuel.

Ibbe had hung on to Alexa and Zachary, one in each hand, till he got to the cauliflower, which it turned out had brown spots on them, but the Brussels sprouts looked as good as Ibbe has seen them, so he tore off a clear plastic bag from a roll, and had almost finished stuffing it with sprouts when he heard Alexa's high-pitched voice scream, "ZACHARY!"

Ibbe turned to see apples, a torrent of Golden Delicious, roll by on the floor past his feet, 93 apples deciding, after Zachary had liberated the one sitting in the bottom right corner, that if *one* of them got to go this was the moment for the rest of them to break out, it was now or never, perhaps if they scattered in all directions the better chance some of them would have to escape or else they'd all end up as pie, dumpling, betty, or sauce.

Ibbe took hold of his grandchildren's hands and was standing in line at the 8-items-or-less counter before the last apple had even come to a stop. When they arrived home Tetty couldn't understand how on earth Ibbe could come home with a bagful of Brussels sprouts when what she'd asked him to pick up was two jars of V-8 juice. Ibbe didn't tell her about the apples. "It's our secret, what do you say," he'd told Alexa and Zachary on the way home. Zachary, only three, sat looking out the car window as innocent as a cabbage, but Alexa was old enough to have absorbed enough Calvinist guilt to think her grandpa's suggestion a good one. "We won't tell Grandma, shall we," she said, the little conspirator.

The chili turned out fine despite the absence of the V-8 juice. After the meal Ibbe read the Bible and then asked Alexa if she would close in prayer. "Lord," she said, "please be with Mom and Dad in Naggra Falls. And we thank you for your Word, even though we know you didn't write it all by yourself."

So taking care of Alexa and Zachary for a weekend turned out interesting. Ernie the dog was another matter. Arlene had bought the thing, a Pekinese, about a year ago because she fell in love with it when she saw it as a cuddly two day old pup in Paula's Pet Store in town. She'd named it Ernie because the dog's pushed-in face reminded her of Ernest Borgnine. "Don't worry about him," Arlene had told Ibbe and Tetty that afternoon when they were dropping off the kids and the dog, "the only thing he barks at is strangers, that and the doorbell. Such a good guard dog. And we didn't even have to train him to do that–isn't he intelligent?"

Not five minutes after Al and Arlene's van had pulled out of the driveway, the dog had begun yapping its head off, a piercing, high-pitched racket sharp enough to rip through a sheet of plywood. He'd started yapping as soon as he heard the grandfather clock in Ibbe and Tetty's living room chime the quarter hour.

"Oh, no, is this what I think it is?" Ibbe groaned.

It was. Ernie, a modern dog, had grown up with quiet digital clocks, not mechanical clocks that chimed, and apparently thought the doorbell was ringing. "Not every fifteen minutes," Ibbe moaned. He was too shell-shocked to think of removing the clock's weights.

Ernie yapped every quarter-hour, on the first stroke of the chimes. Ibbe, who'd replaced the battery in his hearing aid not a day earlier, lasted no longer than an hour and a half. "Either the mutt goes or I go," Ibbe said, banishing Ernie to the basement. What he *really* wanted to do was string the dog up from one of the ceiling joists. It wasn't any good; the dog could still hear the clock chime, and thought he should let everyone know strangers stood on the front porch threatening the place.

During the middle of the night Ibbe got up quietly so as not to wake Tetty, shut the dog in the garage, and managed to grab a few hours' sleep.

Tetty told him next morning she didn't sleep a wink thinking of that poor little dog out by itself in the garage on a cold December night. She rescued him, shivering, by six the next morning. Alexa and Zachary woke up half an hour later.

"Another day," Ibbe groaned, burying his head under the pillow. Al and Arlene better be having a good time in that motel in Niagara Falls, he told himself.

~~~~

What brought about Al and Arlene's desire to get away for the weekend was the state of their marriage, which both of them would have told you was hanging by a thread. Here they were, only nine years married, both of them barely in their thirties, and their marriage sucking canal water.

They'd grown up together in Alfalfa, started going together in grade 10 after Al asked Arlene if he could walk her home after a Young People's bowling party one summer night, which indicated to Arlene he really cared for her since he lived all the way on the opposite end of town a good twelve blocks away. They got to talking heart to heart under the willow in her backyard and discovered they both loved country and western, especially Patsy Cline's song "Crazy," which is a pretty solid basis to start a relationship on, especially when you're sixteen. Five minutes after Arlene's mother had finally come to the back door and told Arlene it was time to come in, Arlene allowed Al to put his arms around her and kiss her and then he backed away so slowly from the screen door where she was standing she knew he didn't want to leave yet and he said, "I'll see you tomorrow," which they both knew meant they were, as of that moment, going steady. Seven years later, after they'd broken up once and gotten back together again, they got married and honeymooned up north where Al put his fist through the bathroom window of a little country motel trying to punch out the peeping tom standing on an apple crate and peering at them naked together in the bathroom.

They discovered that while their mutual liking for Patsy Cline was a pretty good basis for going steady it wasn't enough of a foundation to build a marriage on. During their nine years together a number of significant differences have developed between them. For one thing, Arlene has started attending the Wednesday evening service at Blessed Assurance with a friend because she enjoys the more expressive worship and the praise songs which mean more to her than the psalms they sing from First CRC's psalter ("Let God arise and by his might/ Put all his enemies to flight/ With shame and consternation"), whereas Al doesn't particularly care to sway on his feet and to wave his hands in the air and sing what he calls happy-clappy songs projected on overheads ("Whoa-oah-oh-oah-oh/ Heaven is in my heart/ Whoa-oah-oh-oah-oh/ Heaven is in my heart!").

"If I want karaoke night I'll go to Alf's Tavern," Al told her.

They love each other, that they do, but they have their differences. Al is a night person, wide awake after watching *NYPD* or *Jerry Springer* the nights the Leafs aren't on, while Arlene, who sits reading Catherine

Cookson or LaVyrle Spencer and has started yawning by ten, usually calls down to him in the rec room no later than ten-thirty, "Think I'll head for bed, hon." He sips a brewskie by himself while catching the scores on *Sports Desk*, and joins her an hour later. He tends to be outgoing and boisterous and needs people around him, especially male friends, whereas Arlene is quieter and finds fulfilment in her family, in Alexa and Zachary. She prefers to hang colourful still lifes on the walls, he prefers outdoor scenes, steep snow-capped mountains or waves crashing into rocks. Her favourite comic strip is "For Better or Worse," his "Hagar the Horrible." She tends towards spinach salads with low-cal dressing, he puts away mounds of potato or chicken salad drowning in mayonnaise. She drinks herbal tea, he slurps acrid black coffee. She likes tennis and swimming, he is strictly for winter sports–snowboarding and hockey.

He's been playing for the Avalanche, the town hockey team, eleven years now, left defence and the point on the power play, where he had his front teeth knocked out by a friendly elbow two winters ago and now wears a partial which makes him look like Dracula when he takes it out during games. What has begun to worry him though, more than anything else, is a fear that he has begun to lose five or ten miles an hour on his slapshot, so crucial from the point on the power play. There are young guys five, ten years his junior itching to take his place, and he knows it.

He bought a set of weights last winter which he set up in the rec room downstairs–Arlene took one look at the bench, the barbells, and said, "You're not putting all this in *here*, are you? Where will the kids play?" and Al said "Where else would I put it?" and Arlene suggested he could set it in the unfinished part of the basement beside the furnace and Al looked at her as if she had a screw loose. Since then he's been pumping iron to increase his upper body strength, huffing while the perspiration drips from his face as he works on his biceps, his pecs, his abs. Two months later he measured his upper arms with the plastic measuring tape from Arlene's sewing machine and was pleased when he saw he'd increased his right bicep by half a centimetre. That's one more mile per hour on the old slap shot, he told himself.

Al and Arlene's differences have begun to catch up with them. Slowly they stopped talking with each other, Al's way of coping with conflict being to brood rather than to talk it out. Their conversation at supper is limited to strained, polite talk, like, "Could I have the butter, honey?" or, "Sure was cold out today, wasn't it." One night, slipping into bed after a quiet evening, a *very* quiet evening with little conversation between them, Al asked, "Did you turn down the heat?" and her answer, with a rigid smile and just a bit too much of an edge, was, "Yes honey, I turn it down every night, remember? Just the way *you* like it."

They broke out into an argument then, not the house and garden variety every husband and wife enjoy now and then, the kind that clears out the sinuses, but the knock-'em-down, drag-'em-out kind that plagues your mind long afterward like the memory of a painful toothache. What spurred it was what spurs any doozy of an argument: some insignificant thing that snowballs over time into something as huge and frigid as an iceberg. What lay behind Al's question whether Arlene had turned down the heat, they both knew, was that his preferred temperature overnight is a degree or two short of Arctic, while Arlene prefers a more Caribbean ambiance.

"Maybe you could see it my way if you didn't come up all hot and sweaty from lifting those stupid weights just before you go to bed," Arlene said, arms crossed in front of her flannel nightgown.

"Maybe if *you* weren't half as frigid you wouldn't need all those blankets at night," he said, which struck him as awfully clever before he said it but not as much so as soon as the words were out of his mouth.

"Has it ever crossed your mind–that maybe I'm that way–because *you* are such a lousy lover?" she said deliberately, and then it was gloves off and they said the cruel and shocking things a husband and wife can end up saying to each other and calling each other, until an hour later, bleary-eyed and punch-drunk, they stared at one another from their respective corners, both of them wondering who was going to get the house, the van, the Patsy Cline tapes, who would gain custody of the kids. The *kids!*–had things between them really gone that far?

The thought of Alexa and Zachary not having a mother *and* father living together sobered them. They sat looking at each other at 1:00 in the morning, the rest of the neighbourhood asleep and oblivious to the turbulent little tragedy being played out at Al and Arlene's, who sat numb and silent, each defeated by what the other had said. They sat not speaking for three or four minutes, which is a long time for a couple used to asking polite questions whose sole purpose is to break an awkward silence.

"Do you remember," Al began finally, "the time we broke up that summer?" and Arlene looked at him suddenly, for she could tell by the tone of his voice that this was not one of those break-the-silence questions. "You were the one to break up, do you remember, which in hindsight I admit was probably the right thing to do, the way I was acting." He paused, and Arlene wondered for a moment whether he might actually begin to cry. "Did you know that I didn't eat for the next three days? I was pumping gas at Andy Stokes's Texaco station that summer and I told Andy I was feeling sick, which I was in a way, and I walked six miles all the way out to Wesselinks' farm that day 'cuz you were staying there for a week with Cathy Wesselink, remember? and it was raining pretty hard and I stood inside the bush across from Wesselinks' for two hours getting soaked to the gills, watching Cathy's house hoping I might see you so we could talk, and just before supper when the rain had stopped finally, you and Cathy came outside and I crossed the road and called your name and me 'n you went for a long walk to talk about us and we ended up going together again, do you remember?"

Arlene looked at him. It was the most he had said in one breath since they had taken that long walk together. "I remember," Arlene said, "except I'd forgotten until you told me about it again just now."

"Did you know I'm still as crazy about you as I was then?" and he got up from where he was sitting on the couch across from her chair, and the tears did well up into his eyes then as they held each other, and so did they in hers.

"I've got a secret to tell you," she said after a long silence that was beautiful rather than awkward, "something I've never told you before."

He felt as if he were a guest on *Jerry Springer* about to be told something painful, and he braced himself.

"Do you remember that night you walked me home from bowling the very first time and we sat under the willow in my back yard and talked?"

"Till your Mom said you had to come in?"

"Uh huh. Do you know what I liked about you that night, what I found really attractive about you?"

He wondered whether it was his looks or the snazzy western shirt he remembered he was wearing that night, and he turned his head slightly sideways, pleased by her question. "What?" he said.

"This is not gonna be what you think, so don't laugh, OK? It was–how thin you were, your thin arms coming out of the sleeves of your shirt. I've always thought thin men are sexy," and she burrowed her head into his chest under his chin.

He raised his eyebrows and said, "Oh?", unsure whether or not he should feel flattered.

"Uh huh," she said, "that's what I've always liked about you."

"Just wait till I turn old and fat, then," he said, but she was kissing him in his neck, on the soft part of his skin which she liked, away from the sandpaper stubble of his late-night beard.

Later, after they'd gone to bed and found out again that making love is always best after you've fought and then made up even if it is 2:15 a.m., Al said, "You know, honey, what you and I should do is get away, just the two of us, one of those weekend getaways in Niagara Falls that are advertised in the paper all the time."

"What about Alexa and Zachary? We've never been away from them a whole weekend."

"I'm sure my mom and dad would love to take them. You know how they always use the least excuse to drop in to see them."

"What about Ernie? I get the impression sometimes your dad doesn't like him."

"Ernie won't be any trouble."

"You want to ask them? They're your folks."

"You know what else I was thinking, hon? While we're in Niagara Falls what we should do is pop across the border to one of them outlet malls and get us an electric blanket, the kind that has different temperature controls, one for your side of the bed and one for mine."

Arlene said that was a great idea, if they weren't so darned expensive.

What Al didn't tell her then was that he was thinking he could sell his set of weights to pay for the fancy electric blanket. After all, some things in life are more important to a guy than a blazing slapshot.

Not many, but some.

Avalanche open season with win

Senior B Champions Alfalfa Avalanche took to the ice in their season opener Friday night with a convincing 6-2 win over their arch-rivals the Freemore Flyers.

Captain Howie ("Muddy") Waters took the ceremonial opening face-off before the hostilities began. The teams played a fairly even first period with the Avalanche leaving the ice with a 2-1 lead on goals by Herb ("The Boss") Voss and Lou ("Big Enchilada") Salata.

Things got a mite woolly in the second period when a well-known Flyer took a run at Avalanche goalie Kevin Holland, which led to a "friendly" team meeting behind the net. Pleasantries were exchanged, especially when Frank Perry had a few kind words to say about the ancestry of several members of the visiting Flyers.

Dan Leroux scored the Avalanche's third goal, but the Flyers also potted two to tie the score.

The third period saw furious end-to end action, with Avalanche goalie Kevin Holland repeatedly standing on his head. Both teams took numerous undisciplined penalties, and the Avalanche had to weather several occasions when they were two men short.

The winning goal came late in the third period by veteran defenceman Al ("Dutch") Rozema, who just seems to keep getting better and better. His rocket slapshot from the point on a power play gave the opposing goalie no chance, and the Avalanche had their first well-deserved win of the season.

It's great to have you back, boys! We look forward to another great year.

-news story in The Alfalfa Sentinel-Star

THE CAYMAN ISLANDS

Winter here in Alfalfa is hard on cars, it makes them do strange things. They sneak a look at the thermometer outside the garage window on cold mornings, see that the mercury has huddled at the base of the thermometer trying to protect itself from the cold, and decide all in all they'd rather stay inside. And so they deliberately turn their oil thick as syrup, freeze their tires to the garage floor, and turn their vinyl seats icy cold, all so their owners won't want to bother running to the Drug Pharmacy for that cold remedy after all.

Winter's hard not just on cars but on people too, especially seniors with lots of mileage on them. When the temperature hasn't risen above zero for weeks and daylight slinks off into the west by four in the afternoon already, the joints in old people's artificial hips begin to creak like the rusted door hinges on an old model T, and it's hard for them then to generate any more energy than would a frozen battery. Winter's so hard on old people, in fact, that every year some of the frailer ones have finally had enough and journey to a place where it's always warm and light and where every tear is wiped away. I'm not referring to Florida, but an even better place.

Oetse Kikkert is 79 but he's of no mind to join the people in town who head south for the winter, he'll stick it out here. Oetse still runs the Chevy he bought at Carr Motors back in '78; it reached 200,000 clicks last fall, but may not see many more. Oetse doesn't drive it much these days; in fact, it never really leaves his driveway. He backs it out of the garage winter mornings, lets it run for ten minutes to recharge the battery and get the oil flowing while he checks to see if the direction signals and brake lights still work, then drives the car back into the garage. He figures *he's* old too and has to get up every morning regardless of how he happens to feel, so there's no reason for his car not to. He takes a ten minute walk every day no matter what the weather–give in to the temptation to spend all day inside and next thing you know your pistons seize up and you're brought to Rusty Acres, the rest home for cars outside of town. Oetse plans to still keep running a while.

Those of us who do spend the winter here in Alfalfa do the best we can. Some winters the weather treats us kindly and we may not have to shovel the driveway more than, oh, nine or ten times before Christmas, and if we're lucky we can hang up the shovels again by the end of March. Between Christmas and March, though, is one long dark night of the soul. Particularly if you're a Calvinist. It's one thing if you're an atheist who believes that weather is nothing more than the result of certain atmospheric pressures predictable by multiplying the square root of the barometric pressure of north-south isobars divided by the longitude of the incoming cold front and subtract 32. But if you confess that God's sovereignty rules everything and that it is he who fathers forth the snow, and you get up in the morning and see that he has just fathered forth yet another two-foot drift of it the length of your driveway–well, it can be not just a small quiz but a major test of your Christian faith.

What helps to make winters bearable is that God plays no favourites. Except for maybe a few, like Rev. John DeHeer at First Christian Reformed, where the parsonage driveway is cleaned by Johnny Elzinga because he's there doing the church parking lot anyway, otherwise all of us northerners are in it together. You know, when you're pulling on the mittens and stocking cap and trying to screw your courage to the sticking place to face that driveway full of snow, that the same scenario is being played out at your neighbour's next door and at every other house on your street. You say goodbye to your wife and kids to make sure they show proper appreciation for what it is you're heading out to do, as though you were leaving on a three-week trek across frozen Arctic wastes by dogsled, then after ten minutes of shovelling you stop to catch your breath and notice all your neighbours are leaning on their shovels catching their breath as well, and you experience a deep feeling of community that is just not available to people living in the tropics.

Next thing you know, two or three of you are standing together engaged in deep intellectual conversation about the frequency of significant quantities of frozen precipitation in northern climates. Anything to stall having to shovel the significant quantity of frozen precipitation clogging up *your* driveway.

You can see why it seemed just a bit unfair then when some people here in Alfalfa started using snowblowers, which break the rule that winter plays no favourites. Besides, with all the racket they make, snowblowers just don't promote neighbourhood camaraderie. You'd feel silly crossing over to your neighbour's while he's spewing this magnificent geyser of snow and since he can't hear you above the roar of the snowblower's engine you make gestures to attract his attention making you look as though something terrible has happened, like your family has all been asphyxiated by carbon monoxide coming from the space heater because you haven't opened a door or a window in the house for three days because of the snowstorm which also happened to knock out your telephone so you need your neighbour to call 911, and finally he sees you waving frantically, cuts the snowblower's engine that took him twenty minutes to get going with the pull starter, and all you tell him is, "Some winter we're having eh?" and you know that what he's thinking is that the extreme cold has finally cracked your block.

That's how Dorothy DeHeer was feeling after being cooped up in the house with her husband John and three sons since the evening service on Sunday, five days ago. As soon as Dorothy had turned the Christian Reformed World Missions calendar to December two weeks ago the weather had turned cold, the temperature hardly rising above zero, with snow or freezing rain falling every second or third day. People said they couldn't remember such a December–it seemed hardly fair, especially since it wasn't even officially winter yet.

Then the weather turned bad. On Tuesday a blizzard swept through the region, snow swirling by the parsonage's living room window in solid drifts. Everything in town ground to a halt; the last three days people were imprisoned in their own homes. Then, last night, the blizzard had finally abated and this morning the sun shone so brightly it appeared as if God had gone absolutely bananas with his tube of titanium white, like a kid spraying Dream-Whip on his apple pie with mom not home, and the sky was such a vivid cerulean blue you wonder how only a day earlier it could have held so much snow.

With the cancellation of his Tuesday evening Council meeting and Wednesday evening catechism class because of the snow, John DeHeer had been holed up in his upstairs office all week working on his advent sermon from Isaiah:

> Arise, shine, for your light has come,
>   and the glory of the Lord rises upon you.
> See, darkness covers the earth
>   and thick darkness is over the peoples,
> but the Lord rises upon you
>   and his glory appears over you.
> Nations will come to your light,
>   and kings to the brightness of your dawn.

John was so deep in his study of Bible commentaries on the text that he missed what was happening outside, oblivious to the spectacular show outside his office window. But when you're a preacher in a Reformed church you consult commentaries for what the most scholarly theologians have written about your text, you don't just give your flock twelve minutes of human interest drivel you've shaken out of your sleeve. You may not be a dynamic pulpeteer, but after you've spent thirty minutes covering your three points at least the people can walk out of church saying, "That sure was a Reformed sermon, pastor."

Dorothy walked upstairs to John's office shortly after ten that morning. Books were piled on his desk. "Are you going to spend all day in here again?" she asked. No response. "Would you like me to make you some coffee downstairs?"

John did not look up. "I'll be right there, hon," he said, which Dorothy knew he wouldn't because he hadn't heard anything she'd said. She could have said, "My lover is waiting for me downstairs; we've decided to run away together and start a new life for ourselves running a gay bar in the Cayman Islands," and John would have said, "OK, be right there, hon." Well, he *had* been busy. Advent is hard on a minister; all those extra sermons and then the candlelight services and Christmas pageants for the children–it's usually not until well into January that a minister discovers again what peace on earth is all about.

Dorothy's had a busy time of it as well. Rural churches tend to have fairly clear expectations of what a minister's wife should be like, and these don't always coincide with what *she* feels her life should be like. But she's adjusted, working hard at preparing the children's Christmas program, doing extra baking, visiting some of the shut-ins, and hanging up long strings of Christmas cards she and John receive from present and former parishioners, cards depicting Krieghoff horsedrawn sleighs, cuddly reindeer, bright red cardinals on snowy branches, angels of every age and gender, most of them not the kind that would scare the tar out of any shepherds, and serene portrayals of the holy family that made it look as if Mary just picked up baby Jesus at Wal-Mart instead of screaming in childbirth in a smelly cattle barn.

John and Dorothy's three teenage sons, home because school was closed with the blizzard, spent their time wrestling boisterously in the T.V. room in the basement and wolfing down food to regain their strength for more boisterous wrestling, unaware of their need for forgiveness for the sin of driving their mother crazy. Finally Dorothy let them know, in language that isn't normally heard in a parsonage, not even a Christian Reformed one. Especially by the minister's wife. But there are times when words, unsanctified ones, are the handiest stones to put in your slingshot, especially when you're a 5' 4," 110-pound mother up against three hulking, 190-pound heathens who have learned from their father how not to listen.

Dorothy figured she'd better leave the house before she did something she'd really regret. She had groceries she would need to buy before the weekend–no, groceries she had–what she needed was an excuse to get out of the house. She let John and the boys know she would be going out, but by their reaction she knew she might as well have sent up smoke signals. She looked out the front window and saw that Johnny Elzinga had already plowed the driveway and was busy with his huge yellow machine on the church parking lot next door. Everywhere on their street people were out with snow shovels, their coats bright splotches of colour on an otherwise white landscape.

She checked the thermometer outside the kitchen window and saw it was 20 degrees below zero. Better wear that scarf. She bundled herself up and stepped into the garage. The cold, even in the garage, took her breath away.

The car door on the driver's side wouldn't open, as if the car didn't want her to get in, then as she felt the shock of the cold vinyl seats the car fogged up its windows with her breath so she could hardly see. When she turned the key in the ignition the Pontiac gave a strange sound, like the growl of an angry dog, then a hollow click. She tried again and got only the click, then on the third try not even that. Blank. Nothing. Now what? She'd rather walk to wherever she was headed, even if it *was* all the way to the Cayman Islands, than ask for help from inside the house.

145

She remembered Johnny Elzinga clearing the parking lot next door, he'd know what to do. She walked over, and a moment later Johnny backed his yellow machine onto the driveway. He stepped out wearing a padded green snowmobile suit, a red Montreal Canadiens stocking cap, and a three-day stubble of beard. "We'll have to pull the car out," he said, his breath a white plume in the air, "so we can connect the cables to the battery." He attached a heavy chain to a hook on his machine, then looped the chain underneath the car's rear end. He told Dorothy to get in and steer, climbed back into his machine, and pulled the car out of the garage as if he were dragging out a dead elephant by the tail. In a moment he had attached cables and the car turned over with some deep grumbling, then finally started. "Make sure to keep her running eh, maybe drive on the highway for a while to recharge the battery."

"How come it wouldn't start?" she asked, "the car's not that old."

Johnny shrugged. "Ja, it's the weather, it's murder on batteries."

The car was sluggish in town, complaining with a constant creaking, then gradually became more civil. Dorothy saw Oetse Kikkert, moving slowly on his morning walk. He waved. She'd take being as spry as Oetse was when she had as many miles as he had on him–it must have been all those constructive ideas Oetse had given the worship committee over the years that kept him sharp. You're getting cynical, woman, she told herself. Aw, it was just being cooped up in the house for five days that did it, that was all.

She decided first thing she'd do was take the Pontiac for that drive Johnny Elzinga mentioned, otherwise it would just stall while she was inside Art's Mart. She checked the gas gauge and saw she'd have to fill up soon, trust the guys to use the car and not put in any gas. Or had she used it last? Whatever. When she reached the highway she saw the plows had been out and the highway was clear, its edges heaped with banks of snow so high in places she thought of the Sunday School illustration of the Israelites crossing through the Red Sea.

After five miles or so the car began to give her some warm air, enough to keep the windows clear. She wasn't sure how high to run the heater, afraid it might drain the battery. She looked down at the gauge and saw the needle was well on the charge side. Better keep going a while and charge it up good.

It's hard to know where to go when you're not particular about where you're going, when all you want to do is drive the car for thirty minutes at eighty kilometres an hour, it doesn't matter where. It's especially hard for Calvinists, who figure you're given off two weeks a year for vacation but the rest of the time you better know where you're going, else no telling what dubious place you might end up in. But thinking earlier about having a lover who was going to take her to the Cayman Islands made Dorothy feel uncharacteristically adventurous and before she knew it the car, as if it had a mind of its own, had turned right, taking her off the familiar highway and onto a road she couldn't remember having travelled before.

What had made her think of the Cayman Islands was a couple in their former congregation, Larry and Carol Appeldoorn, who had gone there as a prize because Larry had achieved the year's highest sales in farm implements or something, and they had later shown John and Dorothy pictures of themselves high on a pink terrace overlooking a turquoise bay and also down on the beach lolling in their bathing suits in chaises longues with tall lime-coloured drinks. She and John had never done anything decadent like that, Dorothy realized, John had never won any contest for–what? The CBC's annual best sermon award? The ministerial association's prize for the year's highest number of converts in Classis Dairy Belt? It wasn't even Christmas yet, but Dorothy was about ready for a southern vacation.

The road she was on was narrower than the highway, not nearly as well plowed, with drifts of snow that licked onto the pavement and seemed to pull the car towards the edge of the road. The road curved several times, and Dorothy was afraid to go any faster than she would in town. She shuddered to think of John's reaction should she run the Pontiac into the ditch. She looked into her rear view mirror and saw she was kicking up clouds of white. She wondered if she should turn around and head back to the highway, but she was afraid she'd get stuck in some farmer's unplowed driveway. She could always hang two lefts and arrive back at the highway.

Hang two lefts–she chided herself for adopting the boys' slang. Louts, all three of them. She felt good being away from them, away from the house, away from John buried in his sermon. The car heater finally poured out heat and she took off her leather gloves and loosened her scarf. Driving like this, free to go wherever she wanted, she felt lighter than she had for days, weeks. She could be all the way in Sudbury before she'd be missed. No, the other direction of course, stupid, she would head south for Myrtle Beach, Fort Lauderdale, Puerto Vallarta! for a torrid rendezvous with her secret lover. Pina coladas poolside; suntan lotion slathered where she'd dropped her bikini straps; candlelight dinners in thatched-roof restaurants on the beach; then motel room lamps dimmed for slow, languid, tropical sex. She caught herself. See what happens, Dorothy DeHeer? You start with loose language, next thing you know you've dropped your bikini straps and before the end of the paragraph you're in some motel room in Mexico having sex with a total stranger. And you a minister's wife, a 41 year old mother of three with stretch marks. Keep your car on the road, gal, it's lethal out there.

She came to an intersection and turned left. She'd never seen farmsteads spaced so far apart–in fact, when was the last farmhouse she passed? She looked down at the gas gauge and saw that the needle was resting on the gauge's lowest red stripe. She slowed down to make sure she would not miss the next road heading–what was it, west? but it didn't come until she had driven she did not know how far. She slowed the car, then made another left through snowdrifts blowing across the intersection. Beyond the wire fence running along the edge of the road, empty snow-covered farmland stretched as far as she could see.

Her spirits rose with the thought that she was headed in the right direction. She reminded herself distances always seemed greater when you were looking for something than when you knew where it was. She passed several yellow brick farmhouses hiding behind windrows of tall pine.

She had gone another five kilometres when she saw the sign signalling a stop ahead. She climbed a rise, reached the crest, and recognized the highway up ahead! She looked down and saw that the orange warning light on the gas gauge had come on. How many kilometres did that give her, twenty? Piece of cake, Dorothy, she told herself, I'm headed for the city. How long had she been gone, half an hour? At the most. The gas would be cheaper in the city than on the highway, she'd fill up there, then head back. John and the boys wouldn't even know she'd been gone.

She reached the outskirts of the city in fifteen minutes. Everywhere huge mounds of snow lay heaped along the edge of the road. She thought for a moment whether she should drive to the mall and get in a bit of Christmas shopping while she was here, maybe do some ultra-damage with the credit card. She drove along the outskirts of the city debating with herself, then decided stopping was too risky. Just fill up, gal, keep that car running and go home while you're ahead. Still, it was a shame to waste the opportunity; she didn't feel ready yet to go back to John and the three stooges.

Somehow she ended up in the industrial part of the city, she wasn't sure how, among grimy factories and vacant buildings with gaping broken windows. She drove behind a truck plastered with snow, its exhaust pipe behind the cab sending up a steady cloud into the cold air. She forgot suddenly how far she had driven since the orange warning light had come on, felt a moment of panic, and decided she'd better pull into the first gas station she saw. It came only a block down the street, a bit seedy and she didn't recognize the brand, but gas was gas, right? She would have preferred full service but she'd done self-serve many times, she could handle it. The only thing she disliked was the smell afterward of the gasoline on her hands.

She congratulated herself on remembering not to turn off the ignition, stepped out of the car, and was hit behind the eyeballs by the cold air which took away her breath. She removed the gas cap and inserted the nozzle; when she pressed the handle the gasoline pump shook and wheezed with the effort. The wind blew the exhaust from the car's tailpipe directly into her face; she covered her mouth with the glove of her free hand–no way she was going to stand out here any longer than she had to, her toes were already starting to freeze. She stopped the pump when it reached twenty dollars and ran inside to pay.

It was cold even inside the office, which smelled of engine oil. A short fat man stood behind the till; he wore striped overalls splotched with grease, and a brown leather cap with ear flaps. The stub of a cigarette hung from the corner of his mouth, and Dorothy saw the man had nicotine-stained teeth. "Twenty dollars," he said.

She handed him the bill. She'd needed for some time now to hit a bathroom, but could see herself sitting down on a grimy toilet seat and being grabbed by a hairy hand coming up out of the toilet stool. She decided she'd rather hold it in.

She heard the sudden roar of an engine. She turned around and saw her car tear away from the gasoline pumps, race onto the street, and disappear behind the brick building next door.

The car was gone! It happened so fast she hadn't even seen who was behind the steering wheel; it was as if the car had taken off by itself.

Her jaw dropped–it hadn't happened. It couldn't have happened! She turned around to the fat man behind the till. He shrugged his shoulders and shook his head, as if to say, "It wasn't me, lady." Dorothy dashed out of the office, ran to the curb, and looked down the street. No sign of her car. She raised her hands to her head.

The drive from the city back to Alfalfa was rather quiet, all in all,

Dorothy feeling disgraced sitting between her husband and Johnny Elzinga in Johnny's Dodge pickup. Not much was said in that half hour; a minister and his wife know which issues between them can be discussed in the presence of others, and this wasn't one of them.

John was surprisingly understanding about the whole thing, actually, Dorothy had to admit when she explained later. He threw no accusations, didn't become patronizing or brood in angry silence–if only he didn't look as if he'd just been told there was no God after all, sorry, the idea had been tried and found unworkable. But the fact was, their car was gone. It was out there somewhere gallivanting with strangers, no telling what depraved acts, what monstrous violations were being done to it this very moment. Dorothy felt vaguely as if a close friend had betrayed her, then had to remind herself it was only their car. Still, she couldn't shake the feeling of rejection.

Four days later Dorothy answered the doorbell; she recognized Sergeant Lofthouse of the Alfalfa police. "May I come in?" he said.

Dorothy showed him into the living room. She thought the policeman looked grave, and wondered at first whether something had happened to a person in their congregation. She called John from his study upstairs.

"It's about your car," Sergeant Lofthouse said. "I've got some good news. And some bad news, I'm afraid."

He paused, as if waiting for them to declare which they'd rather hear first. "The good news," he said, "is your car's been located, and it's in surprisingly good shape. You're two lucky people."

Dorothy spoke for both of them, afraid of what she would hear next. "And the bad news?"

"The bad news is, the car's all the way in West Palm Beach." He paused, as if to let the weight of it sink in. "That's right, West Palm Beach, as in Florida. They've been having unusually warm weather there–your car was located sitting in an oceanside parking lot where it had a beautiful view of the sun over the water and of women in bikinis playing volleyball on the beach. It's a bit of a mystery how it got there. The shape it's in, looks like nobody did anything to it, almost–I know this is silly, but like it got there by itself." He took off his cap and scratched his head in puzzlement. "I guess one of you is going to have to retrieve it. If you've kept up your premiums, though, your insurance company should cover the airfare." He rose. "We'll be in touch."

~~~~

150

It was John, actually, who came up with the idea, Dorothy felt proud of him as they were boarding the plane to pick up their prodigal car. With the money from the insurance company, for the price of airfare for one they could both go, spend a week in West Palm Beach, then drive the car back; there was no way John could do all the driving by himself. There'd been only one problem: church. Louis Doornbos, chairman of Council, had scratched his chin, said it was the second time this had happened, there was that wedding in Vancouver last summer, remember, and thought he'd better put it to a vote. John had left the Council room for the discussion. He was called back twenty minutes later. They'd decided they would manage somehow, perhaps Rev. Verseput could fill in again.

Dorothy sat in seat 12A; John had let her take the one by the window. She looked over at her husband beside her, her heart brimming with love. It wasn't the Cayman Islands she was going to, and it wasn't with a secret lover, but this would do. It would do.

Around town with Heloise

Wasn't that some storm Ma Nature dumped on us last week. All over town automobiles wouldn't start, highways were closed with white-out conditions, on top of that we had our first "No Bus" days so that many students were billeted out. Remember harried mothers in our community.

Remember too all operators of snow removal equipment who put in long hours, often thanklessly. Would you believe there are snowplow drivers who get yelled at for filling driveways? Put yourself in their place. Where should they put the snow off the streets, in their pockets? If they take a while getting to your street please be patient. Schools, churches, and businesses need to be done first.

Heard a little incident happened at a certain home on Laurier Lane this past week–true, Rick and Heidi? (Apparently a Christmas wreath caught fire inside the house, it was thrown onto the driveway under the "heat of the moment," where it promptly ignited the driveway! A pickup usually parked in that spot had been leaking oil, which ignited. I'm told folks had an interesting time watching a driveway on fire. Apparently they had a bit of a hard time getting water out there in the cold temperatures).

Our get well wishes to Tony Smart (no pun intended) who slipped on ice, broke his ankle, and now has his leg in a cast.

The Thrupps were supposed to have spent the weekend in Lucknow with Alice's mother, but the severe weather intervened.

That's all for now.

-column in The Alfalfa Sentinel-Star

BRIGHT LIKE STARS

One of the nice things about Christmas Day for a Christian Reformed kid is that more likely than not it will fall on a weekday, and so he can walk out of church after the Christmas morning service and realize he's allowed to do all kinds of things he would otherwise not be allowed to do on Sundays. It's a very liberating feeling. Sundays are tough for a Christian Reformed kid because his family observes Sabbath rules so strict that had Jesus practised *them* instead of the radical ones he did he wouldn't have gotten into all that hot water with the Pharisees.

During the winter there are times a Christian Reformed kid will wish he could have been born into a Roman Catholic or a United Church family, because all *these* kids in the neighbourhood have laced up their skates on a Sunday afternoon and are playing shinny on the rink in the park while *he* has to stay inside and do jigsaw puzzles with his sisters. You can understand why some of a Christian Reformed kid's favourite Bible stories are the ones where Jesus lambastes the Pharisees after they've criticized him for breaking rules that said you couldn't go swimming on Sunday or stop in at Burger King for a Whopper.

This year Christmas Day happens to fall not on Sunday but on Thursday, which is good news for the four Sprik kids. It means their parents, Jerry and Donna, will do their Christmas Day ritual of taking their kids tobogganing down a hill on Jake Vander Molen's farm just south of town. Jerry doesn't always spend as much time with his kids as he knows he should; he teaches seventh grade at Calvin Christian school here in Alfalfa and it seems he's forever making lesson plans or marking science projects on photosynthesis or the structure of beehives or the migrating patterns of Canada geese, if he's not busy at church with deacons' work, that is. But during Christmas holidays things ease up a bit despite all those church services and he can spend some quality time with his kids. Which is what he's going to do today.

They've come home from the Christmas morning service where the Sunday School kids acted out the Christmas story directed by Dorothy DeHeer. Jennifer Sprik wore a robe Donna made from an old white bedsheet, and carried a popsicle stick glued to a cardboard star covered with silver foil, and told the shepherds, most of whom were missing front teeth and wore tea towels on their heads, "Do not be afraid. I bring you good news of great joy that will be for all the people." Little Kyle Sprik, draped in a bright red tablecloth for a robe and wearing a satin turban Donna had fashioned for him out of an old dress, was one of the magi who recited in rhythmic, high-pitched voice, "Where–is–the–one–who–has–been–born–king–of–the–Jews? We–saw–his–star–in–the–east–and–have–come–to–worship–him." The star in the east was represented by four children, each carrying a large white letter of the word S-T-A-R printed on a red poster, but the children lined up in reverse order and spelled out the word R-A-T-S instead, until Dorothy DeHeer wondered what everyone was laughing about and managed to arrange the children in the proper order.

All the grandparents craned their necks to catch a glimpse of their grandchildren, hoping they wouldn't muff their lines, and then the rest of the congregation sang "Angels From the Realms of Glory" and "How Bright Appears the Morning Star." Then, as if the adults were all so busy thinking about deep theological things like the mystery of the Incarnation that they had missed the simple good news proclaimed by the children and therefore needed a booster shot, Rev. DeHeer preached on the second chapter of Matthew, a sermon on God's Word In Creation (the Bethlehem star), God's Word Inscripturated (the Old Testament prophet Micah), and God's Word Incarnate (the Christ-child). Finally, Rev. DeHeer raised his hands and promised everyone God's peace that passes all understanding, then the congregation stood and sang the familiar carol "Once in Royal David's City," its majestic final words accompanied by Jerry Sprik playing a trumpet descant:

Not in that poor lowly stable

with the oxen standing by
we shall see him, but in heaven,
set at God's right hand on high:
there his children gather round
bright like stars, with glory crowned.

Then, after the service, the congregation enjoyed coffee in the basement and, between bites of Christmas cake and homemade cookies sprinkled red and green, wished each other a blessèd Christmas rather than a merry Christmas, which sounds entirely too frolicsome for any self-respecting Calvinist.

Now, two hours later, the Spriks have finished eating their Christmas dinner which Donna started at 6:00 this morning when she got up to peel potatoes, cut up the cauliflower, baste the turkey and pop it in the oven. She's been a bit testy ever since. A week ago she suggested they do glazed ham for a change so she wouldn't have to get up so early, then a day later Jerry came home with a seventeen-pound frozen turkey he'd bought at Art's Mart so she had no choice but to do the thing–what's Christmas without turkey? he said. Ham is for Easter, for Pete's sake.

As for Jerry, he's finally woken up from a two-hour after-dinner nap, which had nothing to do with the amount of turkey and potato and cauliflower he put away. What did him in, he said, was doing the dishes, all those pans and bowls and plates encrusted with cranberry and scalloped potatoes. If Donna is lucky she might manage to squeeze in a bit of rest after they come back from tobogganing and the kids are too exhausted to do anything but watch TV.

The kids–Ronnie, Laura, Jennifer, and Kyle–have been raring to go tobogganing ever since they finished dinner and Donna, that good woman, has had a dickens of a time trying to keep them quiet while Jerry slept. But now he feels rested enough to go and he's about to load up the car with their toboggan and an inner tube from an earth-mover, so huge all six of them can pile on top of it at once. Early yesterday morning three inches of snow fell on top of the snow brought by last week's blizzard, but today the sun is shining and it's only a few degrees below zero, perfect weather for working off a big turkey dinner by forming a human pyramid on top of an inner tube, whizzing down a snowy hill while bumps throw off kids right and left, then tramping back up to do it all over again.

Donna is helping the younger children into their snowsuits and mittens and rubber boots while Jerry steps outside to place the toboggan and the inner tube and two big thermoses holding hot chocolate into the car trunk. If he packs things just right he won't even have to close the trunk lid with a bungee cord; the inner tube will act as a buffer so the lid won't bang against the toboggan that sticks out four feet from the mouth of the open trunk like a long, thin tongue.

It's colder outside than Jerry thought. He's hauling stuff to the car wearing only a sweater, so once he's stuffed things into the trunk he doesn't stay outside any longer than he has to. When he runs back into the house Donna and the kids are all at the front door, anxious to go. "Are you ready?" she asks, without looking at him. What she'd really like to do is send Jerry and the kids off to Vander Molens' farm to go tobogganing while she stays home by herself and experiences a bit of the peace that passes all understanding.

Jerry seems in a carefree holiday mood. "I'm ready," he says, "let's kick ass," then immediately chides himself; his kids are all in his school and he is aware he needs to set an example. Teaching grade seven is tough enough as it is, all those adolescent male glands secreting testosterone and disrespect toward adults; the last thing he needs is for Ronnie or Laura to tell other kids at school, "Bet you wouldn't believe what my Dad says at home."

He puts on his jacket and toque. The car doors will still be locked from this morning and he shouts to Donna, "Honey, will you grab the keys?", then wonders, after what has transpired between them this morning, whether the "honey" was too falsely loving. What should he have said? Something more matter-of-fact: "Would you mind getting the keys?" "Donna, do you think you could grab the keys?" It's hard to know what's the right thing to say when you're walking on egg shells.

Donna goes back into the kitchen to get the keys, where they always hang on a hook inside a closet so they can both use them. They've had to do this because somehow Jerry has lost his keys–he doesn't know how on earth he managed that. Maybe it was the time this fall when Ben Fennema, a colleague at school, borrowed Jerry's car and utility trailer to move a refrigerator he'd bought at an auction, then Ben had placed the fridge too far at the back of the trailer so that the hitch jumped off the ball, the heavy weight snapped the trailer's thin safety chains, and trailer and refrigerator went flying across the road and into a ditch. Afterwards Ben was so discombobulated he must have forgotten to return the keys, or so Jerry thinks. All this year he's been telling himself to stop in at Hardy Hardware to get an extra set made but somehow he always forgets. So far they've managed to share Donna's set.

Donna comes around from the kitchen. "They're not there," she says.

"The keys? They have to be," Jerry says, and walks over to check. When he gets to the closet, however, he sees Donna's right, the keys aren't there–where could he have left them? He's positive he hung them in the closet when they came home from church this morning, but maybe he left them in the pocket of his suit coat. When he checks, though, the keys are not there.

It wouldn't be like him to lock the car with the keys still in the ignition; he might be absentminded but he's not stupid. What he thinks suddenly, with a shock at the possibility, is that he might have locked the car with the keys under the front seat, where he used to place them at church when he didn't want the heavy ring of keys in his pocket. That was because Donna's key ring has a large blue plastic key on it, which makes the ring easier to find if it ever gets lost, she says, but Jerry finds the thing awkward and bulky and, frankly, childish. He used to place the car keys under the front seat but only at church, as if car thieves had agreed that that area was off-limits or that God might zap them for stealing stuff off his property, but Jerry doesn't do this anymore, not after some of the things that have happened here in Alfalfa, especially in the neighbourhood.

Last August Vern and Nancy Winkle three doors down had packed their hard-top camper the evening before they'd left on holidays so they could get an early start next day, then 6:00 in the morning when they were ready to take off, there was no camper on their driveway! Someone had come along during the night and had stolen the camper with everything inside it–camping gear, suitcases, and all. Sergeant Lofthouse was dumbfounded. "Must have backed up a car onto the driveway and just driven off with that camper. Who'da thought it, right here in Alfalfa?" The case has never been solved. Then this spring someone stole some maps and audio tapes from the glove compartment of Jerry and Donna's Chevy during the night. Jerry didn't bother telling Sergeant Lofthouse, but since then he's taken to locking the car, even on their driveway during the day.

It's a bit of a thing between him and Donna. She's more trusting and doesn't always lock the door when she steps out of the car on the driveway, not even when they come home in the evening and they know they won't be using the car anymore. "Lock, please?" Jerry always says–she can predict both what he'll say and the exact moment he'll say it–and she dislikes the too polite way he says it, but Jerry knows if he didn't she wouldn't lock the car door.

Just in case he locked the keys in the ignition, though, Jerry goes out to check, but they're not there. He's not any more absentminded than most people are, but he did forget once to put on the hand brake while changing a front flat tire, and as he was removing the wheel and saw the car begin to slide forward he had just enough time to escape having it come crashing down on his foot. He peers down through the windshield to see if despite himself he's reverted to his old habit and placed the keys under the front seat, but he can't tell if he did. Of course not, that was the whole point of putting them under the seat, right? Duuh, Ronnie would say. His voice hasn't quite started to change yet, and he brings it from deep in his throat to get the desired low effect: "Duuh." Meanwhile, Donna and the kids are standing on the front porch in snowsuits, looking at Jerry. He goes back into the house, wondering where he could have put those–keys. Well, nothing to do but start looking.

"Try all your pants pockets," Donna says, but Jerry knows that's no use, he had those dumb keys this morning driving home from church in his suit and he hasn't worn anything else. Still, it's simpler to do as Donna suggests than to argue with her, so he gives each one of his pants a perfunctory check. He knew it–no keys. He wonders whether one of the kids, maybe Kyle, who's six, has been playing with them but Kyle, wide-open eyes all innocence, says he hasn't touched them. Just to make sure, Jerry looks up and down his bedroom. No keys.

They check all through the house: the fruit bowl on the dining room table, around the tubes of toothpaste and skin lotion and aftershave on the bathroom counter, the dresser in Jerry and Donna's bedroom. Under the red tablecloth on the coffee table in the living room, behind the toaster in the kitchen, underneath the cushions of the couch in the family room downstairs. No keys.

"They've *got* to be around here somewhere!" Jerry wails, aware he's the one who's gotten them into this, although he's still not convinced one of the kids hasn't put the car keys somewhere. Could they have fallen down the toilet? It's about the only place they haven't looked. The kids, meanwhile, are getting hot and impatient bundled up in their snowsuits and mittens. They clump through the house in their rubber boots, halfheartedly going over all the places they've already searched. Ronnie, who's in his father's grade seven class and discovering things there about his father he never knew before, mostly that his father was created a little lower than Captain Marvel, is muttering, "Great, Dad, that's the second set you've lost." Jerry turns his head sharply but thinks this may not be the most fortunate moment to remind his son to have respect for his parents.

Half an hour later and still no keys, they are beginning to realize the inevitable: they aren't going anywhere. Donna starts helping the kids out of their snowsuits. "Some Christmas this is turning out to be," Jennifer mumbles. Jerry stands at the living room window trying to figure out where on earth he could have placed those car keys, then concedes he might as well go outside and empty the trunk. Perhaps they could play a game inside and drink the hot chocolate. *That* would thrill the kids. Ten minutes later, when he's extricating the toboggan and the inner tube from the car trunk, Jerry thinks Jennifer's right: some Christmas this is turning out to be. He reaches up and slams the trunk lid shut.

It closes with a bang–and an unusual rattle, and then Jerry brings his hands to cover his eyes. He doesn't need, nor does he even want, to look–the rattle of the trunk lid is enough. He groans. How could he have been that *stupid*! And what to tell Donna and the kids without looking like an idiot? But they could have known as much as he: how could he have opened the car trunk without keys? Well, nothing to do but go in and face the music.

Half an hour once again and they are on their way to the Vander Molens' farm, all four kids yelling and bouncing on the back seat. Jerry feels laved by their ready and unbegrudging forgiveness, unlike that of adults. He looks over at Donna; she's staring straight ahead, not smiling but not really sullen either. Jerry checks his watch; it's 3 o'clock, a good bit later than they had planned, but they could get in two hours of tobogganing still. Maybe, Jerry's thinking, he should give Donna a break tonight. From the Vander Molens' it's only another twelve miles to the outskirts of the city. It's Christmas Day rather than Sunday, maybe they should treat the kids to hamburgers.

When they arrive at the toboggan slope it seems almost every family in Alfalfa is here–kids of all ages are hurtling downhill on sleds, toboggans, and plastic saucers, others are trekking back uphill, their breaths pluming in the cold air. The screech of children's voices is constant, as if they have stepped into an aviary holding hundreds of shrieking arctic birds. On their first run, Donna and Jerry take Kyle between them on the toboggan; Ronnie and Laura and Jennifer want to ride the inner tube down. "Watch out for the creek at the bottom," Jerry warns them, "it's a good drop."

Then he shoves the three of them off and the toboggan slowly picks up speed. By now the snow that fell yesterday is good and packed; with a sudden hollow feeling in the pit of his stomach, Jerry is forcefully reminded just how fast the trip downhill is. The slope is an uneven one, it's a cow pasture after all, and the ride is bumpy all the way down. Kyle has wrapped his arms tightly around Jerry's legs rather than gripping the rope along the sides of the toboggan and, as if to reward his son for his trust, if not to atone for his earlier suspicion of him, Jerry squeezes his legs lovingly around Kyle's narrow torso. At the bottom of the slope they come to a tumbling halt well short of the creek.

Climbing uphill, they sidestep toboggans and sleds and saucers hurtling towards them. Back at the crest they all pile on the inner tube, Jerry and Donna spreadeagled on the bottom, Laura and Jennifer and Kyle forming a second layer, and then Ronnie, who sits gripping his sisters' parka sleeves on his hands and knees atop them all as if he were king of the hill. But he soon tumbles off the pyramid when the inner tube hits a small dip in the slope. Jerry and Ronnie and Laura bounce off two-thirds of the way down, the hill sending them flying as if it were a horse twitching its skin to flick off the gnats crawling down its back. They scream exaggerated peals of panic while rolling head over heels, then they come to a sliding stop; only Donna and Jennifer survive the inner tube ride all the way down. All of them immediately start the long climb back uphill. The cold thin air has reddened their faces, and after only two trips down the slope their mittens and parkas are already coated with snow. They are no longer a mother and father and four kids, they are transformed into six frolicking children by a few hilly acres of snow.

After they've tobogganed an hour and a half and the sun is a bright orange slit falling rapidly behind the horizon, Jerry, still basking in the glow of a day that has turned out well despite his stupidity, gets a wacky idea in his head. He's never seen anyone do it. Another father Jerry does not know is standing with his kids nearby, and it's a silly, show-off thing. "Ronnie," Jerry says, "I dare you to get inside the inner tube and roll down the hill."

The man turns his head at Jerry. Ronnie looks at his father with a stare that says, I may be only twelve, but if you're thinkin' *that*, I'm smarter than you by far.

"C'mon, go for it," Jerry says.

"No way! *You* do it if you think it's such a great idea," Ronnie tells him.

"I won't fit inside the tube," Jerry says, "I'm too big."

Ronnie pushes him. "Yeah, sure. C'mon Dad, I dare ya. You're chicken!" Jerry is aware of the other father standing near enough to hear.

"Ronnie, don't be silly," Donna says, "your father's doing no such thing." Then, when she sees Jerry considering doing exactly such a thing, "*Jerry*, you'll kill yourself!"

But Ronnie has pushed him too far, and Jerry sees it's a sure-fire way to win back his son's admiration. Besides, there's the other father not ten feet away–how can he back out? And if it was OK for Ronnie to do it, why shouldn't *he*? Jerry still remembers Ronnie's earlier comment, "Great, Dad, that's the second set you've lost."

"OK son, you're on," Jerry says, "piece me back together at the bottom."

"Jerry, don't be *stupid*," Donna hisses.

But while Ronnie holds the inner tube upright Jerry manages to cram himself inside, fetus-like, chin scrunched between knees, hands wrapped around the outside of the tube. "Just give me a little shove to get me started," he shouts to Ronnie, "not too hard!" Laura and Jennifer are making squealing sounds. Donna says, "I don't *believe* this." Everything seems suddenly quiet to Jerry, as if absolutely everyone on the toboggan hill has stopped to watch this crazy man do this crazy stunt.

He feels the little shove Ronnie gives him, then the world turns upside down, as if he might be watching a movie of an airplane pilot doing a roll and the earth is where the sky ought to be. Then he senses the inner tube picking up speed and he can no longer recognize anything, people or trees or even sky, everything is just a spinning blur. He feels his stomach turn queasy–there's no way he's going to stay inside this thing until the bottom, he'll barf first. He's knows he's going to have to bail out, soon.

But now the inner tube is not so much rolling as it is bouncing, landing on the snowy hill every two or three seconds–boing, *boing!*–as if he's a character in a silly Saturday morning television cartoon. He's trying to bail out but the tire is whirling so rapidly he has no leverage point from which to pry himself loose; all he does is extricate his legs from inside the tube so that they swing wildly around. He thinks he hears Donna and the children screaming something at him from very far away. Finally, the inner tube loses its balance and he can feel it skidding, snow grinding sharply along the side of his face, which means he will come to a stop soon. He loses touch with snow momentarily, as if the earth's bottom has fallen out, then comes to a hard, hard landing on his left elbow and hip, and he knows he's hit the ice of the creek at the base of the hill. With a shock he feels that one of his boots, he's not sure which one, his right or left, has filled with icy cold water.

He pulls himself from the creek bed to see Donna and the children half running, half sliding down the hill towards him–at least, he thinks it's them, for the horizon hasn't quite stopped spinning yet. Ronnie is yelling, "Wow! That was *great*, Dad! You *did* it!" Jerry hears a smattering of applause coming from the top of the hill.

Donna is out of breath when she reaches him. "Are you alright, dear?" she gasps. When she can see he is, more or less, she says nothing but she's shaking her head, and her mouth is set in a firm line the meaning of which, despite his lightheadedness, Jerry knows.

"You went all the way down, Dad!" Ronnie yells, "I didn't think you'd do it!" The children are all around him, tugging at his coat sleeves as if disbelieving it's really him or that he's actually still here.

"What do you say we go and pour us what's left of that chot hoklit, gang," Jerry says. The sun has disappeared, and darkness will fall soon. Jerry starts limping toward their car parked on the shoulder of the road, his wet pantleg clinging icily to his calf, and his one boot making a wet, squishing sound. His children, however, are bunched around him, their star, and he knows he has redeemed himself in their eyes.

When they reach the car darkness has almost fallen. One thing about all this tobogganing, Jerry realizes, he's worked off that turkey dinner; he never thought he would, but he's ready for some food. He takes off one glove to reach inside his jacket pocket for the car keys.

They're not there. He checks the pocket again where he knows he put the keys, then checks the jacket's other pockets, one by one. No, he's sure which pocket he put them in. Still, he checks the pockets of his pants. No keys.

He slumps against the side of the car in the darkness closing all around. Not again. He knows immediately what has happened. At some point of the afternoon, in one of his many tumbles, the keys have fallen out. They could be anywhere on the hill, more than likely buried under snow. He looks at Donna. "Now what?" he says. He's thinking maybe they can hitch a ride home, then tomorrow he'll have to call George Hardy to come out and change the locks on the car.

Jerry sees Donna reach into the right pocket of her parka, then hold up the car keys, jangling them.

The kids start cheering.

"Wha–? Where did you find them?"

Donna looks at him halfway between smug and triumphant. "Your little inner tube caper? They fell out of your pocket, oh, I'd say about your third revolution. With this blue plastic key on the ring I couldn't miss it."

Donna does not hand him the keys but unlocks the driver-side door, then they all pile in, Donna behind the wheel while Jerry hobbles around to the passenger side. As soon as he's sitting he starts taking off his wet left boot.

Donna, however, does not perform a U-turn to head back home, but heads onto the road going the other way. Jerry waits a moment, trying to figure out what she has in mind. "Where are we going?" he finally asks.

"To the city. I don't feel like cooking. We're going for Chinese food." In the back seat, the kids start raising a happy hullabaloo. "It's not Sunday today, remember," Donna says, "it's Christmas. We can order some take-out. Can you last that long for dry socks?"

"I think I'll survive," Jerry says. He snuggles down into the warmth of his jacket. Ahead of him, he sees, stars have begun to appear, bright against the dark-blue evening sky.

Calvary prayer breakfast

On Saturday morning, 50 men and boys trekked through heavy early January morning snow to attend the monthly prayer breakfast hosted by Calvary Baptist Church. Special guest was judo expert Jack Larsen of Whitby, who introduced everyone present to the basic principles of judo and gave a wonderful demonstration.

Jack explained that he had always thought Christians were "wimpy" and would not be interested in a sport like judo. Then he discovered that the reigning judo champion of Ontario was a Christian, which challenged Jack to let Jesus be master also of this area of his life. With this new commitment he went on to become Ontario champion himself.

Jack and assistant Dick Chatsworth then gave a lively demonstration of the basic moves of judo. Judo is a Japanese word that means "gentle way." Jack broke an apple with one finger, then broke a board with his right hand. The highlight of the demonstration was when Jack broke three bricks with a hand chop.

Jack Larsen has retired from competitive judo and is presently teaching judo classes as an evangelism outreach of his home church in Whitby.

-news story in The Alfalfa Sentinel-Star

GEORGE AND HILLIE

The way some of the regulars at Lucille's Lunch were talking this week after they heard what a truck had delivered to the home of George and Hillie Droge, and that in the dead of January, you'd think George and Hillie were shameless libertines. But the first thing you've got to understand about George and Hillie is that neither of them is likely to go off the deep end. They're Dutch Reformed, so they're more likely to hang back a ways from the edge of the swimming pool of life and see what happens to others who jump in. Then, when they know there's no danger of sharks, they'll tiptoe in from the shallow end so as to make sure they're never in over their heads in something they might later regret, trying all the while to make themselves as inconspicuous as possible. Which is difficult when you're fiftysomething and sport a tan the colour of a hard-boiled egg on a body whose centre of gravity has for some time been steadily travelling south. As you might guess, George and Hillie don't take their clothes off any earlier than they have to.

George owns George's Paint and Wallpaper in town, and is an elder in First Christian Reformed Church. At First CRC you're not elected elder for life, as you would be at St Andrews Presbyterian, but only for three years. Dutch Calvinists hold to a sober view of human nature, thanks to the doctrine of total depravity, and consider three years about long enough to put any person in office. After that you should perhaps sit down for two and let others do it while you give evidence you haven't turned degenerate in the meantime. George's life is so exemplary that every time after his two years off he is nominated and elected elder once more. Sort of what you'd expect from someone who wears a bow tie in his paint store, raises and sells rabbits for a hobby, dislikes the country and western music he hears around town a lot, and hasn't had a speeding ticket since he was nineteen, although he's honest enough to admit he's deserved maybe one or two.

As for Hillie, she's the chairperson of the Right-to-Life Committee here in Alfalfa, and has more than once written letters to *The Sentinel-Star*, her Conservative member of parliament, and the councils of the six churches in town. She's the kind of person who would make a good elder if First Church approved of women assuming such office; she faithfully calls her widowed mother in Owen Sound every week, and she folds up used pieces of aluminum foil to use again later when she does baked potatoes.

Hillie used to worry about her children, what with all the things she read about in the newspaper–teenage girls brutally murdered, men trying to lure little boys into vans, innocent bystanders shot in the crossfire of drug wars–but with the kids all married and living in cities like Hamilton and Kitchener she not only has them to worry about, but her four grandchildren as well. That's one thing about life: it never leaves you alone. Just when you've finished paying Christian school tuition or your kids have done profession of faith or they've gotten married without having to, God sends you something else to pray for.

As for the violence, you used to be able to say these things happened only in the States, then in Toronto, but now things are coming closer. Even in the churches. Not that Hillie feels she and George are lily-white themselves. There's something that happened quite a while ago in their past which she wishes hadn't, but it did, and they can't change that. It's something she and George have since cleared up, not just with the congregation but also between themselves and God, but Hillie's not sure she's ever allowed herself to feel truly forgiven. Even so, when she sees how their kids have turned out, all still in the church and healthy and with jobs, George and Hillie tell themselves they're fortunate, which is as close as Reformed folks are allowed to get to being lucky, thanks to the doctrine of God's providence.

Their oldest son Harold has three children, and sells computer equipment all over southern Ontario. Linda, the brains in the family, is also married and has just started a doctoral program in medieval history in Toronto–Hillie still can't believe it, their Linda going for her Ph.D., and her with a two year old, Hillie doesn't know how she does it. George Jr., who turned out about as unlike his father as he could, is twenty-six and still single (which is a concern to Hillie), wears a ponytail (which is more than a concern to George–George sells paint and wallpaper and raises rabbits for a hobby, remember), and works in an autoparts store whose showroom is filled with shiny chrome tailpipes and custom carburetors and huge magnesium alloy wheels. Hillie used to worry about George Jr, but less so now that he has sold his motorcycle and bought a car, a '66 Ford Mustang he's restoring. To her it's a sign that any day now he will get serious, which to Hillie means he will start dating a nice Christian Reformed girl. She would even, seeing as George Jr. lives in Kitchener, settle for a nice Mennonite girl, although she admits that that isn't likely.

George and Hillie's life changed somewhat last month on the 24th of January when they celebrated their fortieth wedding anniversary. January's an odd time of year to get married, but there's a bit of a story behind that. George and Hillie had talked about what they would do together to celebrate their anniversary, something special. They could do something romantic like drive to Port Dover and have dinner at the restaurant there on the beach; George loves seafood and has heard they serve great Lake Erie perch. They could drive to Niagara to see the Falls, so beautiful in winter with the frozen spray coating all the trees. They hadn't seen the Falls for some years, not since they'd taken George's cousin and his wife, who were visiting for three weeks from Holland and both of whom they'd never met, but that had been in June. Or they could spend a weekend at some interesting place they'd never visited before, like Corning, New York, to see the glass museum and maybe buy some Corningware.

You might not think those plans too exotic, but George and Hillie are the kind of people whose vacations the last thirty years have consisted of two weeks' camping at the Pinery on Lake Huron with the kids. That's what folks at First Christian Reformed do for holidays, they go camping. They can't afford to go to the Bahamas this year, they tell themselves, that would be extravagant, what would other people in the church think? No, two weeks at the lake again will be sufficient, so they pack up the camper which they bought second-hand, its drawers and cupboards filled with old dishes and cutlery and can openers and spatulas that weren't good enough for in the house anymore, they drive four hours to the provincial park, and for two weeks they sleep on a hard thin mattress, spray their arms and legs against mosquitoes and against black flies, debate whether they should call the ranger and ask him to get those young people two campsites over to turn down their music, wonder if they'll ever get rid of the dirt under their fingernails, and tell themselves isn't camping great, food sure tastes better outdoors. Even with the kids out of the house so they can afford to go to the Maritimes now, George and Hillie are so used to camping they still go every summer, maybe at Killbear now and then instead of at the Pinery just for a change. You can see why a weekend in Corning, New York didn't sound bad, even in January.

Except that's not what they did.

For one thing, they couldn't go away because of the open house. Any couple in First CRC celebrating a milestone anniversary does so with an open house in the church basement; it's become a tradition at First Church as unquestioned as infant baptism, even though the Bible doesn't contain a prooftext for either one. The doctrine of the covenant demands infants be baptised, and the doctrine of the communion of the saints demands an open house for an anniversary–at least, according to Miss Evelyn Krikke, who types the church bulletin and announces all anniversaries, so everyone knows when one is coming. No one is quite sure just how Evelyn manages to get the dates of everyone's anniversary, but since she's been church secretary from before the flood everyone assumes that for centuries she's been making entries in some ledger every time a couple got married: June 17, 1897, Pieter and Martha Vander Wal; July 8, 1923, Akke and Sietske Zandstra. Some people–cynics, assuredly–note that Evelyn announces only anniversaries, not birthdays, and suggest it's because she's doing some vicarious wish fulfilment seeing as she herself is not married. Except that's not how these people put it–they refer to Evelyn as a spinster, which is a word you may still hear around Alfalfa, where not all people have yet heard the glad tidings of political correctness.

So George and Hillie Droge had the usual open house. The weather was miserable, the temperature minus twenty with snow driven horizontally by the wind, but everybody came out. There aren't that many things to do here in Alfalfa in January, especially if you're like a lot of people who figure sliding rocks with handles on them down a sheet of ice is about as exciting as watching a glacier move.

Rev. DeHeer opened the evening with prayer, and a funny thing happened. George and Hillie's kids had bought two bottles of expensive champagne for the head table, wine for all the other guests, and what happened right in the middle of Rev. DeHeer's prayer just as he was thanking the Lord for his covenantal care in the lives of George and Hillie Droge, one of the bottles of champagne, which had been sitting on the table a while slowly getting warmer after being out in the cold, suddenly popped its plastic cork with a loud *pong!* and then bounced off the low ceiling of the church basement with a *whack!* That's exactly how it was: *pong! whack!* and Rev. DeHeer, who was standing near the liberated bottle, was so frightened he looked as if he had been hit by lightning while George apparently presumed that everyone had thought that he was stealing a *slokkie* during the prayer, for he spread his arms hands up in a gesture of I-didn't-have-anything-to-do-with-it, and by that time Rev. DeHeer's prayer had fallen totally apart like a car that had dropped its transmission. So everyone felt the evening got off to a roaring start.

People were served beef croquettes and ham and cheese on *krentenbroodjes* and a glass of red wine. People at First Christian Reformed may be Christian but they're not teetotallers like the people at Calvary Baptist. They know that the same Lord who made such marvels of creation like majestic mountains and sparkling blue lakes and dazzling sunsets and Dutch licorice also made wine, much to the puzzlement and chagrin of the folks at Calvary Baptist. But then, the Baptists return the favour by going to the city for dinner at a restaurant after church on Sundays, which offends the folks at First Christian Reformed who believe strictly in God's command to keep the Sabbath holy, which includes not forcing someone else to work. What it does is make the *women* work, having to prepare Sunday dinner, but that's different. It used to be Dutch women would peel the potatoes and cut up the cauliflower Saturday night but few families do that anymore–I don't know, maybe it's the first sign we're all turning liberal. Living by principle sure gets complicated today, and it's enough to make you wish sometimes that God would have given footnotes for some of the difficult texts in Scripture, or left us a Lifestyle Manual just as he left us the Church Order, and then we wouldn't have all these controversies.

In any case, after people had eaten their *krentenbroodjes* and *gebakjes*, George and Hillie's children did a skit about an elderly couple who come into George's Paint and Wallpaper. If you're unfamiliar with Dutch Reformed people and think, since they're Calvinists, that their weddings and anniversaries are about as exciting as farming, remember that these are people who believe the Lord made wine to make glad the heart of man, and that Jesus' first miracle at the wedding in Cana was to make sure that the guests would feel happy enough to laugh at the skits. Dutch Reformed weddings are not a week long as Jewish weddings are, because Reformed people, being Calvinists, believe it would be a sin to take off work that long. That's why they always understand the part of the fairy tale that says you can go to the party (as long as you don't dance), but you've got to be home by midnight.

In the skit Harold put flour in his hair to make him look old and supported himself with a cane in his trembling right hand while Linda wore a floppy grey wig and carried a black umbrella. George Jr., playing his father, had stuffed a pillow inside the front of his pants and wore one of his father's bow ties. The effect was rather comical: George Jr. with his ponytail, stuffed with a pillow and wearing a bow tie. Almost like a cross between a hippie and a used car salesman. Harold and Linda asked George Jr. if they could look at colour charts, then got into a huge argument about whether to paint the outside of the house orange or turquoise, then when George Jr. suggested teal was a highly popular colour lately, Harold and Linda turned on him and began beating him about the head with their cane and umbrella until all three of them collapsed to the floor covered with tangled rolls of wallpaper.

Then when everyone had stopped peeing in their pants from laughing so hard, Evelyn Krikke, who had typed up the program and thus made sure a slot was provided for her, sang "Softly and Tenderly Jesus Is Calling," a song some people felt was more Arminian than Reformed. Then Harold, who hadn't managed to get all the flour out of his hair, proposed a toast to his parents, after which people clinked their glasses and wouldn't stop until George and Hillie kissed. Then Harold told the joke about an old couple celebrating their golden anniversary and someone asked the old coot, "Now, Cyril, tells us the secret of such a long-lasting marriage," and Cyril said "Well, Agnes and I made an agreement when we married that she would make all the little decisions and I would make the big ones." "What were the little decisions Agnes made?" Cyril was asked. "Well," he said, "little things like what city we would live in, and what house we would buy, and where I would work, and how many kids we would have." "Well, what were the *big* decisions you would make, then?" "Oh," Cyril drawled, "things like what we should do about the Middle East situation, and how to solve the international money crisis. . . ."

They had a good laugh about that one, and then someone asked George, "Tell us the truth now, George, has it been forty years of unbroken marital bliss?" and George said, "More like 40 years of suffering and affliction broken only now and then by marital bliss," but the way he said it with a wink people knew he was exaggerating by a year or two.

At the end of the evening Linda came to the podium to present the gift from the children. People wondered why she wasn't carrying a present but instead set up an easel covered with a white bedsheet. Linda gave a heartwarming speech about how George and Hillie had worked hard to establish the store and then had scrimped for years to send the kids to Christian school instead of having fancy vacations and how they had instilled all the right values in their children and deserved now to experience one of life's pleasures themselves. Evelyn Krikke daubed at her eyes and people thought for sure the kids were sending George and Hillie to the Bahamas for two weeks, wasn't that nice of them; if any couple deserved it George and Hillie did, they certainly had worked hard all these years and been faithful church members. Who would have thought, forty years ago, how good their marriage would turn out for a couple who had had to get married?

Except it wasn't a two week trip to the Bahamas the kids gave George and Hillie. Linda walked to the easel, pulled back the white sheet with a flourish, and there, tacked to the easel, in full colour, hung a large photo of a hot tub. It was filled with bubbling blue water, so blue it looked positively decadent, and in the blue water sat a handsome young couple smiling so happily and looking so at ease and the woman wearing such a skimpy bikini that you knew *they* couldn't be Reformed. Then Linda explained to George and Hillie that first thing next week the spa company would come by their place and set up a hot tub in their basement rec room, compliments of the kids. People were so moved and felt so happy for George and Hillie–certainly it wasn't from envy–that they clapped even though they were in a church.

Sure enough, Monday morning–it was still snowing, a bitterly cold day–a large truck rolled up George and Hillie's driveway, on its side the words "OASIS SPAS" painted in large enough letters to be deciphered almost all the way from Lucille's Lunch. At first people weren't sure just what a spa was, it's not a word used often here in Alfalfa, people here don't exactly belong to the Hilton crowd, but by the end of the day everyone knew George and Hillie were the first in town to be the proud owners of a spanking new hot tub.

They didn't try it out the very first night–when you've been living off potatoes and kale all your life and someone suddenly sets pheasant under glass in front of you, you don't just dig in like a pagan, you allow yourself to salivate a moment or two. Then, on the third night, while a cold wind whistled in the windows of the house, George and Hillie looked at each other and, with the kind of unspoken communication forty years of living together brings, knew this was the night. They rummaged in the closet for their bathing suits–they hadn't worn them since George had gotten a sunburn on their vacation at the Pinery eight years ago–found them underneath layers of sheets and towels, and tiptoed into their bedroom. They felt totally out of place, if not just a little guilty, putting on their bathing suits on a cold day in January with the wind howling.

They looked at each other, no Adam and Eve, no Venus and Adonis, but George and Hillie Droge, 59 years old, of Alfalfa, Ontario. George's hair had thinned on top, while his chest, hairless, seemed almost feminine; his stomach challenged the elastic of his bathing suit, from which his two skinny legs protruded as twin tendrils from a watermelon. The weight of Hillie's arms had begun to sag somewhat, and her breasts, when she was undressed, now enjoyed the luxury of being able to rest on her belly; the backs of her legs had begun to resemble the blue and red lines of a roadmap. Had they not inhabited these bodies all their lives George and Hillie might have wondered if they were the same bodies that had risen with illicit desire for each other forty years ago. They looked at each other, laughed a little self-consciously, then went to enjoy their new treasure downstairs.

They tiptoed to the rec room in the basement, lifted the hot tub's cover, and for a few moments just stared at the water, steaming slightly from its glimmering blue depths. They'd never seen anything like it. George turned on the air jets, and they stepped in, first a foot, then a calf, then a thigh, their skin breaking out in goose pimples despite the water's warmth. Within minutes they were almost totally immersed, basking in the blissful water of their children's affection, this brim-full tub of God's forgiving love.

Everyone should feel so blessed.

OBITUARY:

PALLISTER, CECIL, on Monday, February 2, after a not too valiant fight against diabetes that saw him lose one leg, then another. Was loved more than he deserved by his late wife Eleanor. Affectionate father of Gus ("The Wuss"), and Daniel ("8-Ball"–ask him why), both of Alfalfa, and Crystal Colangelo, R.N., of Sooke, B.C., and too proud gramps of 12 grand-children. Survived by brother Samuel in Penetanguishene, not in what you think, and sister Jean in Sturgeon Falls. Mourned, perhaps, by a few friends here and there. Served in undistinguished fashion in the RCAF. Served 32 years as custodian at Alfalfa Public School and despite that still loved children. Was a member of C.U.P.E., the Masonic Lodge, and Fraternal Affiliate of the Royal Canadian Legion, Alfalfa branch. Was fair to middlin' at euchre and horseshoes, and pretty good at birdwatching, having spotted more than 137 species during his lifetime, most of them in this area. Visitation at Dunwoody Funeral Home Wednesday, from 2-4 and 7-9 pm. Funeral service on Thursday at 1 pm at Grace United Church. Donations to the S.P.C.A.

(Written by the deceased and published in honour of request made by him.)

-notice in The Alfalfa Sentinel-Star

THE BRIDES OF ALFALFA

When winter winds whip along Main Street and everybody's in a hurry to get wherever they're going here in Alfalfa, one of the places they nevertheless can't help stopping at even though it's February is Robert Meyer's photography store three doors south from Lucille's Lunch. That wind may be howling all the way from the arctic ice floes, yet people will stop if even for a moment to look at the photographs of fellow Alfalfans that Robert Meyer keeps in his front window. There, just above the Droge family picture taken last month on George and Hillie's fortieth anniversary, is Neil MacWhinnie, great-great-grandson of town founder Jonas McWhinnie, wearing his kilt on his seventieth birthday–you'd think an old man with such skinny legs and knobby knees would do anything to hide them, as any Dutchman would. And look, there's Laura Matthews who married Tyrone what's-his-name from out of town. Laura's otherwise a rather homely looking girl, how did Robert manage to make her look so good? How come *all* his brides look so beautiful, as if *he* were the groom instead of the out-of-town dolts they marry?

Robert Meyer has been the town photographer so long it will be hard to imagine life here in Alfalfa without him around to record it. He was one of the first Dutch immigrants who settled in Ontario back in the fifties, came here alone as a young man. He landed a job in a photography store in the city, learned all there was to know about cameras and developing film, then figured he'd start his own business. He's a patient and amiable old fellow, exactly the right kind of personality for a photographer. If a mother brings her child in for its first portrait and the baby's screams are loud enough to bring neighbouring store owners to their front doors wondering where the fire is with the town siren going off in the middle of the afternoon, Robert Meyer will smile and sit like a patient grandfather until the mother has managed to calm the child. And Robert can do amazing things with meagre raw material. If a Dutch farmer comes in for a passport photo Robert manages to achieve the impossible, somehow inducing the man to smile in the first place, then in making his portrait look remarkably human instead of like the kind of front- and side-view mugshots you used to find hanging in post offices.

Everyone agrees Robert Meyer's artistry lies in his ability to bring out a certain–*frisson*–in his subject no one else has seen before; he makes even Alfalfans look special. Some people have remarked they even lose their warts and moles in Robert's photographs–they don't know how he does it. Certainly there's a radiance in their eyes no one has seen before; no wonder people insist it be Robert who takes their picture.

Especially brides. Robert is in high demand for weddings here in Alfalfa. When couples decide on a date for their wedding, the very second calculation the bride figures out in advance is to make sure Robert is available that weekend. Many a groom has felt more than a twinge of jealousy that his bride should feel so strongly that it be Robert or no one, and that on the photographs Robert has brought out a look on the bride's face that not even the groom has been able to summon. Everyone agrees Robert must have special insight into human nature to evoke that special quality in people. But such insight, the unthinking assume, comes only to those who have been married a long time–it's a special knowledge they think you acquire as a result of managing to survive living with a spouse for a long time, sort of like battle savvy. So how has Robert managed to acquire it? For Robert Meyer is a life-long bachelor.

To remain unmarried is one thing in a large city; few people notice, let alone care. But being single in a small town like Alfalfa becomes another kettle of carp, for people draw conclusions. They didn't use to, bachelors not being uncommon then, but they draw conclusions now, given what's happening in society. Figure it out: a man who never married, an artsy type, goes by the name of *Robert*? Any normal red-blooded Canadian guy would call himself Bob. But what the town's cynics and mean-spirited conclude about Robert Meyer they won't come right out and say; the current word for it strikes them as being inaccurate, and the former word they won't use, it's too–unpleasant. But they have their reasons. And never mind Robert Meyer's age; perversion doesn't end just because a guy has turned sixty.

Nobody knows and everyone wonders why Robert never married. Did he have an unfortunate love affair in the old country? Was that why he immigrated to Canada? The few people who have been to university and who have taken psychology wonder, did he have a domineering mother, a father who was a wimp? It's difficult for people to understand why someone would willingly choose the single life when it's obvious to anyone that the advantages of marriage are so palpable. Some people at First Christian Reformed feel Robert would make a good match for Miss Evelyn Krikke, sort of like killing two birds with one stone, so to speak.

What people can't deny, cynical or not, is that Robert Meyer has always had the knack to catch the truly significant moments in our town's history. He was there to snap the occasion when Lois Fitch, who had just gotten her license after her husband Oliver died, swerved her car to avoid hitting Jake Vander Molen pulling out of the Beer Store, mistook the gas pedal for the brake, and plowed her car over the sidewalk and into the front of the Royal Bank in a majestic shower of glass. Miraculously no one was hurt since there were few customers in the bank despite it being rush hour, except that Franklin Gilchrist, the bank manager, suffered a heart attack. People weren't sure he had it because Lois Fitch's dramatic entry crumpled his heart like a five-dollar bill that's been through the wash or whether it was because of the scarcity of customers in the bank. Robert Meyer's photograph in *The Sentinel-Star* next day showed Lois' car stopped only inches away from the teller's counter; under the photo was the caption "Alfalfa Gets New Drive-In Bank."

Robert Meyer was there to snap the moment the morning after graduation at Alfalfa High some years ago when students had put rubber tires all the way up the sixty foot flagpole on the school's front lawn. No one will know whether their intent was to erect the world's tallest free-standing Freudian pun or to donate as their graduation gift a work of art worthy of the high school's motto: *"Altius, Etiam Altius"* ("Higher, Still Higher"). Neither does anybody to this day know where the students stole the tires from, nor how they got them all the way up to the top of that flagpole, and their feat of engineering remains one of the town's great unsolved mysteries. What *is* known is that it took the school board three meetings to decide how to remove the tires.

They finally had the head custodian, Walter Pinkney, or Pinky as he was known, cut through each tire with a huge saw used to cut through cement–it took him a full day before he got the job done. Students stood on the school lawn, cheering with a loud roar and counting every tire Pinky removed (*Bzzzzzzzz!* "Thirty-three!" *Bzzzzzzzz!* "THIRTY-FOUR!"), until the principal heard them above the roar of the saw and ordered them to disperse. In any case, the town council would very much like to find out who the pranksters were; council is considering repainting the town's name on the water tower, and thought since it deals with heights they would like the students' advice.

And Robert Meyer was there–I don't know how he manages to know about these things ahead of time–to snap what happened when Blessed Assurance Tabernacle decided to replace the parsonage's septic tank. That was before Alfalfa joined the twentieth century and installed a sewer system–I wouldn't be surprised, given what happened, that it was the Reverend Cecil Stewart who made sure the town installed a new sewer system.

Reverend Stewart was Blessed Assurance's pastor then, a blustery middle-aged man with a raised-eyebrow look on his face that said, You know, life is not really all that complicated, humph humph, believe me, I know. He was a political sort who often wrote letters to the editor and liked to be seen on the evening news in the city lamenting the decline of public morality and civic-mindedness and denouncing the evils of bilingualism or creeping socialism or godless feminism. His sermons extolled the blessing of Biblical womanhood, by which he meant large families, children being a reward from the Lord, and blessed was the man whose quiver was full of them, especially if he had a good wife to do the work.

The Reverend Cecil Stewart's own arrow must not have quivered too often, for he and his wife had just two children–no doubt he felt the Lord's work was more important than his personal blessedness. He ran as an independent in several provincial elections, but never garnered many more votes than he had children, voters being astute enough to recognize gasbaggery no matter how sanctimonious its source.

It was during Reverend Stewart's tenure at Blessed Assurance that the church decided to replace the septic tank at the parsonage and hired Johnny Elzinga and his backhoe, which is how everyone at First Christian Reformed heard about it. Normally the church would have hired one of its own parishioners, especially if it had known what was going to happen, but a Dutchman was the only person willing to do that dirty a job.

Johnny told us about it later. "I spent the first half day just digging around the septic tank with my backhoe eh, so I could lift the thing out while I'm wondering whether we'll have to pump it out first, then the farther I get the more I see that that tank is in sad shape, huge holes rusting through the sides of it–that family might just as well have been peeing into a sieve.

"So I had to get that thing outa there. I hook up a thick chain and loop it around the tank and slowly lift that sucker outa there while it's making a huge slurping sound, and as that tank comes up outa the ground the shit–pardon me–and everything comes sloshing outa there to beat the band. But the thing that was the craziest–I says to myself hey what's that, I take one look, and a second, 'n then a third, because coming out of that septic tank was a whole bunch of little white balloons, somebody has been having a lot of birthday parties I says to myself. Until somebody explains to me what those little white balloons are. That Reverend Stewart must have been flushing 'em down his toilet for a long time, because there were more of 'em than you can shake a stick at. But if you don't believe me, just ask Robert Meyer, because he was there to take pictures of the whole thing."

Robert's photos did not appear in *The Sentinel-Star* the next day.

But that wasn't the end of it. When Stanley McCormick, who owns the Drug Pharmacy in town, heard about it, Stanley decided that was the end of his membership at Blessed Assurance, because he noticed that the Reverend Cecil Stewart had certainly not been making his, um, pharmaceutical purchases at the Drug Pharmacy, and that's one of the cardinal rules of life in a small town: you support your local merchants. Stanley McCormick decided that if the Reverend Cecil Stewart was not going to patronize *his* establishment *he* certainly wasn't about to turn around and patronize the Reverend Stewart's, and Stanley McCormick has not attended Blessed Assurance to this day. He's been a Baptist ever since. Not that it made any difference to Reverend Stewart. He soon felt called to relocate his ministry to a larger city, and a new sewer system was, appropriately, his last contribution to our town.

But Robert Meyer has been taking people's photographs so long that just about everyone here in Alfalfa has his or her own memory of him. My own goes back a long time to one of the church picnics of First Christian Reformed, picnics which are still held every July 1 at a lake. First had a membership of about eighty families then–we don't count souls, that's a pagan Greek notion–and someone said we should take a group photograph. Ja, that was a good idea alright, everyone agreed, but eighty families, large Dutch ones at that where parents don't use funny little white balloons, so probably at least five hundred people, how were we going to shoot a group so large?

We knew if anyone would be able to solve that one Robert Meyer could, so Oetse Kikkert, who was chairman of consistory then, was asked to talk to him. No problem, Robert said. He had one of those cameras that could pan across the group. Pan–what? Oetse Kikkert wondered, what was that? They wanted a photograph, not soup. Then Robert explained that if the congregation grouped itself in a long, wide arrangement and people remained still he could move the camera from left to right and the picture would come out clear as a bell with the whole congregation on it.

Which indeed it did, and with more than everyone on it, for if you look closely at the old scrolled up brown and white photograph now, especially the ends of it, about two and a half feet of photograph apart, you'll see that Billy Berkel has a twin brother, which he in fact doesn't have.

What happened is this. After lunch, when we'd had all the games–the sixty yard dashes, the potato sack races and the long-distance egg tossing competition, and Jack Lammers won the funny costume contest wearing a yellow wig with long pigtails, his wife's brassiere holding two grapefruits, a pair of blue hockey shorts with red suspenders, and wooden shoes, everybody killing themselves laughing–then the congregation was called together for the photograph, and Robert Meyer explained that he would move the camera from left to right, from one end of the group to the other. It would take less than ten seconds. People were told to arrange themselves four or five deep, children sitting on the ground at the front, then the teenagers on their knees, and the adults standing at the back.

I can't recall which one of us thought of it first, probably each of the four of us teenagers who hung around together at the time–Henry Hogeterp, Wally Zandstra, Billy Berkel, and myself–would claim it was him, but we all thought it would be a great idea if one of us would stand at one end of the congregation, then sprint around back of everyone and arrive at the other end in time to be photographed again. One thing we did agree on: it would have to be Billy Berkel, who had just won the sixty yard dash, as he always did, at the picnic.

So that's what we did. We made sure we anchored the right end of the congregation, saw Robert Meyer climb his stepladder, waited what seemed ages for people to settle and shush themselves while Robert fiddled with the focus of his camera, then Mrs. Vander Veen noticed one of her twelve kids missing. Her husband took it upon himself to find the child and located him spending his money on ice cream at the snack bar and gave him a royal spanking so we had to wait for the kid to stop crying and then go through the whole settling and shushing and focusing part again, until we finally heard Robert Meyer holler, "Everyone say cheeeese!" One wise guy hollered, "Edam, or Gouda?"

As soon as Billy Berkel saw the camera begin to move he peeled away from us at the corner and sprinted with his head bowed in order to stay low, which is difficult if you've ever tried it, ran behind the Atsmas, the Vander Molens, and the Winkels, the Droges and TeBrakes and Wimmers, behind the Vander Leeks, Lubbers and Klops–all the old immigrants are there on the photograph if you look–and arrived sliding in the grass at the other end and quickly sat up huffing and puffing but trying to look as normal as possible. He was sure he had made it in time.

Then something happened we hadn't counted on. Robert Meyer announced nobody move, we would do one more in case the first one didn't turn out. Billy Berkel had to sprint forty yards back to where the four of us initially were, catch his breath, and do the forty yard dash a third time.

Except this time things didn't work out. Billy had started to smoke because he figured that if he was old enough to work for his dad on the farm he was also old enough to smoke like his dad, which was the case at that time–all of us smoked, shoot, beginning to smoke was like a Dutch kid's bar mitzvah. So when Billy had to run a third time he exceeded his sixty yard limit, ran out of gas, tripped over Mrs. Vander Veen's baby stroller, and did a kamikaze nosedive into the grass two-thirds of the way there while Robert Meyer's camera panned by. It's a good thing barnyard language doesn't show up on a photograph–there would have been a purple cloud right behind Mrs. Vander Veen. All we could hope for was that Robert Meyer would select the first shot.

Which he did. Apparently Oetse Kikkert, who had hay fever, was caught in the middle of a sneeze and showed up on the photograph as a grey blur, no way the chairman of consistory would approve that picture, so Billy Berkel is recorded for posterity as having a twin brother.

It's been snowing all of this February day, flakes plastered against

185

the sides of black tree trunks. The temperature hasn't risen above zero for several weeks, so that by now the earth has frozen solid, which means that Johnny Elzinga and his backhoe will be needed to dig the hole for Robert Meyer's grave. People will be bundling up in mitts and scarves for the funeral this afternoon.

Les Maslowski, whose insurance office is next door to Robert's photography store, noticed on Tuesday that Robert didn't come in that morning, didn't in fact come in all day, then when he didn't open next morning either Les ran out to Robert's place on Juniper. People do that in a small town, they look after their neighbour; in this case it had nothing to do with the fact that Les held Robert Meyer's life insurance policy. When he got no answer Les called the police. They were a little hesitant to go in because Robert has always been a rather private person. He has no family in town and no one other than the elders from First Christian Reformed making their annual visit can remember ever having gone into Robert's home.

The news of what happened has pretty well gotten around. They found Robert on the floor of his kitchen, dead from a stroke. Later, after the people who needed to go in had finished, they said that what they found strange is that none of the rooms in Robert's house had any of his photographs on the walls. You'd think he would have hung some of the shots he's won prizes for, people said later, like his silhouette of the town's water tower in front of a jagged bolt of lightning at dusk, or his shot of how Hannes Tazelaar's silo that Hannes was demolishing was falling right towards his tractor as he was pulling out the bottom blocks with a chain. They didn't find any of these photos in Robert's house.

Where they did finally find photographs, they discovered, was in Robert Meyer's bedroom. Hundreds of photographs. The four walls of his bedroom were completely covered with them, close-up photographs of every Alfalfa bride of the last forty years, photographs Robert had never shown anyone, photographs the brides themselves had not even seen. There were brides photographed in black and white and brides photographed in colour, blonde-haired Dutch-Canadian brides and red-haired Scots-Canadian brides, blue-eyed brides and brown-eyed brides, brides wearing veils and brides wearing flowers in their hair, every one of them Alfalfa brides. And each bride had an extraordinary beauty, a mysterious and haunting loveliness her husband had never seen in her before, each bride looking down from Robert's bedroom wall with a smile, a luminous, enigmatic smile for Robert Meyer alone.

IV.
The Floods Are Loose!

Though all seems melt and rush,
earth-loaf, sky wine,
swept to bright new horizons
with hill runnel, and gash,
all soaked in sunwash,

far north, the ice
unclenches,   booms
the chunks and floes, and river brims
vanish under cold fleece:
the floods are loose!

-Margaret Avison

APRIL IS THE CRUELLEST MONTH

The wooden booths along the back wall of Lucille's Lunch were rocking with laughter this week after Earl Prior told the story of what happened to Hilbert and Dorothy TeBrake last Thursday. The weather had been warm for a good two weeks and everyone in town thought they'd seen the last of the snow now that it was well into April. George Hardy over at Hardy Hardware had removed the one unsold Toro snowblower from in front of his store, put it in storage, and replaced it with a gleaming new shipment of red rototillers and wheelbarrows, while clerks at Art's Supermart had opened the garden centre selling peat moss and grass fertilizer and flats of annuals that almost caused people driving by to put on their sunglasses, they hadn't seen colours that bright for six months. All over town people had started washing cars on driveways once again, scrubbing away a winter's worth of salt and grime. In people's yards the buds on the forsythia bushes had begun to swell, promising to break out in yellow blossoms soon, while here and there, huddling close beside basement walls and under larger shrubs, crocuses and tulips had sent up their first green shoots. Inside houses all over town, dogs woke up from their winter torpor and began to sniff ceremoniously by back doors, toenails scratching on the linoleum, while at night cats slunk outside, pawed fastidiously in flower beds, and interrupted people's sleep with their amorous wailing.

Then, a week later, came snow. Cruel, unrelenting snow.

Everyone here in Alfalfa felt betrayed, as if God had momentarily relinquished control of the universe and anything could happen. Next thing people knew the town would be overrun by an epidemic of freaks of nature: two-headed piglets, albino babies, grotesque hunchbacks, and spendthrift Dutchmen. The snowfall was not a particularly heavy one, as Canadian winters go, only twelve inches or so; but Earl Prior, who lives opposite Hilbert and Dorothy on Laurier Lane, runs a snowblower so powerful it shoots snow all the way across the road and onto Hilbert's driveway if Earl isn't careful. Hilbert complains about it, but Earl Prior shrugs his shoulders and says he tries not to but he can't control where the wind blows his snow. If that weren't bad enough, running along the north side of Hilbert's driveway is a Chinese lilac hedge which acts as a perfect snow fence so that whenever it snows even a little, the wind blowing in from the northwest dumps the whole neighbourhood's allotment of snow onto Hilbert and Dorothy's driveway – except for a patch of four or five feet right in front of their garage door. The hedge stops there, so the wind comes whistling around the corner of the house and scours that part of their driveway clean right down to the cement when the rest of the driveway lies buried under three feet of snow.

Every time it snows Hilbert is thankful for that little clean patch, let me tell you. It's a pocket of cleanliness and sanctity, a small postage stamp reminder that God indeed has not lost control and that order and normalcy have not fled this world even though the rest of Hilbert's driveway lies clogged with snow. Every year when April finally decides to show up and Hilbert's back aches from heaving a winter's worth of snow over the hedge, he tells Dorothy he's going to cut the stinking thing down, he's fifty-six after all, but every May when they sit on their front porch after supper in their yellow Hardy Hardware lawn chairs and see the hedge's delicate purple blossoms and smell its lovely deep fragrance Hilbert tells Dorothy that, well, maybe he'll keep the hedge one more year. But only one.

Dorothy is smart enough not to say anything.

Hilbert says that what he's going to do about Earl Prior he's not sure yet.

Just about everyone on Laurier Lane uses a snowblower now, seems like once Earl got his, everyone else had to have one too. Except Hilbert. Hilbert and Dorothy are Dutch Reformed, which is like a double inoculation against even the slightest notion of wastefulness, so it's not strange that it strikes Hilbert as too extravagant and self-indulgent to blow snow back into the air with a machine when God gave people muscles to shovel it. Dorothy wisely does not ask Hilbert why he doesn't go back to cutting their grass during the summer with a push mower then, for she knows the joy of Hilbert's life is his 18-horse John Deere riding mower. He sits in its saddle much as King Solomon in all his splendour graced his throne. At least, as much as is possible by someone who stands 5'8" and weighs 220, as Hilbert does.

It's like their argument about central air conditioning. The unit they have now in their living room window Hilbert bought through an ad in *The Sentinel-Star*, and that was a good fifteen years ago. When Dorothy turns it on high, which she has to in order to get the cool air through the house, the thing makes about as much noise as Hilbert's riding mower. You heat the house in winter, she says, what's so crazy about cooling it in summer? Hilbert tells her it's sort of hard to explain, but a window unit doesn't so much try to change nature, as central air does, but modifies it, which makes central air somewhat unnatural. Dorothy surprised herself with the thought that came to her mind then. If that's so, she thought, then hell is the most natural place there is, but she didn't dare say that to Hilbert.

This winter Hilbert had suggested they buy a new television set to replace their old one which has developed bars that swim slowly across the screen so that Hilbert gets dizzy trying to follow the puck when he watches the Maple Leafs play. Dorothy tells him it's easy, just look in the Leafs' net, that's always where the puck ends up. Hilbert gave Dorothy his sad dog look he gets when he feels he's attacked by stupidity and he's stuck for words, so that he resembles a tree stump with a permanent scowl. Actually, Dorothy had preferred they buy a microwave, but Hilbert is not yet convinced that microwaves don't cause cancer, regardless of what doctors say. Now that Hilbert's bought a new Buick LeSabre, however, any discussion of buying anything, let alone a television or a microwave, has had to be put on hold.

Hilbert had bought the LeSabre several days before the snow came. He'd been thinking for some time about buying a new car, hoping he could coax one more year out of his thirteen-year-old Concord whose odometer, as if inspired by the new year, had turned over for a third time precisely on the first of January. He had decided it wasn't the right time to buy a new car just yet, but when the transmission in his old Concord went and Andy Stokes at the Texaco station told him what it would cost to put in not even a new transmission but a rebuilt one Hilbert had decided the car simply wasn't worth spending that much money on. Hilbert knows, he isn't Dutch for nothing.

Next day was one of those beautiful mid-April mornings when you know winter is finally over and every cell of your body tells you something good is about to happen to you, like falling in love, or receiving an inheritance. Hilbert drove over to see what kind of deals Tony Carr was offering at Carr Motors on the south end of town. Actually, Hilbert told himself, if the old Concord was going to break down, it could have chosen a worse time than it did, a month or two ago and everything would still have been locked in the dead of winter, nobody stirring, but now that it was late April with the snow gone for another year people would not have to worry about salt eating away the undersides of their cars anymore and they would be trading up for one of Tony Carr's new Chevrolets.

Normally Hilbert would have narrowed it down to the car he thought he could afford, taken it for a test drive, had Andy Stokes check under the hood, talked with the bank about interest rates, then thought it over for another day or two before finally making his move. But the intoxicating spring weather that April day must have muddled the blood flowing into Hilbert's brain, addling him, for how else to explain that an otherwise sober plumber with a dead Concord would, only an hour later, be the new owner of a racy, jet-black Buick LeSabre just three years old? That's what Hilbert was asking himself driving home that morning, wondering how he could possibly explain it all to Dorothy.

It wasn't until he'd walked around the LeSabre twice on their driveway, showing it to Dorothy and about to take her for a spin, that he read the new license plate, amazed he hadn't noticed earlier. "I'll have to exchange it for another one," he told her.

"Why?" she said, panicking. "How much did the car cost you?"

"Not the car, the license plate. Read it."

She read it three times without seeing anything. "NSB 627," she said, "what's wrong with that?"

"Don't you see? NSB. You remember in Holland, during the War? NSBers? Nazi sympathizers. There's no way I'll use that license plate."

Her voice held reproach. "Hilbert, that was fifty years ago."

"Doesn't matter. I can't drive the car with those plates. Think of what everyone will say," and he jumped into the car, backed it down the driveway, and drove off, leaving Dorothy standing there holding her black purse.

He was back an hour later, with new plates that said DOF 333.

The whole TeBrake clan came over to see the new car that Saturday evening, Hilbert's two brothers and their families from Blyth, and

Hilbert and Dorothy's four kids and their children from London and Sarnia, enough people to make a Dutch church picnic, and their reaction, after Dorothy told them the story of the license plates over coffee, was not what Hilbert had hoped to hear.

"Ja, that's quite an improvement all right, I can see why you traded the other ones in," Hilbert's brother Ralph said, reading the new plates through the living room window. "DOF 333. Has a nice sound to it. Sort of official. Too bad, though, that *dof* is the Dutch word for not too bright. Course, it doesn't apply to the owner, in this case."

"DOF, eh," said brother Clarence slowly, a mock serious frown darkening his face. "You know what *that* stands for, don't you?"

Hilbert was not sure Clarence was serious.

"Stands for the Dutch Order of Fascists," Clarence said, howling. "You'll have to get new plates!"

Hilbert gave Clarence his sad dog look.

Then they all got into the spirit, each drawing more laughs than the last:

"Dizzy Overweight Fanatics," daughter Sally said.

"Dirty Obscene Fellow," son Robert offered.

"Diaphanous Oogamous Fruitflies," said nephew Neil, who had studied biology at university and had increased, if not his respect for elders, at least his vocabulary.

Dorothy walked to the kitchen to serve a second round of coffee. "Doddering Old Fart, if you ask me," she said, but not so loud that Hilbert could hear.

That day when the snow came, Dorothy had made Hilbert his regular breakfast of hot oatmeal sprinkled with a bit of sugar and cinnamon, and a hard-boiled egg on wheat toast, then she herself had left several hours later in the LeSabre for the public high school in town where she works two days a week in the cafeteria preparing lunches, a job she started years ago to help pay for the kids' Christian school tuition but which isn't necessary anymore with all four of them out of the house now, nevertheless the money she earns on top of Hilbert's income is nice.

Somehow they always seem to be short of money, according to Hilbert, and Dorothy wonders at times whether Hilbert doesn't keep extra money in a bank account he hasn't told her about, but she would never ask him that. Dorothy asked Hilbert at first whether she should take a job working in the public high school when she and Hilbert have always sent their children to Christian schools. "Get off the pot," Hilbert said, "we pay our taxes like everybody else."

She didn't think Hilbert would actually let her drive the new LeSabre and she knew it was only because it was to her job. Besides providing a little extra income, Dorothy's job gets her out of the house, she'd go crazy cooped up by herself without the several cats she would like to have but can't because of Hilbert's hay fever, which he claims is brought on by, among other things, cats. Dorothy keeps meaning to ask her doctor whether that is possible, but then thinks it better not to ask. A good relationship like theirs is hard to find, and sometimes takes sacrifices.

When she backed the car out of the garage that morning the snow was just starting to come down in thin wisps, the wind swirling it in white eddies that snaked across their driveway. By the time she pulled into the high school parking lot she noticed the wisps had started giving way to larger flakes. She made chicken salad and grilled cheese sandwiches in the warm cafeteria kitchen all morning, casting nervous glances out the window all the while to see what the weather was up to. The snow kept falling, horizontally it seemed, driven by wind.

Watching the cold weather she wondered suddenly whether she had remembered to take the pork chops out of the freezer earlier that morning; Hilbert never considered anything a meal unless it had a good bit of meat with it. Now if they had a microwave she wouldn't have to worry when she got home. She ate a slice of zucchini bread with her afternoon tea, then wasted no time at the end of her shift, said goodbye to the other women, and stepped outside into the cold air and flying snow to drive home.

She found the LeSabre plastered with snow, which took her some time to sweep off with the flimsy little broom on the other end of the windshield scraper. Freezing flakes blew into her eyes, her ears. Then, as she tried to sweep the pile of snow from the hood of the car, the handle of the windshield scraper snapped in two, and she flung the broken pieces to the ground.

Driving home was treacherous. Perhaps the county had already used up the year's budget of salt during the winter or perhaps the boys at the county shed had decided last month to put away their snow plows for the year, but the result was that the cars passing over the town's streets had packed the snow so that it shimmered under Dorothy's headlights. And snow was still falling, flakes driven sharply against her windshield. The LeSabre felt strange to her, so much more powerful than the familiar rattletrap Concord–if anything should happen to the LeSabre–the thought was so distressing she did not even want to think about it. She hunched forward to see past the mound of snow piled up on the hood of the car. She knew she should have swept it off, even if with the sleeve of her coat.

She turned into their street, careful not to veer too close to the edge of the road and slowly steering around parked cars whose white, rounded shapes loomed large as elephants. Just two more blocks, she reassured herself, and the LeSabre would sit snug and safe in their garage.

When she neared their house she reached up to the sun visor and touched the automatic garage opener Hilbert had bought her last fall for her birthday. She slowed down waiting for the garage door to open, then guided the car onto the driveway and into the knee-deep snowdrift sloping away from the chinese lilac hedge. The depth of the snow and the driveway's upward incline slowed her momentum until her front wheels began to spin and the car stopped well short of the open garage. She would have to back out and take another run at it.

She rolled down her window and leaned out to steer the car back down the driveway. She backed the LeSabre as close to the Priors' edge of the road as she dared, then made another run up the driveway. Her front wheels began to spin almost immediately in the deep snowdrift, slowing down the car to a snail's pace, but this time she made it to within ten feet of the open garage before the LeSabre slowed to a halt. One more try, and she'd be there.

She was about to back down the driveway when she saw Hilbert, bundled up in his blue parka with orange trim, come running out of the front door. She rolled down her window to receive his message, cold air blowing snow into her face, but Hilbert opened the door. "Here, let me do it," he said, "I'll drive it in." He sounded brusque, as if something had angered him. Who was she to argue? She got out of the car and Hilbert jumped in. Later she would tell herself that that was where they'd made their mistake, they should have been content with half a loaf and have left the car right there, but the garage, with its light shining so warmly, made her want the LeSabre safely inside. How could they leave it outside like a stray cat in a snowstorm all by itself overnight?

Hilbert backed the car far enough down the street for him to be able to get a good run at the driveway's slope, he put the car in drive, with its familiar little bump forward, then pushed down the gas pedal. He managed the turn onto the driveway fine, there was nothing like front wheel drive for getting through snow, and kept the gas pedal down as the LeSabre slowly made its way through the snow and up the driveway. And up, front wheels spinning so fast that, had Hilbert looked down at the speedometer he would have seen the red needle hovering at eighty kilometres an hour, the car continuing to edge forward through the snow up the driveway's slope, farther now than Dorothy had been on her previous two tries, just six more feet if he could keep those front wheels going, Hilbert rocking back and forth urging the LeSabre to keep moving, peering over the snow piled on the car's hood while he tried to keep it in the centre of the driveway, the car barely inching forward now, past Dorothy standing at the driveway's edge watching him, only five more feet, the open garage door large and inviting, just four feet away now and he'd be there—when all of a sudden he heard the tires shriek like a stuck pig on the small patch of driveway scoured clean by the wind whistling around the corner of the house and Hilbert felt his head snap back as the LeSabre shot forward, its right front end plowing into the corner of the house with a sickening screech of metal, and stopped.

When he dared to raise his eyes after his head had pitched forward with the collision Hilbert looked up and saw the LeSabre's right front end buried into the brick and concrete block corner of the garage, a geyser of steam billowing up from the car's grille. For a brief moment the thought flitted through his mind that, like a disgraced Japanese general, the only honourable thing for him to do was to commit suicide.

~~~~

"Hilbert TeBrake must have won the lottery or something," Peewee Melnyk was saying over coffee to some of the regulars in Lucille's Lunch next day.

"Why's that?" Bob Tonkin said.

"How else do you explain that right after Hilbert spent all that money on that car he bought, he was in the hardware store just this morning asking to buy a snowblower when winter's over, well practically anyway, and when George Hardy explained to him he'd put away his last snowblower in storage Hilbert insisted he have a look at it because he needed one, he said, a powerful one. I was there, saw the whole thing. Practically forced George to sell it to him. What would make a Dutchman do that unless he'd won the lottery and was lookin' for things to spend it on?"

"His people don't believe in buying lottery tickets," Ben Locke pointed out.

"Maybe Hilbert received an inheritance," Bob Tonkin said.

Peewee Melnyk scratched his head. "That must be it alright," he said.

"Waaait a minute, you mean you haven't heard?" Earl Prior said, and, when he knew all eyes were on him, took several more puffs on his pipe, then leaned forward and took a deep breath to describe what he'd seen from his garage the evening before as he was putting away his snowblower after he'd sent up beautiful huge geysers of snow cleaning his driveway.

Remember when? 30 years ago

A sow on Gordon Harper's farm gave birth to a two-headed piglet, a rare event. The piglet was not expected to live long.

Sunday, April 11 at 2:00 a.m. marked the official change-over from telephone operators to direct dial phones in this area. Those working as operators at the time were Mrs. Pat Leitch; Mrs. Ruth Noble; and Miss Jane Whelpton.

Temperatures dropped to -12 F. on April 12, breaking the record for that day that had stood since 1936.

Mr. Stanley Ott assumed his position as postmaster of Alfalfa. He announced that hours for open wicket service would be extended to six days a week, 8:00 a.m. to 6:00 p.m. Monday to Saturday.

Winning curling team in the annual Farmers Bonspiel was Harvey Taylor, Archie McCutcheon, Walter Broderick, and Larry Lang.

The barn of Mr. and Mrs. Leo Meulendyk went up in flames after a short in electric wiring. Firemen from neighbouring towns were called to help put out the fire. Loss of stock, unfortunately, was heavy: 36 pigs, 28 cows, and 2 horses, not to mention machinery.

Three sets of dentures were stolen from the office of Dr. Neil Weir. They have not been located since.

- column in The Alfalfa Sentinel-Star

GIFT OF FINEST WHEAT

A week or two after the surprise snowfall in April when Hilbert TeBrake plowed his new Buick LeSabre into the front of his house, a couple of the town philosophers meeting in Lucille's Lunch were observing how late Easter was this year. Just like the warm weather.

"What I've always wondered," Ben Locke said, "is who decides what date Easter falls on? Really, now. Sometimes I think God's got this contraption like they have at bingo, with a whole bunch of ping pong balls bubbling inside it like popping popcorn and every ball has a date stamped on it and God takes out one of the balls and says, "Ta daa! It's gonna be April 21 this year, everybody!"

"It's quite simple to figure out, actually," Earl Prior said, lighting his pipe, so everyone had to wait while he finished puffing. "Easter always falls on the first Sunday after the first full moon after the vernal equinox. There, now you know."

"Huh, s'long as you know what 'vernal' means," Ben Locke snorted. "Sounds to me like a guy's name. Like in, 'OK Shorty, you clean out the barn, and me 'n Vernal go to town for groceries.'"

"What I can't see is why Easter can't be the same date every year," Bob Tonkin said, "same as all the other special church days like Christmas or Valentine's Day. That way you'll know ahead of time when to expect all the egg and bunny crap."

"That's easy," Peewee Melnyk observed. "The reason it can't be the same date every year is because Easter can't be just any day of the week. It's gotta be a Sunday, otherwise people wouldn't be able to get off work to go to church."

"Apparently the World Council of Churches or somebody is working on that," Bob Tonkin said, "either them or the Pope, I forget which, except they can't get all the Protestants to agree."

"So what else is new," Bob Locke said. "Pass the sugar."

~~~~

Four of the churches here in Alfalfa worshipped together early Easter morning after Rev. Sandra Oppendahl at Grace United suggested they hold an ecumenical Easter sunrise service. There was some discussion as to where to have it, since traditionally sunrise services are held outdoors, preferably in a picturesque location such as on a hilltop or by water, so on both points the organizers were in a bit of a pickle. The highest point around town is the dump–rather, the landfill–a mile west of town, so that was that. As for water, Ken Schoenfeld of Calvary Baptist said they were free to meet beside his farm pond, but this offer didn't generate a great deal of support. Then someone suggested the golf course outside town, which is where Robert Meyer always took bridal couples for photographs. If it was good enough for wedding photos it should be picturesque enough for a sunrise service. It wasn't exactly a hilltop but at least people would have a clear view of the horizon and the sun coming up. The organizing committee decided on the sixteenth fairway, which has a decent-sized water hazard running through it, especially during April when it is swollen with the spring runoff.

The late snowfall we had this month finally melted only a week or so ago, and the worshippers at the sunrise service found the fairway a bit soggy, especially near the creek, so people kept edging towards dryer ground, and by the time the service ended people were a good eight-iron away from where they had begun. Sunday morning also turned out to be cold, especially at six in the morning with the sun barely up, so that a number of people got up early and checked their thermometers, saw the temperature, and climbed right back into bed. Decided they'd catch a service later on television instead.

At the service Rev. Oppendahl had a homily about the women who got up early to go to the tomb and how, this Easter morning, they set an example for us all to follow, but she cut her message short after she felt water starting to soak through the soles of her shoes. Everyone who was there agreed Stan McSpadden's trumpet accompaniment on "Christ the Lord is Risen Today" sounded wonderful in the cold open air despite the occasional squawks coming out of his horn because of Stan's blue lips and a few misplayed notes caused by the gloves Stan was wearing because of the cold.

~~~~

Sacred Heart Catholic Church did not participate in the sunrise service, the Triduum being a rather important part of the Catholic church calendar. Mass was celebrated on Holy Thursday, then the Good Friday service was the only service of the year at Sacred Heart when mass was not celebrated. Saturday evening after it was dark marked the Easter Vigil service. All the lights inside the church were put out, then the Easter candle was brought into the pitch-black church after being lit from a fire outside. Father Michael carried the candle forward, lighting candles held by worshippers sitting along the centre aisle, who in turn passed on the flame through the pews.

Father Michael's voice is nothing to write Rome about, so David Crossley, the choir director at Sacred Heart, sang the Exsultet, his strong baritone voice ringing through the church:

Rejoice, heavenly powers! Sing, choirs of angels!
Exult, all creation, around God's throne!

People renewed their baptism vows, and after that a peculiar thing happened.

When Father Michael was supposed to recite the next part of the liturgy the congregation heard only a mumbled muttering from the altar, and then silence. Everyone looked up to see what was wrong with their priest–twenty seconds of silence is a long time when for two thousand years you've said the response on cue so that you could do it in your sleep and not miss a beat. Those who attended mass more than once a year at Easter and who therefore knew their Bible thought of another priest struck dumb at the altar, but unlike Zechariah, Father Michael had not spoken with an angel. It wasn't anything that sublime.

David Crossley's young son Nathan served as altar boy during the service. He held Father Michael's red Sacramentary, and, while Father's back was turned, Nathan started flipping through the book's pages–what's a kid to do to pass the time, all those services become the same after a while. Except the Sacramentary wasn't nearly as exciting as Nathan's Superhero comic books. Then his attention was drawn to the coloured ribbons inside the Sacramentary. Nathan pulled all the ribbons out of their pages and bunched them into a colourful tail, then when Father Michael turned to him he handed the book back not thinking Father needed the ribbons to find his place and there they were, dangling from the book like a bunch of coloured streamers so when Father had to recite the next part of the liturgy all he could do was sputter while trying to find his page. It was the place in the liturgy where Father Michael was to say "Lift up your hearts," but what he actually said was, "One moment please," and the people in the pews automatically responded, "We lift them up to the Lord." Meanwhile, Father was frantically riffling through pages for what he was supposed to say next. There was a moment of awkward silence. Father Michael hated to think his parishioners might presume that after only eighteen years as a priest he was already beginning to lose his marbles.

Next morning, Easter Sunday, four catechumens were baptized and celebrated their first mass. After the service, Father Michael wondered whether he'd overestimated the number of once a year regulars, for he noticed that more wine was left than usual. The wine had been consecrated, as always, and Father Michael did what any priest always does, which is to drink the leftover wine.

He entered the rectory office half an hour later, announced he thought he would lie down a while since Holy Week had tuckered him out a good bit (all those extra services wear down a priest, after all), and so he spent a deservedly restful Easter Sunday.

~~~~

First Christian Reformed Church did not participate in the sunrise service either, since they tend not to be big on ecumenical events. "To begin with," Elder Harold Oudekerk said at the Council meeting, "if Rev. Oppendahl is going to lead the service there's the not so small matter of a woman preaching when Paul is clear on the subject, as we all know, in 1 Corinthians 14."

"Not only that," Timon Mulder said, "suppose they decide to have Communion at the service and people from Sacred Heart are there. Would our participation suggest we agree with them that the bread and wine are turned into the actual body and blood of Christ? Furthermore,"

Timon said, getting into second gear, "would our participation imply that we are one with the Pentecostals there in believing the primacy of speaking in tongues when Paul is clear also on this matter in I Corinthians 14? And what about the Baptists, would–"

"But Timon," one of the younger elders said, "look at what Paul says only two chapters earlier in I Corinthians 12, that the body is made up of many parts. Would you really want to say that the Christian Reformed Church makes up the *whole* body?"

"That's right, perhaps the Catholics are a nose," elder Albert Miedema said, "and the Pentecostals are a tongue, whereas we Reformed are only the– the–"

"The *mind*," Timon Mulder wanted to say, "we are the mind of the body, and if there's one thing we Calvinists know, it's how to discern theological error."

Then Rev. DeHeer reminded members of Council that between I Corinthians 12 and I Corinthians 14 lies I Corinthians 13, which tells us that even though we might speak in the tongues of men and of angels, even though we might fathom all mysteries and all knowledge, and even though we might even move mountains–if we have not love, we are nothing more than clanging gongs. Which some thought was what the argument was starting to sound like. In the end, one elder moved they not participate in the sunrise service this year but that they observe what transpired and then assess the situation next year. The wait and see approach seemed wise to Council.

After coffee recess, another elder asked whether Communion should be celebrated on Good Friday instead, which seemed to him more appropriate than Easter, but Rev. DeHeer reminded Council of the document he had written on this issue last year explaining that Good Friday is the one date on the liturgical calendar when Communion is not celebrated. It should not, Rev. DeHeer argued, become a funereal occasion, which, he said, if we are honest with ourselves we have a tendency to make it, brothers, but it should be a celebration when we are fed by the body and blood not of a dead Christ, but of a resurrected and living Saviour.

So Communion was celebrated again at First CRC on Easter.

~~~~

Donna Sprik got up early Easter morning, not to attend the community sunrise service, but to bake bread. Her husband Jerry is the deacon at First CRC responsible for providing the elements for Communion, and Donna has taken it upon herself to bake the bread. The previous deacon who looked after providing it always bought supermarket bread, which Donna thinks has the texture of soggy oatmeal and the flavour of Lepage's glue, and using it for Communion, she feels, is a sacrilege. Donna grew up on a farm where bread is something you bake, not buy in a store, and when you have a slice with butter and cheese you know you've eaten something and not felt you've been the subject in a chemistry experiment. The particular ministry Donna wants to offer her church is to provide bread that is worthy of the sacrament, worthy of her Lord.

She set her alarm for 5 o'clock to give herself time to bake three loaves, and there she was at 5:30 a.m. at her kitchen table, hands coated with white flour, kneading bread. When the loaves were in the oven she allowed herself a cup of herbal tea but had nothing to eat, which she always does the morning of Lord's Supper so that Communion bread is the first food that day to touch her tongue. By eight a.m. the bread sat cooling on the counter, and when Jerry and the kids got up half an hour later the aroma of the Communion bread had spread through their house like fragrant incense.

~~~~

Timon Mulder rose early on Easter morning as well, not to bake bread but to feed his cows. He has 120 Frisian Holsteins which he milks with his two sons, so he's up doing his own sunrise service seven days a week, 365 days a year. His farm is just what you'd expect a Dutch farm to be: white painted fences, white painted stones lining the pea gravel driveway, white painted barn with green trim and Timon's name on the front in large green letters: "TIMON MULDER & SONS. PUREBRED HOLSTEINS." Timon's dairy cows are the pride of the county; other farmers who raise Holsteins concede first prize to Timon every year at the Alfalfa Fair. The cement floor in Timon's dairy barn is clean enough to eat from.

Timon finished milking by eight, showered, and had his usual Sunday morning breakfast of oatmeal and scrambled eggs. At the table he read the Easter story with his wife Margaret, then put on his suit and tie.

At First Christian Reformed that morning people shook each other's hands and wished each other happy Easter. In the Council room before the service Rev. DeHeer asked Timon to be one of the serving elders for Communion. The service opened with the hymn "Alleluia! Alleluia!" Three large pots holding white lilies stood before the pulpit. Rev. DeHeer's sermon that morning was from the Gospel of Luke when Christ revealed himself to the two disciples in the village of Emmaus in the breaking of the bread. After the sermon the congregation sang two triumphant Easter hymns, "The Strife is O'er, the Battle Done" and "Low in the Grave He Lay." Then Rev. DeHeer read the Form for the Celebration of the Lord's Supper and Timon and five other elders moved to the front pew to receive the trays of bread and wine.

Timon received a tray of bread from Rev. DeHeer and walked down the sanctuary's centre aisle and passed the bread into each pew while the congregation sang,

> You satisfy the hungry heart
> with gift of finest wheat.
> Come, give to us, O saving Lord,
> the bread of life to eat.

After he had finished passing the tray of bread Timon went through the aisle with the plastic cups of wine.

When he was back in the pew and about to receive the bread he saw something he had never seen before in a communion service. As Rev. DeHeer took the tray of bread from the Communion table, a piece of bread rolled off and dropped to the floor. Timon wasn't sure Rev. DeHeer had noticed. He looked around at his fellow elders, but most sat with heads bowed and eyes closed. Timon tried to ignore the piece of bread on the floor and focused instead on his own unworthiness that had brought Christ to the cross, but his penitence was broken by the piece of white bread lying beside a leg of the oak Communion table. The bread lay on the red carpet as starkly–and outrageously–as a white marshmallow.

Timon wasn't sure what to do.

Rev. DeHeer moved behind the Communion table and began to address the congregation: "Take, eat, remember and believe. . . ." Timon ate, but his mind was on the piece of bread lying profaned on the floor. He thought perhaps Rev. DeHeer might notice the bread later when he came to give the elders the wine, but after Timon took the offered cup the minister moved again behind the table. "Take, drink, remember and believe," Rev. DeHeer said.

Timon drank. He felt as if the piece of bread on the floor lay burning a hole through the carpet. It's just bread, he told himself.

Just bread? he found himself thinking, just bread? Why was he sweating then? Something holy was being profaned, he thought, Christ's risen and glorified body defiled. Or was it merely his mania for tidiness? He looked again at the other elders but none had apparently noticed the bread.

He could not sit any longer. He rose from his seat, walked toward the Communion table, and picked up the bread; then he placed it on the tray with the rest of the leftover bread. He felt the eyes of the whole congregation on him as he walked back to his seat.

~~~~

That afternoon Jerry and Donna and the kids ate their Easter dinner of roasted rabbit and green beans and scalloped potatoes. White and purple lilies graced their table. Jerry had wanted to eat ham–"Rabbit? We always eat ham on Easter!"–but Donna had good childhood memories of eating rabbit. "Hey, might as well kill the old Easter bunny once and for all," Jerry said, and after that the kids, whose minds were filled with images of soft cuddly pets, wouldn't eat any rabbit.

After dinner Donna took two of their kids to her parents' farm while Jerry did the cleaning up. Half a bag of pieces of bread had been left over from the Communion service that morning, and as usual when Jerry brought it home, Donna asked the kids, "Who would like to go and feed Opa's ducks?"

"Yeah!" the youngest two shouted.

"Duh, big deal," twelve year old Ronnie said.

"I have history homework," Laura said.

"Not on Sunday you don't," her father said. "Besides, it's Easter Monday tomorrow, there's no school."

"Well, Jennifer and Kyle and I will go then," Donna said.

She put on their coats and boots, they trooped into the car and drove to her parents' farm. A hundred yards behind the house and across a stretch of grass lay a pond ringed with stones.

Her father met them before they had a chance to knock on the back door. He was wearing his farm jacket over his white shirt and tie. "Knew you'd be coming," he said.

"Hi Opa!" Jennifer and Kyle shouted, "are you coming with us?"

"Wouldn't miss it if you paid me. C'mon, let's go see if the ducks are still there. Did you bring the bread?"

Jennifer held up the plastic bag with a mittened hand.

Six ducks swam toward them as they stood on the grass at the edge of the pond, the ground soggy under their feet. The sky was a cloudless blue; above the trees the sun stood bright but without the heat yet of summer. "Not too close, Kyle," Donna warned.

"They remember us," Jennifer said, "they know we're gonna give 'em bread."

"Got 'em trained have ya?" Donna's father said.

The ducks swam serenely, treading water with orange webbed feet. Kyle threw a piece of bread toward them and three ducks dove forward with surprising quickness, the first duck gobbling the bread with jerky motions of its head, the others swimming rapidly after it.

Jennifer tossed a piece of bread into the water and again the ducks dove. Several tiny feathers of grey down, Donna noticed, floated on the surface of the dark green water. The blue on the tops of the male ducks' heads shone in the sun; below their eyes their feathers were a brilliant green, down to the narrow white band that ringed the base of their necks.

"Here, watch," Donna's father said, placing a piece of bread in his palm and holding it out to the nearest duck, a brown female. The bird swam towards him and gobbled the bread from his hand. "That's Queenie," he said to the children, "and that one over there is Duke."

"How can you tell them apart, Opa?" Jennifer asked.

"Well, Duke there has just a bit crookeder lower beak than all the others, see that?"

The children continued throwing bread into the water, the ducks lunging after it. Donna stood watching the birds as if she had never seen them before, transfixed by their colours radiant in the sunlight. She marvelled at the beauty and care that had gone into creating them and then she was filled with a sense of divine presence all around her: in the crisp spring air, in the grass and water, in the bread, above all in the blue and green iridescence on the ducks' heads glittering in the sunlight with the very effulgence and glory of the risen Christ.

Too much religion?

Dear Editor,

If you ask me I'm starting to wonder whether you aren't a little heavy in your coverage of religion. Take last week for instance. Six church reports, all saying the same thing. Why not have one church report on behalf of all the rest? Why not give equal space to the local Elks or the Orange Lodge?

While I'm writing anyway let me say, that maybe the men who are on a first name basis with God wouldn't mind clearing something up that I couldn't help noticing from the sermon reports lately. About Judas, Rev. Findlater at Calvary Baptist is reported as stating that in Matthew 27 Judas "went away and hanged himself" yet, if I remember right somewhere else, it says that he fell and his intestines spilled out. So which is it? He can't hang himself one gospel and spill his guts in another.

Similarly, we're told in one place that the two thieves on the cross both mocked Jesus, but in another gospel Jesus tells one of them today, you will be with me in paradise. Which is it, can't God get his story straight?

Maybe our esteemed ministers should clear up some of these questions we common folk have.

Edward Hopp
R.R. 3

-letter in The Alfalfa Sentinel-Star

THE FRAGRANCE OF HYSSOP,
THE AROMA OF THYME

I n a pleasant spring morning," a certain bean grower named Henry
David once said, "all man's sins are forgiven. Such a day is a
truce to vice." It's a notion more Transcendental than Calvinist, of
course, as Henry David's friend Nathaniel pointed out, but Harry Olthof
of Alfalfa would know what Henry David had in mind.

Harry's 32, has already lost much of his hair on top which he makes
up for by wearing it long at the back, and sports a thin blond mustache
you can see only because it plays against the red backdrop of his upper
lip. He's the television specialist at Ernie Elphick's E.E. Electronics
store here in Alfalfa, and for some years now has been walking the half
a block to Lucille's Lunch every day to join five or six cronies there for
coffee, some stimulating conversation about the deep things men talk
about over coffee, and a smoke. Especially a smoke. The stimulating
conversation doesn't always happen, so when it does it's a bonus. The
conversation may run as follows:

Click of lighter.

Sound of inhale, then exhale of smoke.

Pause.

"Peewee get his hay in before the rain yesterday?"

Slurp of coffee.

"Yup, but only by a tit hair."

Slurp of coffee, exhale of smoke.

"Supposed to be nice rest of the week, though."

"'bout time." Exhale of smoke.

"Whadja think of the Leafs' game last night?"

"All I can say is, it's a good thing the season's over next week." Slurp of coffee.

As he can after passionate lovemaking or a prolonged nap, a man can keep going a long time after a satisfying conversation like that.

But it's the cigarette Harry goes for–there's something about nicotine cruising darkly through a Dutchman's veins; it's the mercury in his thermometer. It may have been a Frenchman who introduced tobacco to Europe back in 1560, but it was the Dutch who said, "Nikki baby, awfully glad to make your acquaintance, waddya doin' tonight?" Nicotine is the element in which Harry lives and moves and has his being. If his plane crashed in the bush up north in the dead of winter Harry could survive three months on nothing but a carton of cigarettes–what would kill him would be having to ration them that long. Harry doesn't normally walk any farther than he has to, but he'll walk half a block to Lucille's for a cigarette.

You can see then that it would have to be a fairly special miracle rather than your no-frill, house-and-garden variety for Harry to quit smoking. He'd started when he was fifteen and has been a good pack-a-day man for twenty-two years. If you didn't already know, nicotine is found not only in cigarettes; it's a toxic alkaloid that may be mixed with water and used as an insecticide. That means Harry has imbibed enough nicotine in twenty-two years of smoking to kill off the weeds in a thirty-acre cornfield, not to mention his wife Tina and their three boys. Tina has been urging him to quit, although not lately; she knows he knows how she feels. She's never heard a reformed smoker say, "Thank you for pointing out once more how disgusting my habit is. That was really helpful. I needed that."

But she also knows how to locate his achilles heel on the subject. They keep their money for the week in a small metal box under their bed–on his side, not hers, which is only fair. After all, he's the one who bows down to it more often. Tina will make subtle hints. "Honey," she'll say, "I thought we still had two twenties in there."

"We did, but I was out, so I bought a carton." Harry does not use the word cigarettes, it's best to be somewhat indirect about your vices.

"Oh," says Tina, "I was going to get some pyjamas for Bobbie. Well, the weather's not too cold yet. He can last till next week, I suppose." This occurred in November.

As usual, the hint is lost on Harry. After sixteen years of smoking the convolutions of his brain have become encrusted with nicotine the way zebra mussels cling to a submerged wreck. Next week he and Tina will have the same conversation.

Now, if I said that a Dutchman quitting smoking is not just your run-of-the-mill miracle, it's not the crème de la crème of God's miracles either, not like the parting of the Red Sea or Christ feeding the five thousand. After all, what's one man prevented from slowly killing himself compared to the saving of thousands of lives? Let's keep some perspective here. No, it's just a bit less of a miracle, more on the level of Joshua commanding the sun to stand still. Don't laugh–Harry knows that if he could give up smoking it would add ten or twenty years to his life, which *is* like the sun standing still, in a way, and who's to argue with that?

Harry's thinking about quitting didn't come easy to him. Nor was his decision to quit a snap decision; Reformed folks like Harry tend not to act rashly. No need for you to jump into the ditch just because everyone else is. When the crusade choir starts in on "Just As I Am, Without One Plea" and thousands start filing to the front you like to think about the idea a while; you want to make sure it's something you'll be able to live up to later. If you do finally feel moved to make a decision you tell yourself, well, perhaps I will, and you rise from your seat and start down the aisle, except by this time you notice that the stadium lights have all been turned down and everywhere around you ushers are sweeping up the crumpled-up song sheets and the empty KFC buckets used for the collection.

So Harry, like a stone at rest, would have to be subject to Newton's first law of motion, appropriately called the law of inertia: no way he was going to move unless he was acted upon by an external force. He had been aware, all the while, of the medical statistics, which he respected. On this point he was not in agreement with whatever sage it was who said there are lies, damned lies, and statistics. He knew their validity alright, he just told himself they applied not so much to a mere pack-a-day guy like himself but to *heavy* smokers like Clarice Sacco, who keeps Ernie Elphick's books at a desk in the back and inhabits a permanent pall of blue cigarette smoke. As anyone knows, that is about as clever as deciding the law of gravity will apply only to others.

The first nudge towards Harry's quitting occurred three years ago when Ernie decided the store should be smoke-free. It had nothing to do with his being Baptist, Ernie said. It was true, Harry and Clarice had to admit, Ernie had been amazingly tolerant, for a Baptist, about their smoking in the back of the store. "It's the way society's going," Ernie said, "government buildings, airplane flights, your better restaurants– even Tim Horton's–they've all banned smoking, it's what our customers expect."

Grabbing a smoke outside in the alley back of the store with Clarice was pleasant at first during August and even early September, being outdoors seemed healthy, like taking a walk. October, most days, was tolerable–with a good jacket. November was arduous leaning toward decidedly cruel despite the jacket. Then came December. Clarice lasted three more days, drew the line at wearing a hooded parka, and decided smoking was no longer worth the hassle. She had four sessions with a hypnotist in the city and quit, just like that. Harry wasn't even envious; after all, who's to say this hypnotism stuff didn't border on the occult?

He began walking the block and a half to Lucille's.

But like mice gnawing at a block of cheese, the statistics kept gnawing at his peace of mind, until finally there wasn't much left of the cheese but the holes. He saw himself twenty years down the road, his lungs a pulpy mass of charcoal, his breath no more than a rusty, asthmatic wheeze, and he knew he would have to quit or it was curtains for him. But the distance between knowing and doing can be as far as walking the road from Alaska to Zanzibar, and that's a long way for a fellow like Harry.

Facing such a formidable challenge as quitting smoking, Harry must have figured he'd better take several practice runs at it, for he had three rehearsals at quitting, a year or so apart; the longest lasted four days. He was so irritable Tina could have used mental cruelty as sufficient grounds. But what are you gonna do–she loves the guy. Besides, she used to smoke herself before they started having kids, and was able to quit only because of her morning sickness, so she knew what Harry was going through.

Harry's last attempt happened two years ago when Tina was pregnant with their latest and was in her first trimester. She suffered a triple dose of heartburn every day: one from the baby, and a double dose from Harry's irascibility. His breath smelled like a Dutch import store from all the peppermints he was eating to help him get through the day. He normally watches a fair bit of television, he's a video specialist after all, so when you think he's just being a couch potato he's really doing pretty high-level research, but he couldn't sit in front of the T.V. longer than fifteen minutes and he'd get up, pace around the room, and slam the cupboard doors in the kitchen looking for nothing in particular, or with a loud clatter straighten out the kitchen drawer holding the soup ladles and spatulas and barbecue utensils. Tina thought he might go to the tool shed outside and straighten out *his* stuff, screwdrivers and hammers and chisels or whatever, but no, he had to horn in on her turf as if it was her life that needed straightening out.

After this third failed try Harry resigned himself to his addiction, even if it meant it would kill him before he was sixty. "Just order me a plain metal casket," he told Tina, "not one of those expensive burnished oak jobbies, no sense putting that much money straight into the ground." He'd like them to play The Righteous Brothers singing "Unchained Melody" at his funeral, if he could get away with it at a Reformed service.

He smoked for the rest of Tina's pregnancy. The baby was born three days before Christmas and was named Noelle Irene, which means "Christmas Peace." Tina's parents flew in from Edmonton to give Tina a hand and to witness the baptism, which was set for the first Sunday in January. Harry, clad in plastic cap and bootees, stood not five feet from Tina during the birth. An hour later he held his new daughter for the first time, and when he saw how utterly beautiful she was, each tiny fingernail perfect, her hair delicate as gossamer, he cried. He hadn't done that since he was eleven when he was riding his bicycle and his foot slipped off the pedal and his crotch came down on the crossbar. Holding his daughter he knew that she would need a father, not some physical wreck with emphysema. This realization proved to be the irresistible force of Newton's first law of motion: that very moment Harry made a holy vow he would conquer his smoking.

January 1 would be the day, no sense rushing things. It would be his gift to his new daughter. He told no one. There would be no fanfare, he decided, he would surprise everyone and just quietly up and quit.

Tina came home from hospital the day before Christmas, in time for the family to open presents together next day. Tina's parents began the process of spoiling their new granddaughter early: every other present seemed labelled Noelle. Harry gave Tina a sapphire ring, her birthstone, in gratefulness for giving him a daughter and in celebration of his new, soon-to-be-smoke-free life.

From Tina he got a video set of John Cleese's *Fawlty Towers* and a T-shirt that said "Does anal retentive have a hyphen?" The boys, with Tina's help no doubt, gave him a present shaped like a long, thin tube, and Harry went through the silly family ritual: "Looks like a basketball." It was a poster with all the letters of the alphabet photographed in brilliant colour from actual patterns on butterfly wings. Harry looked at Tina nursing Noelle, then at the boys playing with their new toys on the floor, their faces flushed with excitement. He sipped his eggnog and felt life had treated him better than he deserved. In five days, when he would quit smoking, he would deserve it even more.

One package in shiny red wrapping paper, its shape vaguely familiar to Harry, remained. It bore his name. He recognized his father-in-law's handwriting, the Dutch H, the two exaggerated r's. Lifting it and feeling its weight he knew immediately what it was. He tore off the wrapping paper and held up the gift, afraid his surprise was too enthusiastic, too phoney. It was a carton of cigarettes.

It took him only a week to finish it off. After all, a gift is a gift, you can't just spurn it. But a vow is also a vow, and Harry had made two of them. One was at his daughter's baptism, a vow that would take him and Tina a lifetime to fulfil. The other he made good on as soon as his father's gift had gone up in smoke.

It's early May now here in Alfalfa. Spring was late this year and everything's growing as if to make up for lost time. Harry hasn't smoked for a year and four months. He's put on about twenty pounds in that time. It's been hard for Tina too, but for different reasons. Harry has come to realize that with quitting smoking he's not only added years to his future, he's gained a heightened sense of the present as well, all because of his new sense of smell. Tina's not sure it's so much a *heightened* sense of the present; to her it's more that Harry's become omniscient—as in God. The moment he steps into the house from work Harry knows what Tina is cooking, whether it's curried chicken and green beans spiced with nutmeg, or roast beef and asparagus with cheddar cheese sauce, or lasagna seasoned with oregano and a green salad tossed with tarragon and chives.

There's a tall lilac bush outside their bedroom window that has just broken out in bloom, and the heavy scent of its purple blossoms sends Harry off to sleep every evening. During the night when he gets up to change Noelle's diaper now that Tina no longer nurses her, he experiences an interesting bouquet of aromas: the first sour stench rattles his sinuses as if he's had a whiff of smelling salts; then there's the lemony scent of the towelette he uses to clean between the creases of Noelle's thighs, and the sweet talc aroma of the Johnson's baby powder he sprinkles on Noelle to finish the job. Then he lays her back between the sheets of her crib that carry just a trace of the pungent bleach Tina washed them in. Finally he slips back under the comforter with Tina and the familiar smell of her wool nightgown. Next morning he wakes to the aroma of scrambled eggs and coffee and blueberry muffins.

Harry also finds himself remembering things from his past, moments forgotten but triggered back into memory because of their smell. Reaching down into the cupboard under the kitchen counter where Tina keeps odds and ends he catches the tangy odour of shoe polish, and what flashes into his mind suddenly is the smell of the shoe polish he used every Saturday evening when he was a kid and his chore was to polish the shoes of every member of his family for church next Sunday morning, all the shoes standing in a long row: his father's large black shoes and his brothers' brown ones, his mother's blue shoes and his sisters' slim pointed white pumps. He'd forgotten that.

Or when he and Tina take Noelle outside to sit in the sun and he smells the sunscreen Tina spreads on Noelle's arms and legs, what he suddenly remembers is the smell of Noxzema. He tells Tina about it: "I must have been eight or so and our family was camping at the lake where we went every summer. I'd gone swimming and afterward I lay down on my stomach to dry in the sun and I fell asleep. I slept so long the backs of my legs got burned, so bad the muscles of my legs cramped, and every hour my mother had to slather the backs of my legs with Noxzema cream. You remember how it smelled, sort of sweet and oily with camphor in it?"

These are the memories that come back to him. Everywhere he goes now, smells leap out at him. Leaving their house to drive the three miles to work he's a split second too late to beat the school bus–again. Now he'll have to follow the reek of its diesel fumes all the way into town. Despite his closed windows he soon picks up the musty scent of the dust the bus kicks up from their dirt road ahead of him. Then, as he hits the intersection at the highway, he opens his side window and there's Johnny Elzinga working in the ditch with his backhoe, the smell of the ditch rank and foul. On the highway, the rich fecund odour of spring grass is everywhere.

Harry's olfactory sense has become so acute he can smell things a mile off, things other people don't notice, things other people don't think Harry's smelling either.

"What's that smell?" he asks Tina, sniffing his nose.

"What smell?"

"Were you painting today?"

"No."

"Must be Fred next door."

Tina looks at him. They live in the country, Fred and Helene's house is a good thirty yards from theirs.

"I think it's the smell of wood stain," Harry says, nose slightly raised as if he might be about to sneeze. "Wood stain and pine. Must be Fred's decided to put wainscoting in their downstairs family room."

Tina gives him a look as if Harry has just said he's decided he no longer believes in infant baptism. She gets this from him all the time now–she's not married to Harry, she's living with Supernose.

That Saturday Fred and Helene invite Harry and Tina over for a game of darts, they'll send their daughter Pam over to babysit, but it turns out the invitation is just a pretext for Fred and Helene to show them the new pine wainscoting in their family room.

Later, as they cross the lawn back to their place, Tina expects Harry to look smug with the I-told-you-so expression he's starting to wear a lot. Instead, he looks serious. "That sweater Helene was wearing was new," he says, "I could tell. And did you notice the garlic on Fred's breath? Must be taking it for high cholesterol."

That's the way it's been going for Harry. In fact, some people think he's become a bit of a nuisance, the way he detects things, personal odours. He has stopped drinking coffee because he has come to dislike its stale smell on other people's breath. He keeps opening windows in the store to gain fresh air and Clarice, who has traded smoking for hay fever, keeps closing them. He takes two showers a day now, and shakes Noelle's baby powder all over himself afterward.

"What's wrong with Harry?" his cronies at Lucille's ask, "he doesn't drop in like he used to." It's not that Harry's tempted when he does go–he's not–no, it's the smell of countless cigarettes, acrid and musty, that has seeped into the very walls of the restaurant, its booths, wood tables and chairs, which whacks Harry across the nose now when he steps in. He doesn't even miss the stimulating conversation.

In fact, some people feel Harry's turned into a bit of a hermit. They wouldn't be surprised if he went and built a cabin by a lake in the woods somewhere.

It's true that Harry has become an outdoors kind of guy. He takes his family on long walks, Noelle strapped to his back, and he points out various trees and wildflowers to Tina and the boys. He rubs his hand along the trunk of a pine tree and lets the boys smell the sharp odour of the pitch on his fingers. He explains how Queen Anne's lace smells different from buttercup.

Harry's become especially interested in herbs because he likes the way they smell. He's built a small greenhouse in the back yard where he's started growing herbs. He grows chives, with its pungent odour and grasslike tufts, and dill, whose flowers look like a small yellow explosion. He grows purple basil, with its bitter aromatic smell, and fennel, its anise scent reminding Harry of when he was young and he had a stomach ache and his mother gave him anise milk to drink. He grows rosemary, lemon balm, and sage. Tarragon, oregano, and mint. Harry takes a lawnchair out there in the evenings with a book, and sits down right in the middle of the greenhouse. It's not quite a cabin in the woods, but Harry feels as cleansed there as if he had immersed himself in water. Every few moments you'll see him raise his nose slightly and close his eyes, savouring the pungent fragrance of hyssop, the minty aroma of thyme.

It's better than television.

Local man charged

Police were called to Lucille's Lunch this past Thursday after a rowdy altercation broke out.

Eyewitness reports indicate a patron of the restaurant apparently had trouble getting ketchup out of a bottle when he inadvertently sprayed some onto a woman sitting nearby. The woman's husband took exception to this action, words were exchanged, and it is reported that one man sprayed the other with the contents of the bottle.

Charged later with assault was Ross Danks, 34.

-news item in The Alfalfa Sentinel-Star

BENEATH THY CARE
THE SPARROW

Rocking slowly in the wooden porch swing one May evening on the deck behind his house on St. Laurent Street on the western edge of town, Harold Droge sits watching his newly planted tomatoes and green peppers grow while the sun goes down a fiery red beyond the cornfield stretching away from back of his house, when he knows suddenly that he smells skunk.

He sits up, lifts his nose and sniffs calculatingly, as a Dutchman might who has cut the cheese in church and wonders if anyone has noticed and even so he knows it'll be the kids who get the angry stares. It's the unmistakable musk of skunk alright, directly beneath the deck. Harold gets up from the swing slowly as if he might be balancing a glass of water on his nose, and walks into the house to find his wife Marilyn, who is sitting in the family room in the basement reading a novel for her book club.

"Honey," he asks her, "where are the kids?" Alison is seven, twins Daniel and Michael five.

Marilyn looks up slowly from her book, then shrugs. "Probably at the Ferrettis, why?"

"Shouldn't we know where they are?"

"Honey, this is Alfalfa, that's why we moved here, remember?"

"Is Angel with them?"

"She always is."

"Isn't it the kids' bedtime?"

She looks at her lime-green watch. "Oh, give them another five minutes or so."

Harold nods uneasily and goes back upstairs to see how the Blue Jays are faring against the Red Sox at Fenway. He doesn't feel much like sitting out on the deck any longer–the sun will have to manage setting without him. Maybe by tomorrow the skunk will have decided to take up residence at the Foleys next door; Murk will know what to do. He's in his early sixties, retired from farming four years ago, a rustic sage who knows the answer to all the weighty enigmas of life, such as how to prevent your pipes from freezing in winter or how to keep the rabbits from eating the young pea shoots in your garden. He and his wife Bernice came over to introduce themselves the day Harold and Marilyn moved in; Bernice carried a basket of fresh green beans and a snow-white head of cauliflower.

Harold is the son of George and Hillie Droge; Marilyn's parents are Frisians named Ennema–that's not the reason Marilyn decided to get married, she loved Harold, still does, enough to sacrifice retaining her maiden name. Harold and Marilyn used to live in the city twenty miles away, but moved back to Alfalfa two years ago after a series of events convinced them there was more to life than a beautiful old brick home in a war zone. Harold sells computer software in the city, and agreed with Marilyn that he could do so just as well commuting from Alfalfa and save the kids and the dog to boot.

Both Harold and Marilyn grew up here in Alfalfa; they started dating while they were in university. The first years after they'd married they both got jobs in the city and lived in a small two-bedroom house built during the war, but when the twins were born the house suddenly grew too small and pinched, like a corset on an opera diva. Marilyn was for moving back to Alfalfa where the kids would have room and also get to know their grandparents and Angel wouldn't have to be outside on a chain, but Harold had always dreamed of living in a stately old brick home. Marilyn acquiesced and they bought a brick house, a couple hundred thousand short of what you could call stately, but it was all they could afford with interest rates as high as they were back then.

The house was in the east end of the city on a street the real estate salesman told them was "in transition," and would soon be an "upscale neighbourhood," one for "discriminating buyers" such as themselves; all the house needed was some "loving attention." Marilyn thought it wasn't loving attention the house needed as much as mouth-to-mouth resuscitation. It obviously required major remodelling and she didn't relish the thought of the kids' lungs coated white from breathing drywall dust. The basement was unfinished and dank. The house had no garage, which meant they would have to park on the street. If anything was stately it was the trees in the neighbourhood, huge maples on both sides of the street–which meant no doubt the gutters were clogged. Marilyn thought Harold's judgment of the house was coloured by the third floor loft, where he envisioned his office, although Marilyn did admit she could plant a nice border of perennials along the backyard fence. What made her capitulate finally to Harold's wish to buy was the little park behind the house, where the children would be able to play. So they bought and sixty days later, on the 1st of August, moved in.

Harold attacked the remodelling with gusto; Marilyn felt herself swept along in the slipstream of his energy. For a while a huge dumpster took up their front yard. They removed the oil furnace, which rumbled flatulently at night and, as old and huge as it was in the dark basement, resembled a baleful mastodon hibernating in a paleozoic cave; they replaced it with a modern high efficiency gas furnace. On the main floor they stripped off layer after layer of wallpaper, so many layers the corners of the rooms were round; when Harold punctured a corner with a pencil, it went in a good inch. They stripped the wood throughout the house of its light blue paint, sanded it, and restored its natural finish.

The surprises began soon after they'd moved in. The beginning of September, eight students moved into the house next door, four of whom had cars so that invariably a Firebird or Camaro would be sitting in Harold's parking spot in front of the house when he came home from work. Afternoons, the street looked like the site of a frisbee-throwing convention. At night the students sat out on the dormer roof listening to music blaring from open windows–Harold and Marilyn didn't hear the music as much as they *felt it*: the music seemed to have little melody, in fact, just the deep thump of the bass reverberating through the very walls of their house. The water in their glasses vibrated as they sat eating dinner. Their knives and forks tinkled on the table. Marilyn cast a look at Harold that said, I hope you're enjoying your dream home, as for me and my house I'm miserable.

There were other–inconveniences. During the first six months their car was vandalized three times. The first time a window was broken and the radio ripped out, the second time all four hubcaps were stolen, the third time someone scratched a gouge in the side of the car all the way from headlight to taillight. If he'd owned a store Harold might have thought the Mafia were giving him a not so subtle message–listen, I'm just a poor schmuck selling software trying to provide a home for my family, he wanted to tell them, leave me alone. When Harold called their insurance agent after the third incident the secretary said, "Oh, it's you." And the house diagonally across the street, Harold was sure, was either a cathouse or a crack-house judging by the steady parade of men who came and went, especially at night. There was never anyone Harold saw more than once at the house, no one he recognized. Monday mornings no garbage bag ever stood at the curb.

The most shocking surprise occurred six months after they moved in. Harold and Marilyn were awakened one morning by the clank and snarl of heavy machinery; they looked out of their second storey bedroom window and were shocked to see bulldozers tearing up the soft green grass of the small park behind their house. Harold called city hall and was told the space was slated for a high rise. "Slated by whom?" he asked.

"It's been in the works for a long time," he was told by a woman who sounded as if she wore a clothes pin on her nose. Her voice was about as empathetic as the computer voice that gives you the telephone number when you call information. "Be thankful you had the park as long as you did," the voice said, "the building's two years behind schedule."

Harold felt thankful alright, as thankful as someone in an alley with his pants around his knees, his hands in the air, and his wallet gone. "How many storeys will the building have?" he asked.

"Sixteen."

He did not dare tell Marilyn. The real estate agent who had sold them the house Harold murdered at least twenty-four times over the next several days, each killing more novel and violent than the last.

They watched the building rise behind their back fence, floor after floor–Harold stopped counting after twelve, realizing there were still more to come. When the bricklayers finally arrived Harold and Marilyn winced to see that the brick was white. When the bricklayers were done the back of the high rise towered into the sky only feet away from their back fence, its facade steep as the wall of a canyon. What Harold and Marilyn saw from their kitchen window now no longer was blue sky and green space but a massive wall, white and cold, as if a huge iceberg were bearing down on them. Their back yard lay in dark shade now as early as 1:00 in the afternoon, when the sun disappeared behind the building. Harold felt as if he'd bought them all tickets on the *Titanic*.

If he had, even more disaster lay ahead. One June evening not long after the high rise was completed Harold was mowing the lawn of their back yard in the shadow of the apartment building, its wall of glass and white brick looming ahead of him, when a beer bottle came plummeting out of the sky, landed five feet in front of him with a whump!, and exploded on contact. Harold more than doubled his personal best for the standing broad jump, backwards at that. His heart paradiddled. His first thought was that the bottle had come from the students next door, then he realized the bottle's trajectory had been straight down. He looked up at the high rise and saw the undersides of rows and rows of balconies. He wondered, when he'd gotten over his anger, whether he was in a filming of *The Gods Must Be Crazy III.*

The beer bottle was just a portent of things to come. In July Alison stepped into the house and told Harold, "Daddy, there's a magazine with bare naked ladies in the back yard." Harold went out to investigate and saw a well-thumbed copy of *Hustler* magazine lying in the grass. He thought he'd save it in his toolbox in the basement in case he needed it for evidence. In August, Marilyn discovered a rusty bread toaster in the garden when she went out to cut some roses. In September they saw that an aluminum lawn chair had fallen into their yard, in October the grate of a hibachi. Harold decided he didn't need to save any more evidence.

Then came winter, the winter that almost broke the record for snow, and Harold and Marilyn thought the rain of donations from the gods of the high rise had ended, for they noticed no further objects. But when end of March came and the snow that had been deep enough to hide the four foot high blue spruce on the back lawn had finally melted, they found that over the winter an eclectic inventory had fallen into their yard: a bicycle pump (no hose), a package of soggy chicken drumsticks wrapped in cellophane, a shiny blue ceramic ashtray (a wad of pink gum stuck inside), a green corduroy pillow, half a pair of jumper cables, a U2 tape cassette (the thin tape stretched like a streamer away from the cassette and high into the bare branches of the maple beside the fence–Harold had wondered during the winter what on earth it was in the tree that glinted in the sun), a red clay flowerpot, an A&P plastic grocery bag filled with garbage, some twenty assorted empty pop cans, a hardcover copy of a Ken Follett novel from the downtown library (a year overdue, and too soggy to read), and six more beer bottles (not shattered, because of the snow).

They were shocked. All that stuff raining into their yard without their being aware of it! How long before one of their kids got brained by a falling object? Maybe the hibachi itself was next.

That wasn't so far off. Harold had let Angel outside one afternoon and shortly afterward they heard the dog yelp. Harold opened the back door and the dog sat cowering against the house as if it had seen Martians. He walked out into the yard to find out what had scared the dog and thirty seconds later he too almost ran in terror back to the house. What he saw, half buried in the lawn by the back fence, was an old black bowling ball. He looked up at the high rise but no face peered from any balcony. He was stunned. He didn't think a person could heave a bowling ball that far. What kind of animals lived up there? He left the bowling ball where it was and called the police.

When he went in to tell Marilyn what had happened the look on her face told him he had to decide between keeping his dream of a brick home or his marriage. Within a week he'd put the house on the market. But he and Marilyn felt caught in a moral dilemma: how much to tell prospective buyers? For all they knew a microwave oven–a refrigerator, even–might come plummeting from above while they were showing the house.

As it turned out they need not have worried. Within a week they'd sold to the owner of the house next door, who was looking for more rental space for students. Harold figured the man knew the risks of life in the neighbourhood.

They were faced now with the question of where to move. They couldn't afford the area of the city where they really wanted to live, and Harold did not think Marilyn would want to move to the suburbs: she just wasn't the vinyl siding and asphalt driveway type. All that was left was somewhere out of town. But where?

The answer came to Harold clear as glass: Marilyn had been right, how could he not have recognized it? He suddenly realized the truth: they'd become prodigals who had wandered too far from home, eating the corn husks of strangers when all along there had been but one place for them: Alfalfa. Safe, clean Alfalfa.

That night Harold dreamed they'd bought a home in Alfalfa, a place so down-home it looked like a vacation lodge. Along the front of the house ran a deep veranda on which stood a batallion of rocking chairs all in a row, bright red and blue and yellow and green rocking chairs waiting for people to sit in them and tell each other stories, a place so *gezellig*, as the Dutch would say, so homey it could never exist in real life but only in a dream.

The Blue Jays are leading the Red Sox 2-0 when Alison, Daniel, and Michael burst into the house just after eight. "Dad, there's a funny smell outside," Daniel says, lifting his nose. Watching the game, Harold has forgotten about the skunk. He rushes outside to bring Angel in before something happens that he will not be able to undo.

He does not want to tell Daniel what the odour is, certain the word "skunk" will throw the house into pandemonium. "Sshh," he says, not wanting Marilyn to hear, "we'll find out tomorrow what it is. C'mon scout, let's get you guys ready for bed." The game is in the sixth inning by the time they finish bathing the kids and putting them to bed.

He knows he should not worry about Marilyn; she's been doing small-town life as though she's never been away. She drives Alison to her soccer games at the park, the boys to Little League games. She's joined a book reading club with eight other women. She picks up their milk from a dairy farm, freezes the vegetables given to her by Bernice Foley next door, and cans relish and applesauce. Harold has discovered the joy, the texture, the pure sweet passion of vegetables cooked as they are meant to be. His mother Hillie cooked the Dutch way: boil the vegetables until they cry uncle.

Eating fresh vegetables inspired Harold to plant a garden this spring. He secretly envied Marilyn's success with the perennials she had planted in the yard, purple bellflower and white stonecrop and orange cowslip and yellow foxglove and blue lavender in front of the house, dark red roses along the garage in the back–all that lush vegetation, such a riot of colour. But he didn't want to grow perennials because they were, well, perennials, and he doesn't want to be a pansy. A vegetable garden is more–functional, he tells himself.

He figured he should talk to Murk next door, whose garden is about the best looking patch of vegetables Harold has seen here in Alfalfa. "Tell you what your garden needs, is a load of manure," Murk told him, and went on to explain that the people who'd lived there had neglected the garden, the soil was depleted and what Harold should give it was a good shot of nitrogen. "My son Kevin took over the farm a mile or two over," Murk had said, "anytime you want to borrow my pickup just let me know." Last fall Harold did just that, gave the garden several loads of cow manure, then it rained, and for the next three days the smell was so potent Harold was afraid it would set off the smoke alarm inside the house. The kids pinched their noses exaggeratedly to remind him.

Living on the edge of town and planting a vegetable garden, Harold has also discovered the world of little creatures, which forage into their yard with regularity. He has encountered a splendid variety of animals: sparrows have built a nest in a crook of the rainspout, rabbits zigzag crazily across the lawn in the evening, even deer can be seen in the winter at the edge of the cornfield. Last week Marilyn planted impatiens in an old wooden barrel Harold had sawn in half, and for the next two nights raccoons burrowed in the dirt, tearing out the flowers.

Harold asked Murk about it next day. "Did you put any bone meal or blood meal in the soil?" Murk asked. Marilyn said she had. Murk nodded. "Thought so. That's what they're going after. Next couple of nights run an extension cord out there–let me know if you need one–and plug in a radio. Tell you what you do. Tune it to a French-speaking station, I suspect if these raccoons are anything like most people around here, they're anglophone raccoons who dislike the distinct society clause and won't come anywhere near that radio. Just keep it playing the next couple nights, not too loud, mind you, Bernice doesn't sleep well nights as it is. But I think you'll see your flowers'll be fine."

Turned out Murk was right. They've exchanged life in a city war zone for life in a zoo, though, Harold thinks–have the animals invaded his world, or has he invaded theirs?

And now a skunk has taken up residence under their deck. So far Marilyn hasn't noticed, he thinks. Tomorrow he will talk again with Murk. Murk owns a .22, he'll know how to get in a shot so the skunk will never know what hit him.

That night he watches the late news with Marilyn in the family room, then they get ready for bed. Undressing in the bedroom, Harold sees Marilyn coming over to him wearing her white nightgown, a strange look of purpose on her face. Except for a slight smile, he detects trouble. But she takes his hand and leads him to bed. "Honey," she says, "I've been thinking. The twins are five already, I think it's, you know, about time. . . ."

They slip into bed. He's not given it thought, but if Marilyn feels ready for more, why not? But ready or not, it is the right time for this, and he is willing to accept whatever this will lead to, to accept whatever Marilyn feels is right.

Afterward, lying in the dark beside her with the scent of their lovemaking still in the room, Harold thinks back to their brick house in the city and their life now here in Alfalfa, and then it comes to him that what Marilyn has wanted all along is simply home, wonderful woman, a safe place for their children, and then he is struck by how deep and innate is the search for shelter, for home, and how every creature, human or animal, instinctively seeks sanctuary.

It's as if a light goes on inside him, and then he feels blissfully warm and unafraid and free. Maybe he won't ask Murk Foley to come over with his .22 after all. Tomorrow, he will suggest to Marilyn, they should stop by Lindemulder's Nursery to buy some perennials, peonies or something, fragrant red and purple flowers to plant around the deck.

Calvary Baptist news

Congratulations to Donald Arbuthnot and Lynne Walton who were united in marriage at Calvary Baptist Church at 2:00 pm on Saturday, May 16, Rev. David Findlater officiating. The newlyweds plan to honeymoon in the Maritimes.

"See the Conqueror Mounts in Triumph" was one of several hymns performed by a children's handbell choir next day during the Sunday morning service at Calvary.

-notice in The Alfalfa Sentinel-Star

THE BEAMS OF OUR HOUSE
ARE CEDAR

I don't know what the weather's been like for you, maybe where you live it's a perpetual balmy 22 Celsius, trees never lose their leaves nor flowers their blossoms, and pleasant music fills the air–if so, it's time you leave that mall you've been hanging out in and find your way back home, but here in Alfalfa, after a record-breaking late snowfall drove the farmers stir crazy with nothing to do but slurp coffee if not something stronger in the booths in Lucille's Lunch and grouse about what they wouldn't do if better weather didn't show up soon, spring finally decided it should perhaps put in an appearance after all, and since then the weather's been lovely, so warm that the pink and white blossoms that appeared on people's fruit trees have all given way to minty green young leaves and now it's the first week of June and most people have managed to push out of their minds the bitter memory of a winter which had kept going and going like an interminably long sentence some amateur writer has completely lost control of.

June is wedding month here in Alfalfa, and tomorrow Virginia Wiebinga is getting married. At long last, her mother Florence thinks. I will have to wear a suit, her father Harm thinks.

Virginia turned 39 a year ago. She's not marrying Sam Tinklenburg, a long-distance trucker who took a fancy to her, nor Albert Zomer, a chicken farmer who tried to win her hand, tried hard but didn't get very far. No, Virginia's marrying Paul Moffat, a freelance photographer who rescued her one night during a thunderstorm. Tomorrow they're getting married, they'll honeymoon two weeks on the islands of Greece, then settle here in Alfalfa where Virginia will keep working in Bob Miller's Travel Agency and Paul hopes to open a photography business. Alfalfa needs a photographer after Robert Meyer died last winter.

Virginia has asked her father to escort her down the aisle tomorrow, despite the fact she's not lived at home a long while. "Hey," she told him, "you're still my father." Harm's tickled pink to be asked, just think, their oldest daughter Virginia finally getting married–he wasn't sure he would still be standing by the time she finally got around to marrying. Harm thinks the world of her, likes her spunk, perhaps because she has more of it than he does. In other ways he thinks she takes after him–her intelligence, for one; her looks for another. Harm also likes her cautious nature, how she doesn't rush into anything–take her approach to marriage, for instance, how she didn't settle for just any bozo, not until Mr. Right finally came along. Deliberate, that's what Virginia is, and that's how Harm lives life too–although the word deliberate might be a bit flattering to describe Harm; procrastinating might be more like it. Harm goes fishing a lot, has the temperament and the patience of a fisherman. He generally doesn't do anything until he pretty well has to. He doesn't so much live life as he waits it out, as if it were a twenty-pound lunker he will eventually catch if only he'll sit and watch his line long enough.

Take the matter of their yard, for instance. Most Saturdays Harm's contemplating the meaning of life sitting in his boat up at the lake while his neighbours are slaving away here in Alfalfa in their yards. They don't just keep their grass short, they manicure it. Their flower beds are clean, their hedges clipped, as if every one of them is competing for the annual Trillium Award. They're out there on their hands and knees with a nail clipper the moment any blade or stalk or twig has the audacity to grow a millimeter too long–You! Who do you think you are! *Snip!* Into the compost for you, where there is weeping and gnashing of teeth.

Harm doesn't always get to things as soon as he knows he should, although he assures himself it's better for foliage to be a bit longer during the dry summer months. Then last week a woman he didn't recognize came by their house and asked him whether he needed someone to mow his grass. Harm wasn't sure whether she was in the lawn mowing business or whether she had drawn the short straw and was now belling the cat on behalf of the neighbourhood. "That's alright," he said, "I take care of it myself." The woman shot a glance at his unruly lawn, turned back to Harm, then said dryly, "I see that you do," and walked off.

Harm has gotten along famously with Virginia's fiance Paul. It's not just that Paul had the good sense to recognize Virginia for the catch that she is; no, for as everyone knows, fathers tend to be very possessive of their daughters. Even if they are 39. Perhaps, after four daughters, Harm sees Paul as the son he's never had, or perhaps it's that Paul also likes to go fishing. Or it may be the way Paul takes pictures that reassures Harm; he likes the way Paul manages to photograph a thing as it is rather than attempting to change it or impose his will on it.

In all the photographs, both formal and informal, that Paul has taken of them in the eight months they have known him now, Harm likes it that not once has Paul asked him to put on a suit and tie. When all the family is telling him, "Dad, this is for our *Christmas* card for Pete's sake," Paul would say, "Oh, that's alright, Harm's fine as he is," and there Harm would be on the picture, wearing his favourite cardigan with everyone else looking dressed up for Sunday. There was one thing Harm did have to get used to, though, and that was Paul calling him by his first name–it seemed a bit presumptuous to him at first. In their circles, a young man refers to his girlfriend's father respectfully as Mr. so and so; then, after marriage, will call him Dad. Now that he's gotten to know Paul, however, Harm secretly enjoys the camaraderie, the intimacy, even, between them, so that Paul calling him by his first name makes him seem more like a friend than a son-in-law.

He will probably have to wear his suit at the wedding tomorrow, though, much as he would like not to. He will wear it for Virginia's sake. He hasn't worn his suit in, how long? Must be five years ago, when Vivienne got married. Hasn't found any reason to wear it, not even for church when they have Communion. It's made him stand out a bit at First CRC, where suits and ties are the general rule on Sundays. "Just think, if you were going to visit the Queen in Buckingham Palace you'd dress up," people are in the habit of saying, "so all the more if you're going into *God's* house." Harm knows there's a fallacy lurking in the weeds in that argument somewhere, but he doesn't quite know how to haul it out. All he knows is that he has no desire whatsoever to visit the Queen in Buckingham Palace, or anywhere else, for that matter. But tomorrow, at Virginia's wedding, he will wear his suit. If the mice haven't made nests in the pockets in the meantime, that is.

One thing about Virginia being as old as–uh, being the age she is, turns out Harm doesn't have to pay for the wedding as he did with Valerie and Veronica and Vivienne. Set him back a good bit, each one.

He'd just finish paying for the last one, then whack! another whopper of a bill would hit him across the back of the head like a two-by-four. He was more than willing to do it a fourth time, too, fair is fair. He'd counted on it ever since Vivienne was born, knew that a man like himself was destined not for wealth but for happiness–think of it, four beautiful daughters, what a gift–while others less fortunate were destined for mere wealth. So he'd offered to pay for Virginia's wedding too. But she declined. "Dad," she said, "I'm 39, I've lived on my own since I was twenty-three, I've paid off my house, there's no way you're paying for my wedding." You can see why Harm admires her spunk.

Another advantage to Virginia's living on her own is that there hasn't been the usual commotion and mayhem around the house the days before the wedding. The first three weddings were a bit hard, especially Valerie's, maybe because it was their first and they weren't good at it yet. For one thing, Valerie wanted the wedding ceremony held anywhere but at First Christian Reformed–"It's nothing but an ugly wooden box built by a bunch of Dutch farmers!" she'd wailed.

"Well, where do you want it then?"

Valerie preferred St. Andrews Presbyterian with its beautiful stone architecture. Florence rolled her eyes, put her hand to her mouth. How could she think such a thing, what would people say, Valerie getting married in a Presbyterian church. "Talk some sense to her, Harmen, talk to her!" Then there were all the other details: baby's breath or edelweiss for Valerie's bouquet, pink taffeta or turquoise organza or yellow chiffon for the bridesmaids' dresses, and whether to serve salmon sandwiches at the reception–"Salmon! What's wrong with soup and buns?" It was a war, such a headstrong girl Valerie was; where did she get it from? Harm spent much of the time down in the basement making new leaders for his tackle box while above him women's voices shrieked like skillsaws.

This time, however, with Virginia taking care of everything from her house, it's been positively serene–people should always get married in their thirties, Harm figures. It's been so calm he can even put up with having to dress up. Tomorrow, at Virginia's wedding, he will wear his suit. And a tie, the blue one with spawning salmon leaping up a waterfall on it, which, if Harm absolutely *has* to wear a tie, is the one he'll put on. He knows how the salmon feel. There are times his own life seems like a long swim upstream.

Later that morning Florence is after him again to try on his suit, she's been reminding him for weeks now. Harm knows why–what she really wants is for him to buy a new suit. He can't see the use of buying something he wears once every five years, if that.

"I can't *believe* you're actually going to wear that thing to your own daughter's wedding," Florence says of the old suit, "you probably can't even get into it anymore." Harm looks left and right to see if there isn't something around the house that needs to be done, a leaking faucet washer or a wornout cupboard door hinge to replace. Usually when you don't have time for it every faucet in the house is leaking, but now when you need one there's nothing. He gets up from his chair with the clenched mouth he wears when he feels put upon. "Well if you twist my arm, Mother, I suppose I'd better."

In the bedroom, he pushes aside hangers filled with work shirts and cardigans and twill pants to reach his suit shoved to a corner of the closet. When he pulls it out he sees that its shoulders are covered with a layer of dust. He'll have to get Florence to give it a good brushing, then it'll be as good as the day he bought it. When he pulls the pants off the hanger he can see he hasn't hung it on the crease, so that now the pants sports a double crease. Oh well, once he's worn it an hour or so the old crease will come back.

When he tries on the slacks, however, he knows immediately he's in trouble. He can hardly get them up over his hips. The cotton-pickin' thing must have shrunk or something just hanging there all those years–do suits do that? And when he tries to close the pants over his waist he can hardly bring the button to meet its hole; it's not until he breathes in and pulls in his stomach, hard, that the button will close. When he lets out his breath his belly hangs out like a sack of oats over the top of the pants. Better try on the coat. The darn thing gives him just as hard a time–his shoulders feel cramped, his arms are tight in the sleeves, which ride high on his wrists, and the coat button–he might as well not even try to close it. The whole suit is threatening to split every one of its seams. Had he gained that much weight? No wonder the girls got together to buy him a mountain bike for his last birthday, a not so subtle hint he should get more exercise. When he looks at himself in the full-length mirror he sees that a corner of his denim shirt bottom is sticking out of his still open fly. Hmm, maybe Florence was right, he thinks. But he can't let her know that, she'd never let him forget it. He doesn't know whether to laugh or cry.

Florence, when she steps into the bedroom, does. She takes one look at him, puts her hand to her mouth, and breaks out in stitches of laughter, giggling so hard she's doubled over. Here Harm had just steeled himself for her to take a strip off his hide and she ends up laughing. Harm can't remember her laughing at anything like this since the time at the lake when he had his hands full with fishing gear, standing with one foot on the dock and the other in his boat while the distance between the two slowly widened beyond his ability to bridge them no matter how hard he tried and he ended up in the water with a prize-winning belly flop. Then, however, as soon as Florence has stopped laughing they both remember that Virginia's wedding is tomorrow afternoon and realize suddenly that if Harm is going to walk Virginia down the aisle they're faced with a little business they will have to transact, and that right soon.

There are times when living in a small town has its advantages. Can you imagine going into a department store in the city, finding a suit that fits both you and your budget, and then, when you're standing there looking debonair with pantlegs puddled around your ankles while the tailor is down on his knees pushing the end of a measuring tape up into your crotch and you tell him, "We need it done by this afternoon, please–umphh!" But when Harm and Florence explain the situation to Michael Verner at Michael's Men's Wear in town early that afternoon, Michael winks reassuringly and says, "Leave it to me. Check back with me today about four," and Harm is the owner of a new navy blue wool suit with handsome vertical stripes, on special summer sale at that. You can't put a price on personal service like that.

At home, he's so relieved, all that tension happily released, that he feels a rare energy. He fires up his lawnmower and starts cutting his lawn, no telling if Paul and Virginia might want to take some nice pictures tomorrow under the maples in the back. Maybe hoe some of the flower beds so the pictures will show that good, black Alfalfa soil.

Two hours later, however, his adrenaline rush is replaced with fatigue, and Harm tells Florence he's just going upstairs to stretch his legs a while. "You go ahead," she tells him, "I'm gonna sit here and read." Florence is an avid reader, a devotee of the historical romances of world-renowned writer Euphemia Custance Brown. Harm lies down upstairs meanwhile to thoughts of his favourite Jiggin' Frog cast right on target under willow trees hanging over the marge of a lake, and of leaping largemouth bass.

But he can't fall asleep for the life of him, he's too excited thinking about Virginia getting married tomorrow and how he will walk her down the aisle in his new blue suit, and after only ten minutes he decides to get up. He combs his hair in the bathroom, wetting a cowlick that will not sit down. When he goes to town to pick up his suit he'll drop in for a quick haircut if there's not too long a wait at Melvin's Barber Shop. Downstairs, everything is quiet, very quiet. Looking, he sees Florence has fallen asleep, mouth open, in her chair. Outside it's a beautiful afternoon, sunshine dappling the trees, not so much as a breeze ruffling the leaves. Predictions for tomorrow are the same. The weather fills Harm with the exuberance he felt earlier: no man should drive a car in such beautiful weather, he should walk, it would be good for him. If it weren't two miles to town he would. Tell you what, he tells himself, now would be a good time to ride that bike the girls bought you.

And that's exactly what he does, slipping out of the house without waking Florence. She'll be conked out another hour, he knows. Out on the road, though, the mountain bike feels strange to him, it's been a long time since he's ridden a bicycle. All those complicated gears, nothing like his old one-speed when he was a kid and all he had to do was hit the pedals backwards to apply the brakes. He loved to come to a skidding stop in gravel, turning the handle bars slightly so the rear end of the bike would come slewing around. Now, he's sure the neighbours must be watching, peeking from behind living room curtains and making smartass comments: "Hey Marge, come here and take a look! Wiebinga's out there ridin' a bike. Look at him. Ha ha! Whatta sight!"

Never mind. A man improving his health is a splendid thing. Bands of angels would be cheering, if only we had the eyes to see. A mere thirty minutes later–the lineup at Melvin's was too long for him to get his hair cut–he's on his way home victorious, his new suit in its plastic yellow wrapper flapping from his left hand held behind his shoulder.

Ah, but the law of gravity is a cruel, cruel thing. Fledglings drop out of nests to splatter on cement sidewalks below. Autumn leaves of scarlet and gold inevitably fall to the earth. Airplanes plummet out of clear blue skies to churn nose-first into cornfields. Harm Wiebinga, approaching a street intersection with one hand clutching his suit, the other the bicycle's handle bars, sees a car coming and turns the pedals backwards to apply the brakes as he used to when he was a kid with his one-speed, but nothing happens. He remembers, fumbles for the brake handle with his right hand, loses his grip on the handle bars altogether, and manages to stay on the bike a second or two more just as a bronco rider will stay on his horse a moment longer even though he's already lost hold of the rope, then will most certainly and cruelly fall.

Florence is in the middle of dreaming of the travails of Modesty

Culloden, beautiful and headstrong woman resisting, yet falling prey to, the rugged manliness of Robert McDougall, lord of Broadmoor Castle, when she is startled awake by a knocking on the front door. She recognizes it's one of the Alfalfa police.

No woman should have to be awakened from a deep nap to see an officer of the law on her front porch. Sudden panic sweeps over her like a cold wave hitting a pier, and the first thing she thinks is, Oh no, what's the old coot gone and done now, then, with relief, remembers he's sleeping upstairs.

The policeman tips his hat, and says, "Mrs. Wiebinga?" When Florence nods he asks, "May I come in a moment, please?"

Florence knows immediately the worst has happened. Is it one of the children? Grandchildren? She opens the door and the officer steps into the vestibule. He takes off his cap. "I'm Sergeant Lofthouse, ma'am." Florence nods. "I have a little bad news, I'm afraid. But it's good news, too, in a way. The bad news is your husband has had a little bicycle accident. The good news is, it could have been much worse."

"Harmen?" Florence points back into the house. "That can't be, I'm afraid you must have the wrong house. My husband is upstairs, taking a nap."

He gives her a patronizing smile–she hates that benign smirk policemen have, then hand you a hundred and fifty dollar ticket. "Don't think so, ma'am."

"Oh yes, he went up no more than fifteen minutes ago," and she checks her watch–oh my goodness, somehow it's after four. "Just a minute, I'll run up and call him. You'll see."

Upstairs, however, the bed is strangely empty. No Harmen. What did the policeman say, a motorcycle accident?

The rest she hears numbly: a bicycle accident, just missed being hit by a car, it could have been much worse. He'll be OK; fortunately the break in his right ankle was a clean one. Then she focuses on the policeman's face again, his voice telling her, "He's at the hospital right now, Mrs. Wiebinga, Doc Summerall is putting his leg in a cast. They'll give you a call when he's ready to be picked up. Better yet, perhaps you should go there now."

Purcell's "Trumpet Voluntary" is a stately piece, just the right tempo for a man with his leg encased in a plaster cast and hobbling on crutches to navigate a sanctuary aisle with a bride on his arm. Florence has just been escorted to her seat in a front pew, and as the organ music begins, pealing up toward the beams of First Christian Reformed Church of Alfalfa and all the congregation rises, she turns to see her daughter gowned in white satin, her countenance radiant behind a white veil, so beautiful that can it really be Virginia?

And there is Harm walking beside Virginia. Florence had suggested this morning that, what with her father's broken leg, maybe Paul should accompany her down the aisle, but Harm said he'd escorted every one of his daughters, no way he was going to miss escorting Virginia, broken leg or not–if she would have him, that is. "Daddy," she said, kissing him, "I'd hate to see that brand-new suit of yours go to waste."

So now there Harm is, stumping down the aisle to the cadence of the music, white cast covered to his ankle by the pant leg of his new wool suit Michael Verner was kind enough to take apart at the seam so they could hem it up with safety pins, the whiteness of the cast matching the brilliant whiteness of his shirt and Virginia's gown. Harm's wearing his tie with salmon leaping wildly upstream, silly man. His hair, she notices suddenly, is too long, spilling over his ears, over the collar of his suit. He should have gone to Melvin's for a cut before the wedding, but you try to get him to do *any*thing. And yet, come to think of it, it looks good on him, the long hair, a bit rakish, the old rogue.

As she looks back up the aisle she believes First Christian Reformed Church has never been this full for a wedding; the whole congregation has come out, it seems, this Saturday in June: George and Hillie Droge are here, Hilbert and Dorothy TeBrake, the Tazelaars, younger couples like the Winkles and Olthofs, oldsters such as Oetse Kikkert and Evelyn Krikke, sniffling into her handkerchief; Albert Zomer is here, and Sam Tinklenberg, standing in the back, right behind a strange young man with thick-lensed glasses whom Florence has never seen before, and look, even Jerry and Bonnie Shivers from Lucille's Lunch are here; she didn't know they were churchgoing people. Then, at the thought of all these friends who have come here for Virginia's wedding, Florence too takes out her handkerchief and begins to daub at her eyes.

Through her tears she sees Harm and Virginia come closer until Virginia separates to join Paul in front of Rev. DeHeer, then Harm stands by Florence's side. When she turns to the front and the triumphant wedding march subsides, she realizes, for the first time perhaps, this town, these people, this sanctuary, are *home*. She could dwell here all the days of her life.

ACKNOWLEDGEMENTS

My thanks to Harry Cook, who knows a good story when he hears one and thus got this book started. Thanks to good friends Douglas Loney and John Levesque, who read the manuscript and whose suggestions and encouragement were extremely helpful. A special thanks to my wife Judy, who is both astute critic yet sympathetic reader, and whose good advice has strengthened this book throughout. I also owe a debt to a number of newspapers, small and large, who have provided material for this book. To document each instance would be difficult, nevertheless the debt here and there has not been insignificant, and I express my thanks.